CHARLOTTE
SAYS

For Lauren Griffiths – one of my most very favourite humans.

STRIPES PUBLISHING
An imprint of the Little Tiger Group
1 Coda Studios, 189 Munster Road,
London SW6 6AW

www.littletiger.co.uk

A paperback original
First published in Great Britain in 2017
Text copyright © Alex Bell, 2017
Cover copyright © Stripes Publishing Ltd, 2017

ISBN: 978-1-84715-840-6

The right of Alex Bell to be identified as the author
of this work has been asserted by her in accordance with
the Copyright, Designs and Patents Act, 1988.

A CIP catalogue record for this book is available
from the British Library.

Printed and bound in the UK.

10 9 8 7 6 5 4 3 2 1

CHARLOTTE SAYS

ALEX BELL

RED
EYE

Chapter One

Isle of Skye – January 1910

"Don't be frightened yet," the voice says. "I'll tell you when it's time to be frightened…"

I turn, looking over my shoulder, but there is nobody there and I am alone once again at Whiteladies – that house of confused spirits and cracked china dolls and slaughtered horses. From somewhere downstairs a grandfather clock counts down the six hours in deep, melancholy tolls and, like a magnetic force, my eyes are drawn with a terrible irresistibility to the door at the end of the corridor. Nothing else exists in the entire world but that door. It is closed but I can hear someone sobbing behind it. Sobbing, sobbing, sobbing. On, on, on. I must help them. I must open that door. I must do something. Now. While I still can.

I walk down the corridor, and the soot and blood mix together in swirls of black and red – on the walls, on my skirts, on my hands and in the fine grooves of my fingertips. The closed door looms before me, and it hides a secret that will be the end of everything I know and love. Yet still I move closer. I reach for the door but I can never get to it. No matter how many steps I take, the door is always further and further away. My fingers grasp at nothing. Grief makes the air thick and heavy, and I choke on smoke and, all around, there is the smell of burning human hair…

Flames lick at my skin as my hand reaches for the doorknob.

"Charlotte says you shouldn't open it," a voice remarks, almost conversationally.

I turn and, through the fire, see little Vanessa Redwing sitting on the floor of the corridor with her back to me. She's playing with her dolls' house and I see that she's wearing her riding habit, her dark curls drawn into a low bun beneath her top hat. From this angle I can't see her face but I do see the scarlet streak of blood running slowly down her neck from her ear. She hums as she moves her doll from one room of the house to another.

"Charlotte says don't open the door," she says again, not turning round.

"Why not?" I ask, my voice a croak.

"Something bad happened in that room," she says.

"But I must know," I say. "I have to remember."

"Charlotte says you'll regret it if you look," Vanessa whispers. She turns her head slightly and I sense she is watching me, but her face is hidden by the netted veil attached to the stiff brim of her riding hat. "Charlotte says there are some horrors that burn," she says.

The fire leaps taller, crackling with spite as it devours the house around us. The heat is almost unbearable; the smoke makes my eyes water; it hurts to breathe.

Vanessa holds the doll up to her ear, as if it's whispering something to her. Then she giggles softly. "Charlotte says let it burn," she says, giggling some more. "Let it all burn right down to the ground."

"Wake up!"

I turn away from her, finally managing to wrap my fingers round the brass door handle embossed with the Redwing coat of arms, the hawk emblem with the cold, cruel eyes that blaze red hot. The brass smokes, burning and blistering my skin, but I don't care. At last I will get to see what lies beyond, to find out what happened in this room...

"Wake up, miss," a man said again. "We've arrived. We've reached the school."

His fingers pressed against my shoulder and I shoved his hand away before I could stop myself. In those confusing moments between sleeping and waking, it was another man standing before me, another hand on my arm, purple bruises blooming under cruel fingers. But then the image faded and it was only the carriage driver, shivering in the gloom and giving me a reproachful look.

"I'm sorry for waking you, Miss Black," he said, his lilting Scottish accent making me feel a long way from home. "But we've arrived at the school."

I looked out of the window but night had fallen while I'd been sleeping and there was nothing much to see except the glow of lanterns shining through the fog. The tang of salt and brine reached right into the carriage, telling me that the ocean was somewhere close. There was no scent of smoke or ash or burning hair. And when I looked down at my black kid gloves, they were not sticky with blood.

"Miss Black," the driver said again, starting to look a little vexed. "We've arrived at—"

"I heard you," I snapped. I had been so close to the door that time, so close to remembering. But it was not the driver's fault, so I shook my head and added, "Please forgive me. It's been a long journey and I am fatigued."

"Of course," the driver mumbled, already turning away to see to the removal of my luggage.

The cold had bitten deep into my bones while I'd been asleep, and the blood rushed painfully back into my hands and feet as I got up from the uncomfortable bench seat. I was absolutely famished. I'd used my last pennies on a pot of tea and a plate of crumpets while waiting for the ferry in Mallaig but that had been hours ago and now I was dreadfully hungry.

The heel of my boot crunched on the frozen gravel as I stepped out and saw the horses steaming in the lamplight, snorting and shuffling their hooves, anxious to be on their way. The driver must have been eager to leave, too, for he had barely set my trunk down on the ground before climbing back into his seat.

"The school is straight through those gates," he said, pointing with his whip. "If they'd left them unlocked then I could have dropped you off at the door. But you can get in through them side gates just there easy enough."

He paused and I wondered whether he was waiting for a tip. Perhaps if I offered him one then he might even get down from the driver's seat and help me with my luggage. But I had no money left in my purse and I was damned if I was going to beg. So I simply offered him a tight-lipped thank you. He shrugged in response, flicked his whip at the horses, and the carriage trundled away, taking the warm lamplight with it. I was left shivering in the dark outside the black iron school gates, scowling after the retreating carriage as I reached down to grip the handle of my trunk.

It was devilish heavy, and my arms and back ached with the effort of dragging it along behind me. Thanks to the boats running behind schedule, I was later than I had said I would be in my letter, but I thought they might have left the gates open for me just the same. I looked up at them, tall and imposing, with the words *Dunvegan School for Girls* spelled out in the ironwork at the top. *An exclusive industrial school, founded to provide for the maintenance and training of destitute girls not convicted of crime*, read the job advert that Henry had sent me. It was, in other words, a place for those who had nowhere else to go.

I found the side gate the driver had mentioned and passed through to the school grounds. The building was larger than I had expected and loomed overhead. The wind whistled through the open tower in the centre, causing the faint echo of a ringing bell to carry through the air. Most of the school was cloaked in darkness, the nearby black windows lifeless and opaque with ice, but a light glowed here and there in the otherwise dark façade. I searched the windows for faces but saw none. The building seemed without warmth or pity or interest in me of any kind. Well, that suited me perfectly. More than anything, I wanted to be left alone. To be invisible.

Unfortunately the fog chose just that moment to turn into misty rain that clung in droplets to my travelling cloak, soaked through the soles of my boots and dampened my gloves, causing them to shrink and cling tightly to my hands.

I had no idea which way I was supposed to go, so decided to make for what looked like a main entrance. My breath smoked before me, and the hem of my black mourning dress became bedraggled and wet from the frosted stones as I dragged my trunk to the doorway. There was no answer when I knocked, so I tried the handle but the door was locked fast.

I sighed and gazed around hopelessly. There wasn't a soul about, and the night seemed to become colder and colder by the second. It had been a long, tiresome journey – I was bone-weary and hungry, and now I was locked out in the dark. It would easily have been enough to make most other seventeen-year-old girls weep in my place, but I knew what real horror was and this was nothing on that.

I straightened my shoulders and glared at the closed door before me. If I knocked long and hard enough, eventually someone would have to hear and let me in. And I would knock all night until my knuckles were bloody stumps if I had to.

I gripped the brass knocker and brought it down on the door relentlessly, over and over again, as hard and as loud as I could, channeling all the fear and frustration and grief I'd felt over the last few weeks, relishing the aching muscles in my arm and back. At least the pain told me I was still alive, which was more than could be said for my mother...

I felt a fresh wave of longing. I would have sold my soul to have been back in our little rented townhouse with her. Mother could play the part of mysterious medium, purveyor of séances and communicator with the dead extremely well but in private her default was always a ready smile, a cheerful nature and a boisterous laugh. For a moment I could see her so clearly in my mind's eye, plump and pretty in one of her flamboyant flowery bonnets, her head thrown back as she guffawed at some joke she'd probably made herself.

But then the image dissolved and blew away, like little pieces of ash plucked apart by the ocean wind.

I swallowed down my sorrow. Now was not the time to fall apart.

"The Black women are strong," Mother had often told me. "The Black women don't give up, Jemima, no matter how bleak things may seem..."

The front door was suddenly yanked open, startling me. I found myself face to face with a maid, probably a year or two younger than myself. She was extremely pretty, with green eyes and glossy blond hair tucked beneath a white cap. I disliked her immediately. She had a sulky look that many pretty girls seemed to suffer from, and I could tell she wouldn't hesitate to make things difficult for me the first chance she got.

"Yes?" she said in a hostile tone.

"I'm Jemima Black," I said. "I've come to take up the assistant mistress post. I believe you're expecting me?"

"You're late," the girl replied with a sniff. "We thought you'd be here hours ago."

"The boat was delayed," I said. "Because of the weather. There was nothing I could do."

The girl sighed. "I'll fetch Miss Grayson," she said, beckoning me inside.

I stepped over the threshold into an entrance hall. Although nowhere near as grand as Whiteladies, it was nevertheless more impressive than I had expected, with a sea-green tiled floor and a tall wooden staircase that led steeply up to the first floor. I thought of the portrait hall that had formed the entrance to Whiteladies, with its magnificent stained-glass window filled with hawks and all those glistening oil paintings, the face of a dead girl staring back at me from every gilded frame. No matter how unwelcoming the school may be, I was glad to be here, hundreds of miles from London.

I'd grown accustomed to the new electric lighting that had been installed at Whiteladies and had forgotten how gas lamps sucked all the moisture from the room, making the air as dry as old paper. Even the potted plants by the front door were wilting. Gaslight produced a much softer glow than electricity and much of the room flickered in shadow. I could make out the exposed gas pipes, though, running along the ceiling, marring the elegant décor.

"Wait here," the maid said, then turned and disappeared through one of the side doors.

I had expected the place to be noisier, considering there were twenty or so girls boarding here, all seven to ten years old. But the place was silent. *Silent as the grave*, I thought, and had to stifle the sudden urge to giggle. I longed for bed and hoped I wouldn't be kept standing around in my wet clothes for too long.

I took out my pocket watch and was shocked to see that it was almost eleven o'clock. No wonder the place was so quiet. All the girls would be asleep by now. I hoped my knocking hadn't woken any of them. I glanced up at the staircase to the first floor, where I imagined the dormitories would be, and immediately saw the flash of white nightdresses, pale fingers curled round the balustrades. The knocking had clearly woken the girls after all, and now there were perhaps two or three of them up there, watching me.

I raised my hand in greeting, but there was a startled gasp as they saw I'd spotted them and then the girls vanished, scattering like birds. At just that moment the door on the side of the entrance hall opened and a woman came striding out. I realized this must be Miss Grayson and, despite the fact that Henry had provided me with a colourful description of the schoolmistress in his last letter, my heart sank at the sight of her. She wore a dressing gown, implying that my arrival had roused her from bed but, strangely, her grey hair was arranged in a perfect pompadour – swept up on top of her head and then pinned in place around hidden hair rolls to add extra height and bulk. Her hair must have been long enough to sit on when it was loose, and the elaborate hairstyle did not match the sternness in her watery blue eyes or the pinched expression of disapproval around her mouth. She was in her mid-fifties and life's many disappointments had clearly twisted her features into a shrivelled look of bitterness. I'm quite certain that she'd resolved to hate me before she ever set eyes on me.

"Miss Black, I presume?" she snapped.

In my heeled boots I was tall for a girl but Miss Grayson still loomed a head taller than me in her itchy-looking woollen slippers.

"Yes," I began. "I'm—"

"You're late, miss." She cut me off sharply. "I'm Miss Grayson, the mistress here, and I must warn you that lateness will not be tolerated at Dunvegan School for Girls. Timeliness is next to godliness, and I run a punctual school."

"I'm very sorry," I said. "But the boat was delayed and—"

"I will overlook it this once but a second occurrence will lead to your wages being docked. Am I clear?"

"Abundantly," I replied coolly.

"I will show you to your room," she said. "The servants have retired for the night. Your trunk will be carried upstairs in the morning."

She kept her eyes fixed on me and I could tell that she wanted me to protest. There were things in my trunk I needed – my nightdress and my slippers and my wash kit – but I refused to give her the satisfaction so I simply said, "Very well."

The schoolmistress turned away to pick up a candlestick from the sideboard, lighting this before she extinguished the lamps.

"This way," she said, already heading for the staircase, guarding the candle's flame with her hand.

The heels of my boots seemed to click too loudly on the wooden boards as I followed her up to the first floor. I glanced at the balustrades as we went past, but the girls had obviously hurried back to bed and I wasn't about to get them in trouble by mentioning them.

"My quarters are here." Miss Grayson gestured to a nearby room. "The girls sleep in a dormitory at the far end." She pointed into the gloom. "Your room is located there as well, at the top of the servants' stairs. This will enable us to keep an eye on the girls between us, in case anyone gets it into their head to start running around the place at night."

"Is that something that happens often?"

"Last week I caught some girls trying to sneak down to the kitchen to steal food," Miss Grayson said. Her thin mouth tightened. "Needless to say they were all whipped and sent to bed immediately. Dishonest behaviour will not be tolerated here."

You horrid old shrew, I thought, disliking the schoolmistress even more intensely. *We are not going to get along at all.*

Miss Grayson led the way down the corridor and opened the door to my room, the bare wooden boards creaking under her slippered feet as she stepped inside. By the light of her candle I saw that the little space was every bit as spartan as I had expected it to be, simply comprising of a washstand, a bedside table, a chest of drawers, a dressing table, a rickety chair and a narrow bed. A single coal smouldered in the fireplace but the room was icy cold.

"The fire was made ready for your arrival but I'm afraid you've missed the benefit of it, given your tardiness," Miss Grayson remarked.

If she expected me to apologize a second time for something that was not my fault then she was going to be disappointed. I walked into the room behind her. "Thank you for showing me up, Miss Grayson," I said, peeling off my wet cloak. "Please don't let me keep you from your bed any longer."

Seeing my bombazine mourning dress, trimmed in itchy black crepe, Miss Grayson pursed her lips and said, "Please accept my sympathies for your loss, Miss Black."

I inclined my head but said nothing. I couldn't talk about it, not without breaking down, so I was relieved when the schoolmistress let the matter drop and lit the candle on the bedside table with an obvious show of reluctance. "You'll be provided with one candlestick per week," she told me. "If your use exceeds this then you must pay for any additional candles from your own private funds. I'd urge you to do without as far as you can. Candles lead to wax drips on the floor and they are also, of course, a fire hazard."

I gave her a sharp look, wondering if this was a reference to my past. Surely news of the fire would not have carried as far as the Isle of Skye? That was part of the appeal of coming here in the first place, after all. To leave all of that behind.

"You will have one day off per month, on the last Sunday," Miss Grayson went on. "The bathroom is down the corridor, the third door on the right. And there is a chamber pot beneath the bed. Lessons start at eight and breakfast is at seven. Please present yourself for a prompt start."

"Of course."

At the mention of breakfast, hunger rumbled again in my stomach and I briefly considered asking Miss Grayson whether it might be possible to get some refreshment sent up from the kitchen. But she'd already told me the servants had retired for the night and I couldn't bear to receive another lecture about my lateness.

"If that's all, then I'll wish you goodnight, Miss Black."

And with that she was gone, leaving me alone in the room.

I headed straight to the fireplace, hoping to add some more coal to the fire, but the scuttle was empty. Clearly this was another thing that was rationed. I sighed. There was nothing for it but to go to bed.

By the feeble light of the single candle, I struggled out of my wet clothes, draping them over the chair by the fireplace so they could start to dry out. Once I had stripped down to my undergarments, my teeth immediately started chattering. But mere physical discomfort barely had the power to touch me any more.

I sat on the edge of the bed and ran my fingertips lightly over the many cigarette burns that scarred my arms and wrists, all the way up to my shoulders. My arms were a mess of scar tissue – ugly, ruined skin that felt tough and leathery to the touch. I recalled how some of the original burns had become infected, bleeding and weeping, and these scars were even uglier. As they'd healed, the skin had tightened around the scars, which now made it difficult for me to bend my arms at the elbows. I couldn't properly feel the material of my mourning dress, or the touch of my fingertips brushing over the scarred surface.

I tried to think back two weeks, to the night of the fire but almost at once I could feel my heart speeding up, my breath turning shallow in my throat, my chest constricting as if an iron weight were pressing down on it, hard enough to crush my ribcage.

Don't be frightened yet, his voice whispered in my mind once again. So clear and close and loud that it was like he was really there in the room, taunting me. *I'll tell you when it's time to be frightened…*

I tasted cigarette smoke on my tongue, breathed in the overpowering scent of his hair's Macassar oil, felt fingers digging into my skin hard enough to leave bruises. The smell of blood filled the air.

Sit here, the voice went on inside my head. *And hold this doll—*

"Shut up! Shut up!" I gasped. "You are not here. You are not here."

I opened my eyes, pushed Whiteladies from my thoughts and concentrated on breathing slowly until my heart rate finally returned to normal. I was out of London now, escaped from that dreadful place. Jemima Black was not a medium any longer, she was a schoolmistress, and life was to be plain and ordinary from now on. Completely plain and ordinary.

I went over to the washstand and poured icy water from the jug into the bowl, then quickly splashed it over my face. Crawling between the freezing sheets, I wrapped my arms round the black grief I carried with me everywhere, trying not to mind the sting of its claws and teeth as I cried myself to sleep.

Chapter Two

Isle of Skye – January 1910

The cold woke me early the next morning – it felt like my tears had frozen to my face during the night. It was still dark outside so I knew it must be early and yet I was ravenously hungry. As I climbed out of bed I wondered whether there could be anything more wretched in all the world than having to get up, shivering, in the early hours by the light of a single candle, especially when that candle was cheap and greasy and filled the room with the scent of animal fat.

The school had an air of misery about it and I was reminded of my grandmother telling me that buildings could be haunted by human sadness as well as by ghosts. Unlike my mother, who cheerfully accepted she was a fake, Grandma had believed herself to be a genuine medium right up until the day she died. She was quite convinced that she regularly conversed with the dead and that she had once even made contact with a demon.

It was trapped inside a painting, she'd told me. *A painting of an old woman in a wedding dress. The family were terrified of that painting, Jemmy, because sometimes the old woman would weep and wail, and scratch at her face at night. She moved around inside the frame, too. They thought they should just toss the painting straight on to the fire but luckily I was there to stop them. Destroying the painting would have released that devil and who knows where we would have been then? The only safe thing was to lock it up in a trunk and toss away the key.*

Oh, Mother, don't scare Jemima with those bedtime stories! my mother had said with her customary laugh.

I sighed and pushed all thoughts of family from my mind. Instead I gazed around the little bedroom. No servant had been to light the fire and, when I went over to last night's washing water, I saw that it had frozen in the bowl. My eyes went to the bell pull behind the bed and I wondered whether I was permitted to ring it to call a servant. Finally I went over and gave it a firm tug. Even if a fire was not allowed, I needed to ensure my luggage was brought up so I could change into a suitable dress for the day.

25

No one came and I had to ring the bell twice more before the same blond girl from yesterday finally knocked at my door. She scowled at my requests but I was firm with her and felt a petty sense of victory when she finally left, taking with her my wet clothes from the night before to be cleaned.

I was forced to break through the ice in the bowl in order to wash. After that there was nothing to do but wait for my luggage to arrive, my sense of triumph rapidly turning to panic. It was almost seven o'clock, the hour when I was supposed to present myself for breakfast. I tugged at the servants' bell again but it was another twenty torturous minutes before my trunk finally arrived.

I dressed as quickly as I could, pulling on another black mourning dress, but then there was the problem of my hair. I had always worn it loose or in a simple plait but this would be improper now that I was seventeen. I was not yet accustomed to putting my hair up myself, there had been servants for that at Whiteladies, and it took me several clumsy attempts before I managed a half-decent chignon, secured with a jet hair comb. Upon looking at my pocket watch,

I was horrified to see that it was now a quarter to eight.

I hurried downstairs, back into the entrance hall, wondering where the breakfast room was and how I was supposed to get there, cursing myself for not asking Miss Grayson last night. I finally located the main hall just as the girls were filing out of it, looking neat and tidy in their matching dresses, all giving me curious looks as I passed by.

I entered the room and saw that the blond maid was clearing away the porridge bowls. It was a vast space, cold as an icebox, with large windows that would let in plenty of light once the sun finally came up. The smell of burnt toast lingered in the air and the odd plate of blackened bread remained on the two long trestle tables that took up much of the room.

Miss Grayson was standing beside a raised stage at the far end. Her hair was fashioned in the same fussy pompadour as last night, only now she wore a high-necked blouse and long skirt instead of a dressing gown. A vicious-looking tawse dangled from a loop round her wrist.

The mistresses at my own school had used canes to punish the pupils but Henry had mentioned in one of his letters that Scottish schools seemed to prefer the tawse – a long strip of leather with the striking end split into thick individual strips. These strips, I noticed, were not edged, meaning that they could easily draw blood if enough force was used.

"Very kind of you to join us, Miss Black," Miss Grayson said as soon as she saw me. Her mouth twitched, just slightly, and I wondered whether she was suppressing a smile. She was probably delighted to have this opportunity to reprimand me again so soon.

I walked slowly over to her, preparing myself to take whatever was coming.

"There was a delay in my luggage arriving in my room," I began. "I couldn't get dressed until—"

Miss Grayson fixed her gaze on me and I instantly fell silent. There was nothing in her expression but anger and it was startling to be looked at with so much open dislike.

"Miss Black, I will tell you the same thing I tell the girls," she said. "I am not interested in excuses or hearing you blame others for your own shortcomings. I thought I made myself quite clear on the issue of punctuality last night. You are late for the second time in a number of hours and your wages will be docked accordingly."

I gritted my teeth against the injustice of it. What would she have had me do? Come down in my petticoats?

"I will be frank with you, Miss Black. It was not my idea to have an assistant mistress here," she went on. "I told the board I thought it unnecessary. Besides which, I have enough to do looking after the students, without adding another girl into the mix."

"You won't have to look after me, Miss Grayson," I said. "I'm willing to work hard and I—"

"Do not interrupt me, miss!" the schoolmistress replied, her nostrils flaring. "I will not tolerate rudeness. Furthermore, I have been informed that you continuously rang the servants' bell in your bedroom this morning and kept the servants from their duties with your various demands."

I glanced over at the maid, who smirked at me before disappearing out of the door with the empty bowls.

Miss Grayson's pompadour wobbled as she drew herself up to stare down her nose at me. "I fear you're under a great misapprehension if you think the staff are to be at your beck and call. I understand from your friend, Mr Collins, that you were accustomed to a rather grand lifestyle before you came here, but you'll have to drop all of those airs and graces if you hope to maintain your position. Our generous benefactors employ the servants to take care of the school and its pupils, not to cater to your personal whims."

I felt a slow pulse of anger deep in my stomach and lifted my chin to meet her gaze. "Miss Grayson," I said firmly, "I'm sorry, but it simply was not like that. I rang the bell because I needed my clothes brought upstairs and could not leave my room dressed only in my petticoats, as I'm sure you will concede. I apologize if I delayed the servants this morning, but I really don't know what else you could have expected me to do in the circumstances. If there was an alternative course of action that would have been more appropriate, then by all means let me know so that I might bear it in mind for the future."

For a long moment there was utter silence as the schoolmistress and I stared at each other. Perhaps I should simply have accepted her chastisement meekly, saying nothing, but I had faced down worse monsters than Miss Grayson.

She didn't blink once and yet her eyes remained as watery as ever, while my own seemed to burn with dryness. Finally the silence was broken by a scuffling from the doorway and we turned to see a few of the girls standing there, watching the scene eagerly.

"Go to your classroom and take your seats," Miss Grayson snapped.

The girls fled.

"Hold out your hand," she said, the moment they'd gone.

"What for?" I asked, startled.

"Hold. Out. Your. Hand," Miss Grayson repeated in a low, harsh voice, "or pack your bags and leave the school this instant."

Slowly I held out my hand. The schoolmistress gripped it at the wrist, turned it over so that it was palm up and then administered three sharp strikes of her tawse across the soft skin of my palm. It smarted and stung like anything, leaving several angry red welts, but I refused to let any trace of pain cross my face. She could whip me for speaking my mind but she couldn't stop me from speaking it, and I would rather take a hundred thrashings than allow myself to be bullied. I'd said what I wanted to say, I knew I was in the right, and nothing she said or did could take that from me.

Miss Grayson dropped my hand and took a step back. "An ignoble beginning, Miss Black, I'm sure you'll agree," she remarked. I noticed she'd gone white around the lips. "I fear your career here is destined to be a short-lived one. While you are here, though, and taking payment, you will do your fair share of the work, I assure you. Please accompany me to the classroom and we will begin."

She turned and strode from the hall. I followed, trying to get control of the anger that was bubbling up inside me, threatening to burst out. Hunger did not improve my mood; I had missed dinner last night and now breakfast, too, but like it or not I needed this job. I had no formal training as a governess and, if I was not to be a medium any more, then poorly paid work at an industrial school was the best I could hope for. The alternative was to rely on the charity of some poorhouse for destitute women.

I followed Miss Grayson down the corridor to a large classroom, filled with individual roll-topped desks. A big blackboard stood at the front of the room, and the windows were set high enough to prevent the pupils from looking out and becoming distracted. A small fire burned in the grate but it was still chilly, and the place smelled of paper, chalk and cold wood. The tall desk by the blackboard must be Miss Grayson's. I noticed that it had a big brass bell on it, presumably to ring for quiet, but the schoolmistress didn't even need to look at it. I'd expected a bustle of activity as we entered but the room was silent, with all the girls sitting at their desks, facing forwards, pens in front of them ready to begin.

"Good morning, girls," Miss Grayson said.

"Good morning, Miss Grayson," they chorused back at her.

"This is Miss Black," the schoolmistress said, gesturing at me. "She will be helping you with your lessons. One at a time, I'd like you to stand up and introduce yourselves. Starting with you, Felicity."

A girl of about seven stood up. "My name is Felicity," she said in a soft whisper. "And the magistrates sentenced me to an industrial school because I was found begging in the streets."

She sat down and Miss Grayson pointed to the girl next to her, who stood up and said, "My name is Olivia and the magistrates sentenced me to an industrial school because I was found wandering in the company of reputed thieves, which they said was one of the worst things for a girl of my age."

"My name is Alice, and I got took before the courts for not having no home to go to."

Miss Grayson gave a great sigh. "Please speak properly, Alice. You were brought before the courts for vagrancy."

"Yes, miss," Alice mumbled.

Next there was another girl of the same age. She was a tiny little thing, with pretty, honey-coloured hair and huge brown eyes.

"I'm Bess," she said, twisting the front of her dress with both hands, clearly anxious at having to speak in front of everybody. "And the magistrates sent me here because they said my father was too much of a drunkard to look after me."

After Bess took her seat, a girl of around ten stood up. She was thin, with extremely pale blond hair and a sickly look that spoke of long-term ill-health. And yet there was a spark in her eyes, a sort of smouldering defiance that made me like her at once. "My name is Estella," she said in a strong, clear voice.

"And why are you here?" Miss Grayson said.

Estella did not look at the floor as most of the other girls had but instead raised her chin slightly. "The magistrates sentenced me to industrial school because my parents declared me to be beyond their control."

There was almost an element of pride in her voice.

"And why did your parents finally have to wash their hands of you, Estella?" Miss Grayson pressed.

The girl stared right back at the schoolmistress. "They called me a compulsive liar."

"That is not correct," Miss Grayson replied.

Estella glared at her. "Yes, it is."

"You were not sent here because your parents *called* you a compulsive liar, you ignorant girl," Miss Grayson replied. "You were sent here because you *are* a compulsive liar."

Estella shrugged. It was the first open show of rebellion I'd seen since arriving. All the other girls seemed remarkably well behaved, probably because they were all terrified of the schoolmistress.

"Sit down," Miss Grayson ordered.

To my delight, Estella paused just a moment before doing so. When she glanced at me, I smiled at her. She looked surprised but offered me a small smile in return.

Once the rest of the girls had introduced themselves, Miss Grayson pointed to a pupil in the second row and said, "Georgia, for the benefit of our guest, can you please tell us what one of the two objectives of Dunvegan School is?"

"To provide pupils with the skills they'll need to support themselves through honest, hardworking labour," Georgia immediately said.

"Correct," Miss Grayson replied. She turned her gaze on me and said, with obvious pride, "We are particularly noted for the excellence of our training programme here and girls educated at Dunvegan are highly sought after as domestic servants once they leave. Bess." She turned back to the girl with honey-coloured hair. "The second objective?"

Bess looked startled to have been chosen and replied so quietly that no one could hear her.

"Speak up!" Miss Grayson ordered.

The girl tried again but as soon as she opened her mouth water poured out of it, an endless stream that soaked her shoes and splattered the boards at her feet. Her eyes had a dull, vacant look as her mouth opened wider and wider. She was soon soaked from head to foot, her clothes dripping wet, her hair sodden. Clumps of black sand fell from her mouth, landing on the floor with wet thumps, along with a tangle of weeds that the girl had to drag out of her throat, gagging all the while...

"Speak up, Bess," Miss Grayson said again.

And suddenly the water was gone, and the girl was dry and normal-looking once more.

"To reform the child's character," Bess whispered.

I bunched my hands into fists and kept them carefully clenched in front of me. I must not react, not in front of everyone. Was I going mad? I must not allow myself to lose my mind. I was overtired, that was all, and hadn't eaten in what felt like decades.

"Correct," Miss Grayson said, bringing me back to the room. "You have all come from reduced circumstances and many of you have fallen in with bad crowds as a result, but any undesirable behaviour will be swiftly stamped out here."

She looked directly at me as she said the last sentence. The lesson, which turned out to be a writing one, consisted of Miss Grayson handing out Bibles to the girls and having them copy out verses into their exercise books. She marched back over to me at the front of the room and handed me a large wooden ruler.

"If you see any student writing with her left hand you are to strike her immediately with this," she told me. "You may sit on that stool." She pointed to one at the front of the class. "But please keep an eye on them. There are several girls here who will insist on using their left hands."

I took the ruler and sat on the stool, praying that I wouldn't have to use it. The writing activity was carried out in silence and seemed to go on for an eternity. After the first half hour I was so bored I could have screamed. Being a medium may have had its downsides but at least it was never dull. In fact, I had rather enjoyed accompanying Mother to some of London's most fashionable homes, sitting in their elegant parlours and dazzling the assembled guests with our carefully staged display of table-tipping and wall-rapping, our 'ghostly hands' tricks and levitating candlestick illusions.

Really, darling, it's not much different from walking the boards at the theatre, you know, Mother used to say. She had done a bit of stage acting in her time, before the séance business. And although she couldn't really speak to clients' dead loved ones, I always thought Mother performed a valuable service anyway, as her kindly nature gave her a knack for comforting the bereaved. It always seemed to me that people could carry their grieving burdens a little easier after she had been to see them. No doubt that was why she created such a glowing reputation for herself as a gifted medium.

I had nothing to do but reminisce for the rest of that lesson. I was almost falling asleep by the end of the hour when I suddenly spotted one of the students, who'd shyly introduced herself as Martha, writing with her left hand. The last thing I wanted to do was go over there and hit her with the ruler for an offence so trivial, so I pretended I hadn't noticed, hoping Miss Grayson wouldn't see and that the lesson would soon be over. But moments later, the schoolmistress was on her feet, snatching the ruler from my hand and marching up towards the girl. Hastily Martha put the pen into her right hand but it was too late. Before she could even dip it in the inkwell, Miss Grayson had dealt her a stinging blow across the wrist.

"Martha, I do not know whether you are deviously stubborn or intolerably stupid, but I have told you countless times to write with your *right hand*!"

Martha mumbled an apology, gripping the pen tightly, her knuckles whitening.

"Proceed!" Miss Grayson snapped. "And, this time, do it correctly."

Biting her lip, Martha started to write but, almost at once, Miss Grayson had seized the exercise book from her and was holding it up to show the class.

"Disgraceful," the schoolmistress said. "This is easily the worst penmanship I've ever seen. You do not show any improvement at all, Martha. None! You will sit in the stupid corner for the rest of the lesson."

She gripped the girl by the shoulder, pulled her up from her seat and dragged her, stumbling, past the desks to a stool at the front of the room. Then Miss

40

Grayson reached behind her desk and drew out a tall, cone-shaped white hat, which she passed to Martha.

"You will wear the imbecile's cap for the remainder of the lesson," she said.

Martha put it on without a word, staring miserably down at her feet.

"Miss Black, while I inspect the others' work, would you please record Martha's punishment in the Punishment Book?" the schoolmistress said. "I trust this task, at least, is one you might be able to perform?"

She proceeded to deposit the most enormous tome on the desk. I'd never seen such a gigantic book in my life. You could have beaten someone to death with it, if you'd had a mind to. As Miss Grayson walked up and down the rows of girls, I went over to the desk and saw that letters spelling out *The Punishment Book* were stamped across the leather cover in dark, curling script.

I opened the book and found it was already more than halfway full of punishments doled out to various students over the years. There were columns for the date, the girl's name, their offence and the corresponding punishment, all written out in small, precise text bunched up as tiny as possible, as if the writer had wanted to squeeze as many misdeeds on to the page as they could.

Running my eye down the page it seemed to me that most of the offences were trivial enough – writing with the left hand, being five minutes late to class, performing poorly on a test, daydreaming during lessons. The punishments, though, were anything but trivial. I saw cane lashings and leg whippings and withheld meals, as well as hours and even days spent in 'Solitary'.

Gritting my teeth, I picked up the pen and copied out Martha's name, offence and punishment in a straight line beneath the others. Finally the lesson came to an end and the girls filed out quietly for their fifteen minutes of designated 'playtime' outside. During this time, Miss Grayson gave me a tour of the school, albeit with a reluctant, long-suffering air.

We began upstairs with the girls' dormitory, which consisted of rows of narrow beds with threadbare blankets. We took the servants' stairs back down to the kitchen, where Miss Grayson introduced me to Cassie, the pretty but hostile maid I had already met, and the second maid, Hannah, who looked a few years older and had straight brown hair and a timid expression. Miss Grayson said that Cassie had been a student at the school herself and had only been employed as a maid a couple of years earlier. Now that I looked at the girl closely, I realized she couldn't be more than fifteen. There was also a cook, named Mrs String – a thin woman with a straggle of greasy hair scraped back on her head.

"And that there is Whiskers," Hannah said, gesturing at a grey tabby curled into a contented ball by the fire. "The school cat."

"Whiskers keeps the mice and the rats at bay," Miss Grayson told me. "Everyone has their role to play, you see. And that is the entire household, apart from Henry, who I know you are already acquainted with."

"Oh, are you related?" Cassie asked, in rather a hopeful tone.

"We knew each other as children," I replied.

Growing up as neighbours, Henry and I had been practically inseparable. It helped that his mother was a costume seamstress for the theatre, which was how she and my mother had first met. Mrs Collins often came to our home to measure Mother for the elaborate gowns she wore when playing the part of a medium. But then, to my dismay, Henry's mother returned to her birthplace on the Isle of Skye when I was eleven and Henry twelve.

Of course we'll be married, he'd often said to me in that joking way of his. *As soon as I can make myself worthy of you, that is.*

It all seemed a long time ago now. We had written to each other periodically ever since and Henry's latest letter, containing the job advert for a place at the school where he worked as a drawing master, couldn't have come at a better time.

There's nothing keeping you in London, after all, he'd written. *And I would love to see you again, my dear old friend…*

Part of me dreaded our first meeting. I knew I had changed a lot in the past six years and Henry was bound to notice. And then he would want to know about what had happened to me and that was something I couldn't share. With him, or anyone.

"Mrs String comes in to prepare the meals but Cassie and Hannah are the only other live-in staff," Miss Grayson said. "They have every third Sunday off, so we organize the meals ourselves on those days.

I should make you aware now that we never prepare any food with nuts in it. One of the girls, Estella, mustn't eat them. It's extremely serious. We had an incident last year when she had a funny turn and almost died. The physician had to be called – at great expense to the school, I might add. He informed us that we were extremely fortunate on that occasion but, if there were to be a repeat occurrence, then the result would surely be fatal. For that reason we don't cook with nuts at all. You must bear this in mind when you run the cookery classes."

"Will I be doing those on my own?" I asked, a little nervously. When Mother and I lived alone I had sometimes helped her in the kitchen, but I was no accomplished chef by any means.

"Yes, I thought you could manage to take those lessons," Miss Grayson said, although she gave me a dubious look as she spoke. "I need the additional time to catch up on my correspondence. It needn't be anything too fancy, mind. The girls simply need to learn how to become decent housekeepers. You may peruse Mrs Beeton's book for recipes."

I was relieved to hear there would be a recipe book, at least.

We continued on with the tour. Miss Grayson showed me the remaining classrooms as well as the basement, which contained the luggage rooms where the girls' trunks were stored during term time.

"Of course, many of them remain here for the holidays," Miss Grayson said. "Their parents are supposed to contribute to the fees but some can't and most wilfully don't. Whatever money they get is probably frittered away in gin palaces and dog-fighting dens." She sniffed loudly. "The girls are better off here. This school represents the one chance at a decent life that many of them will ever know. If they can obtain employment in a respectable household then they can raise themselves out of the slums from which they came."

We had reached the entrance hall once again and Miss Grayson stopped at the foot of the stairs. "I suggest you take the rest of the morning to acquaint yourself with the school and unpack your belongings," she said. Her mouth twisted and she added, "No doubt you hoped one of the maids would see to your unpacking for you but I'm afraid you will have to learn to look after yourself."

"I did not expect anything else for a moment," I replied.

"Lunch is served in the hall at twelve o'clock," the schoolmistress went on, as if she hadn't heard me. "Lessons resume at twelve forty-five. Please present yourself promptly."

With that she turned and left me, and I was more than pleased to see the back of her.

Chapter Three

Isle of Skye – January 1910

When I returned to my room I found that the servants' bell had been removed in my absence, no doubt under Miss Grayson's orders. I was not surprised. Clearly she was determined to make life as unpleasant as possible for me.

I unpacked my luggage quickly. It did not take long, for the simple reason that my possessions were few. Most of my things had been destroyed in the fire at Whiteladies. After the funeral expenses had been taken care of, there was just enough money left to see to my wardrobe and procure a few personal items. My clothes were all identical mourning dresses; my shoes and hats were plain and cheap.

After tidying away my things and glaring one last time at the brass hook where the bell pull should be, I put on my cloak and decided to take a turn around the grounds. I was keen to get out of the school, enjoy some fresh air and get my bearings.

On my way down to the kitchen I took the servants' stairs and, to my surprise, almost collided with a maid who was humming to herself and dusting the banisters. She was a thin girl of about my age, with mousy hair tucked into her white cap.

"Oh," I said. "Hello. I thought I'd already met everybody."

The girl abruptly stopped humming and whirled round to face me, her brown eyes wide. She stared at me with such a look of shock that I began to think she must be rather a simpleton.

"I'm Jemima Black," I said. "The new assistant mistress."

The girl said nothing. I wondered whether perhaps Miss Grayson had neglected to inform her that I was arriving.

"And your name is?" I pressed.

"Dolores," the girl whispered, her voice so quiet that I had to strain to hear her.

"Well. How do you do?" I said feebly. I went down the rest of the stairs, leaving the maid staring after me, the feather duster dangling from her hand.

By now the girls had returned to their lessons and I had the place to myself. I ran into Cassie outside the kitchen. She scowled at me and I gave her my coldest stare right back. The cat, Whiskers, was poking around outside the kitchen door and I distinctly saw Cassie aim a bad-natured kick at him as she went past.

Shaking my head, I turned away from the schoolhouse and set off to explore. I quickly found the well-tended vegetable patch, as well as the chicken coop, where a collection of plump chickens pecked and scratched at the frozen earth. The grounds were neatly landscaped and I could hear the distant roar of the sea. I followed the noise right to the cliff edge and saw that the roiling ocean seemed to be in as restless a mood as I was. I had never laid eyes on the sea before yesterday and I didn't think I'd ever quite get used to the incredible hugeness of it. There was something soothing about all that water, as well as the deep rumbling roar of the surf swirling around in the hidden caves below.

I'd been standing there for a few minutes when a dog arrived. I didn't hear it approach; suddenly it was just there and it was without doubt the ugliest creature I'd ever seen. For a start, it only had three legs – one of its front ones was missing, causing it to hop along in a most ungainly way. And it had a scar running down the side of its face that caused its left eyelid to droop. It looked like some kind of terrier, small and wiry, with a patchy grey coat and ears that flopped about all over the place. It seemed terribly excited to see me, hopping up and down on its sole front leg in an absurd fashion as it did its best to lick my hands.

I'd never had much contact with dogs, and wasn't really quite sure what to do, but this was certainly the warmest welcome I'd had from any living soul since arriving on the Isle of Skye.

"Hello," I said, tentatively reaching out and patting the dog's head. "You're an excitable little fellow, aren't you?"

The dog licked my hands and wagged its tail, looking ecstatic.

"Murphy!" a voice called. "Murphy, darn it, where are you?"

I turned to see a young man appear round the corner of the chicken coop. He was wearing a long, rather shabby, brown coat and sturdy walking boots, a blue scarf tied at his throat. His chestnut-coloured hair was just a little too long to be fashionable and curled loosely over his ears and the back of his collar. He stopped dead when he saw me, then a huge grin spread across his face and he hurried over with long strides.

"Mim, my darling!" he exclaimed, coming to a stop before me. "Good lord, you look so ... well, so grown up!"

Henry had changed, too. He still had one of the most honest, open faces I'd ever seen, but he was much taller and broader now. There were smile lines at the corners of his green eyes and his nose had clearly been broken at some point in the last six years because it was bent at the bridge. There was a faint shadow of stubble on his jaw, too. To my surprise, my heart ached at the sight of him. So much had changed since we'd played together as children.

He moved forwards as if to hug me but I quickly stepped back before I could stop myself. The scars on my arms started to itch beneath my bombazine sleeves and I cringed at the thought of anyone touching me.

"Hello, Henry," I said, forcing a smile. "It's good to see you."

His arm, which had been reaching for me, dropped to his side. He seemed to falter for a moment but then recovered himself and said, "It is gloriously wonderful to see you again, old girl." He glanced down at the dog. "I hope Murphy wasn't bothering you? Oh fiddlesticks, I think he might have slobbered on your dress! Gosh, I really am terribly—"

"It's quite all right," I replied. "Black dresses are good for hiding stains."

"I'm so very sorry about your mother," Henry said, in a quieter voice. "I could hardly believe it when I received your letter. How on earth did the fire start, Mim?"

I can't remember, I wanted to tell him. *I can hardly remember anything about that night at all.*

All I knew was that I'd found myself in the grounds with the servants, choking on smoke, watching the house burn and trying to work out exactly how I had got outside in the first place.

The physician who examined me afterwards said that the female mind was a delicate thing that could seek to protect itself in strange and mysterious ways, including causing a person to forget the reason for their grief. Some things were just too painful to remember, he said. The memories might come back on their own but, then again, they might not. I would just have to wait and see.

I went along with his explanation but I could not shake the feeling of dread, the feeling of danger, the urge to flee. Besides, I already knew full well why I could not remember what had happened at the house that night and I wasn't about to share that explanation with anyone. Whiteladies had been a forsaken place for my mother and I from the beginning. God, how I wished that I'd never set eyes on that house.

I cleared my throat and said, "They think perhaps a paraffin lamp got knocked over in the study. The servants all got out but Mother and Mr Redwing both... They both died."

"I'm so sorry, Mim," Henry said again.

I shrugged. What was there to say? The dog, Murphy, poked his snout into my hands, still hopping in excitement.

"Where on earth did you find this ugly creature?" I asked, scratching the dog behind his ear. "He looks like he's been through some kind of battle."

"Well he has, in a way. They have dog-fighting

and rat-baiting at the Mermaid Tavern in town, you know."

I was sure the distaste I felt must have shown on my face and I made little attempt to disguise it. Although I'd never had the misfortune to see one myself, I'd heard of the dog fights that took place in London. They were savage affairs, soaked in blood, with dogs ripping each other to pieces in the ring.

"You haven't taken up the sport?" I asked.

Henry had always been such a kindly, gentle soul; it was what had made me so fond of him in the first place, and the thought that he could have changed so entirely, in such a short space of time, made me feel strangely distressed.

"Good heavens, no!" Henry exclaimed. "No, I can't abide it. And Murphy was never much of a fighter at any rate. They could see he didn't have any natural skill in that department so they were going to use him as bait."

"Bait?"

"Sometimes they put a weaker dog in the ring to be killed by one of the fighting dogs," Henry explained. "To get their blood up, you know. It didn't seem like much of a fair fight so I took him home with me instead."

"And his owner did not object?"

Henry laughed. "Oh, on the contrary, he made his objections known in the only way he knew how." He tapped his nose. "And it's been bent like this ever since. Mother was most put out about it. When I returned home, she scolded me thoroughly and informed me that my new nose made me look 'rakish and suspicious'. So I said to her, 'Mother, old thing,' I said, 'a chap can tolerate being called rakish but I won't be accused of being a suspicious character, not under any circumstances.'"

I couldn't help a small smile at the mention of Henry's mother. I'd been very fond of her as a child. She had often looked after me at her house in the years before Mother deemed me old enough to join her in her séances.

"She'd love to see you again," Henry went on. "You must come for tea on your day off. Perhaps we might make a day of it and visit the Fairy Pools?" He gave me the most endearing, hopeful look. "It's so beautiful there, Mim. We could take a picnic with us…"

He trailed off, floundering at my lack of response.

"Perhaps," I managed. "Although I expect we'll both be very busy."

"Well, bear it in mind," Henry said. He reached out and patted the dog on the head. Murphy sat down at his side, wagging his tail and staring up at him adoringly. "The only problem with this scruffy little hop-a-long is that he's surprisingly fast," Henry went on. "He can nip about like anything. And there's something quite ridiculous about a three-legged dog giving you the slip, wouldn't you agree?"

"Quite," I replied with a smile.

I had forgotten how deeply I had cared for Henry. Now those feelings seemed to come back in a rush that rather winded me.

"Still, there are worse things in the world than being a little ridiculous, I'm sure," Henry went on cheerfully. "Did you arrive last night?"

"I did."

"I went to the port to meet you but they told me the boats were delayed due to the weather and probably wouldn't get through till the morning."

"You didn't have to do that," I said.

"I wanted to," Henry replied. He gave me a searching look and I knew he could tell that something had changed. The old me would have been truly delighted to see him and yet here I stood, rigid as a rod, not even able to so much as shake his hand.

Henry seemed to hesitate and for a moment I feared he was going to ask me what was wrong. But then he must have thought better of it because he simply said, "Are you settling in all right? The old dragon isn't giving you too much trouble?"

"Miss Grayson?" I raised an eyebrow. "She seems determined to hate me."

Henry gave me a sympathetic grimace. "Very probably," he said. "You're not the first assistant mistress we've had here, you know. Many of the local girls have tried their hands at it, only Miss Grayson made their lives so intolerable that they all left within the month. I think you were the only person who applied for the job this time."

"Well, I won't be leaving," I said at once. "I need this job and no one chases me away."

"Oh, yes," he said, with a little nod. "I knew you'd be different. You're made of sterner stuff."

For an awful moment I felt tears prickle the back of my eyes. I wanted to tell him that I wasn't made of sterner stuff, at all – that I was weak and useless and had allowed something dreadful to happen that I could never make up for.

"It would be nice for the girls to have someone around who's a little less … austere," Henry went on. "Someone who could be on their side a bit. Everyone needs at least one person who's on their side, I always say."

"It's difficult if everyone's against you," I replied, immediately thinking of Whiteladies again. "I would've thought Miss Grayson might have pursued a different line of work if she hates children so much, though."

"She doesn't hate children, exactly," Henry replied. "She's a tough old stick but, in her own way, she really is trying to do her best for them, I think. She probably dislikes you, though, I'm afraid. She doesn't want another teacher here, you see. It was the idea of the school's board and, whatever she may tell you, they're the only ones who can dismiss you." He glanced towards the school and said, "I'd better get back. I'll catch the sharp edge of Miss Grayson's tongue myself if I'm late for the drawing lesson. Let me know if there's anything I can do to help you settle in, won't you? Anything at all."

"I'm sure I'll be perfectly all right, thank you," I said. I hated myself for the cool tone but it seemed best to keep Henry at arm's length. We could not simply pick up where we had been before. And I knew I'd never be able to pretend with him like I could pretend with everyone else. The safest thing was to not allow him to get too close in the first place.

A confused look crossed his face, mixed with hurt.

"Well," he said, with what seemed like forced cheerfulness, flashing me one of his crooked smiles. "I'll see you soon."

I watched as he strolled back to the house, hands in pockets, with Murphy hopping briskly along at his side. As Henry had remarked, the dog's missing leg certainly didn't seem to slow him down much. It was, after all, amazing what you could adjust to, what you could learn to live without.

Mother was gone and there was no changing that now. Like it or not, Whiteladies was in my past. The Dunvegan School for Girls was my future. I walked back with a renewed resolve to be successful here, to make friends with the girls, and to prove to Miss Grayson that I could do this job and do it well.

Over the next week I slowly settled into the rhythm of life at the school. I learned the girls' names and began to get to grips with who was good at writing, who struggled with needlework, who showed a natural aptitude for cookery. Miss Grayson decided that I should be in charge of the nature walks the girls had at the end of each day. Having grown up amid the soot and dirty stones of London, I had to educate myself first, and was forced to carry a picture book to begin with in order to identify the plants and wildlife we saw on our coastal walks towards Neist Point.

I enjoyed being out in the fresh air, learning about nature with the girls, searching for a glimpse of a basking shark's fin in the water or the wheeling shadow of birds passing by overhead. There was a wonderful variety of them, from brindled guillemots to red-throated divers.

My favourite part of the nature walks was definitely the sea itself, though. I just adored the clean scent of it – a combination of salt and shells and seaweed that carried along on the wind.

Henry would sometimes join us on these walks with Murphy, and, although I'd resolved to keep my distance from him, I found myself looking forward to his company with a keenness that dismayed me. I was settling into life at the school well, however, and was pleased to have my first few days behind me.

A week after my arrival, I was heading for the breakfast room when the postman came. There wasn't much post normally, just one or two letters for the girls from family members, or perhaps an item for Miss Grayson. Today, though, there was a package – a fairly large box wrapped in brown paper.

I glanced at the address to see who it was for and my breath caught in my throat, my clothes were too tight, the walls of the school shrank around me. I recognized the handwriting on the label. I knew that slashed, spiky scrawl and it belonged to a person I'd been quite certain I would never see again – a person who should be dead.

Chapter Four

Isle of Skye – January 1910

The arrival of the post had the unfortunate consequence of making me exactly thirty seconds late for breakfast. Miss Grayson walked out of the hall and found me standing there with the parcel in my hands. Her mouth immediately thinned into a line of disapproval.

"Ah, there you are. Late again, I see. If I dock your wages any further, Miss Black, there will be nothing left to pay you at the end of the month," she told me grimly. "And so an alternative punishment must be found. Would you prefer five raps across the knuckles with a ruler, or the confiscation of this parcel that I see has just arrived for you?"

I tried not to glare at her. It was terribly degrading being struck with a ruler in such a manner but I was desperate to see what was inside the parcel so, through gritted teeth, I said, "The ruler."

"In that case, I shall take possession of your parcel

for the time being," Miss Grayson replied, holding out her hands for it.

"But you said I could choose—" I began to protest.

"On the contrary, I asked which you would prefer," she replied. "It would hardly be a punishment if you were given what you wanted, would it?"

None of this is what I want! I was tempted to scream at her. *You intolerably stupid woman, I have lost everything!*

"But you can't confiscate my post!" I said, my hands tightening round the box. "It's not right!"

"I've warned you about time-keeping before, Miss Black," the schoolmistress replied. "I won't have tardiness here and you will learn to be punctual, even if it requires special and unusual punishment to drive the lesson home. Sadly some people are incapable of learning any other way, it seems. Hand me the parcel at once."

I had no choice but to pass it over, silently fuming as it was taken off downstairs to be stored in the locked luggage room. The knowledge of its existence burned in my mind for the rest of that day and I knew I couldn't leave it there. When Miss Grayson went to have her lunch, I seized the opportunity to creep into her study and look for the key. It was a mad, risky thing to do, but my efforts were rewarded when I yanked open a desk drawer and discovered the school's collection of keys, all attached to neatly labelled tags to identify the doors they opened. Throughout the afternoon's lessons, I feared Miss Grayson would discover the absence of the luggage-room key at any second. But my crime passed by undiscovered and, finally, evening arrived.

As soon as the school had gone quiet for the night, I tiptoed from my room. The floorboards were like slabs of ice beneath my bare feet and my entire face ached with the effort of keeping my teeth from chattering as I made my way down the corridor. The candle in my hand shook but I couldn't quite tell whether this was due to the dread I'd felt since the morning or the ghastly chill of the place. My nightdress and dressing gown felt like they were made from paper, for all the warmth they offered. The school was still and silent in the gloom, and a coat of frost clung to the black windows, threatening to crack them.

I longed to return to my bed, climb beneath the covers and huddle there until the blood returned to my fingers and toes. But I had to know what was in that box. I simply had to. Perhaps I'd imagined that handwriting. I'd only seen the parcel for a moment before it had been taken away, after all. But I needed to be sure.

I could feel the weight of the brass key to the luggage room in my dressing-gown pocket as I made my way down the steep wooden staircase, shielding the flame of the candle against the icy draughts that kept trying their very best to extinguish it. I didn't dare light the gas lamps in the hall, for fear of drawing attention, and I remembered that there was no gas supply to the luggage room anyway.

I was just reaching for the door handle when I heard a muffled giggle. I stopped dead. The laugh had come from inside the luggage room. I stifled a groan. One of the girls must have got in there and decided to hide. Now I would have to deal with her and send her back to the dormitory before I could investigate the package. That's if Miss Grayson didn't wake up first and come storming downstairs, brandishing her tawse at us for being out of bed.

I put the key in the lock and turned it. The door creaked as it swung open and I peered into the darkness, the candle in my hand doing little to illuminate the room. The giggle came again, louder and sharper this time.

"All right, come out," I said in a clear, firm voice. "I know you're in here."

Nobody answered and I was about to speak again when I looked back at the door, the key still stuck in the lock, and frowned. The room had been locked when I arrived, so how could a pupil have got inside in the first place?

"Hello?" I called again.

In return there was nothing but thick, dusty silence.

Perhaps I had imagined that giggle after all. Or it might have been a mouse squeaking. One of the girls had said she could hear mice scrabbling in the walls just the other day.

I lifted the candle a little higher, straining to see through the shadows. The room was mostly filled with travel trunks. The outline of a horse's head loomed out of the corner, giving me quite a start until I realized it was a hobby horse. There were some teddy bears next to it, along with a couple of dolls and a toy clown. No doubt Miss Grayson had confiscated them from their owners as punishment for some trivial offence or other. There definitely wasn't a girl there.

I lost no time in locating the package, which was still wrapped in brown paper, the school's address spelled out on the label in that hateful scrawl. It was definitely familiar. I swallowed hard, set the candle down on the floor and reached out towards the box with trembling hands. I'd intended to open it carefully, so that I could attempt to wrap it up again, but now all I could think of was ripping it to shreds as quickly as possible to find out what was inside. My whole body shuddered with the possibilities.

I tore open the brown paper and it fell away to reveal a beautifully made toy chest, painted silver and black. *Jemima* was written across the front in carved wooden letters. I could feel a sob rising up in my chest at the sight of it. The nightmare was meant to be over. This school was supposed to be my fresh start.

My fingers fumbled with the clasp and I could

hardly breathe as I lifted the lid. If there had been something as wretched as a severed limb or a rotting corpse inside I wouldn't have been surprised. So when I raised the candle, I was startled to see that the box was filled with dozens of little china Frozen Charlotte dolls, their naked bodies and painted hair smeared with dark soot and grey ash. A note, in the same spiked handwriting, lay on top of them, consisting of just four words:

Let's play a game...

My breath caught in my throat as I stared at the dolls. Of course they were Vanessa's – I recognized them from Whiteladies. They must have survived the fire somehow. Their painted eyes stared straight up at me as if they recognized me, too. They were all as pale as death, as white as corpses – all almost identical but for one solitary male doll right on top of the pile – a Frozen Charlie. I reached out towards it but as my fingertips brushed against another doll, I felt a sharp stab of pain and hurriedly snatched back my hand.

A bright bead of blood welled up on my finger and dripped on to a Frozen Charlotte, landing right where her heart would be, if she had one. I realized then that the dolls hadn't been well-packed for the journey and many of them had been damaged – an arm or a head or a leg snapped off, broken pieces rattling about at the bottom of the chest, like bones. I'd managed to cut myself on one of the jagged edges of the porcelain.

Suddenly I frowned. My eyes darted around the chest, looking for the male doll, but it was nowhere to be seen. It had been right on top before, standing out starkly among the female ones, and yet now it seemed to have vanished. There was a noise behind me and, this time, there was no mistaking it for anything other than what it was – a giggle.

I twisted round, still half crouched on the floor. "Who's there?" I cried.

The candle flickered, shadows shifting against the walls. There was someone in the room with me, I was quite certain of it. I turned back to the dolls and gasped. The male doll was right back where it had been before, perched on top of the others. I stared at it, my heart beating too fast and too hard in my chest.

Then I heard a voice, small and strange and shrill.

"Hide and go seek!"

There was the sound of breath being blown out in one puff. The candle was extinguished, filling the room with the scent of smoke and the cold horror of total, black darkness.

Chapter Five

Isle of Skye – January 1910

I leaped to my feet in the dark, my whole body trembling as I stumbled blindly towards the door of the luggage room.

Before I could reach it there was the scratch of a match being lit and a small girl all in white appeared before me in the doorway. For a wild moment I thought it was Vanessa Redwing but then the girl giggled and said, "Did we frighten you, miss?"

There was a second girl behind her in the corridor outside. My eyes focused and I saw I was looking at Martha and Bess, both dressed in nightgowns. Just a couple of students up past their bedtime, causing mischief. My breath came out of me in a relieved *whoosh*.

"Girls, you scared me half to death!" I exclaimed. Recalling that excited squeak of a voice in the dark – *hide and go seek!* – I realized one of the girls must have uttered those words and I was immediately

72

irritated with myself for giving in to the foolish fancy that the dolls had spoken. "It's extremely late and you shouldn't be out of bed. Now is certainly not the time for hide and seek!"

Martha frowned, looking confused. "Hide and seek, miss?"

"One of you said 'hide and seek' just now. I heard you," I said.

The girls shook their heads. "We didn't say anything. We only just got here."

"Please don't lie to me," I said with a sigh. "Look, it doesn't matter now. The important thing is that we get back to bed before Miss Grayson catches us and there's really trouble. What are you doing out of bed, anyway?"

"Estella woke us up," Martha said. "She woke everyone up."

"She said she had a nightmare," Bess put in. "About a doll who wanted to kill her."

"Goodness!" I exclaimed. "That sounds dreadful. But it doesn't explain why you two are down here in the basement."

Bess shuffled her feet, looking embarrassed, and it was Martha who spoke.

"We came to get George," she said. "Bess's teddy bear. Miss Grayson took him away because Bess made too many mistakes on her spelling test but she can't sleep without George, miss! And he was probably lonely down here all by himself. So we thought we'd just come and ... take him back."

I sighed again. "Don't you girls know the luggage room is kept locked? And won't Miss Grayson think it's odd that the teddy has just reappeared?"

"She's probably forgotten that she took him away in the first place," Bess said. "But if I ask for him back then she might hurt him." Her eyes suddenly filled with tears. "She killed Toby."

"Who's Toby?" I asked, startled.

"Bess caught a little mouse and named him Toby," Martha said. "But when Miss Grayson found out about it, she stamped on his head, miss."

I winced and Bess let out a sob. "She cracked his skull!" she said. "Sometimes I still hear the noise as I'm falling asleep." She really started to weep then.

"All right, all right." I hurriedly used Martha's candle to relight my own, held it up and said, "Can you see George in here?"

"He's there." Bess pointed with a trembling finger.

"On top of that suitcase."

I reached up for the bear, which was fat and fluffy and had warm, brown eyes – just the thing for making you feel less alone. I couldn't help wishing I was young enough that a stuffed teddy could do that for me, too.

I crouched down in front of Bess and held the bear out to her. "Here you go," I said. "And if Miss Grayson notices then you must say I gave him back to you, so you don't get into too much trouble."

Bess took the bear from me and then, to my surprise, threw her arms round my neck in a tight hug. I couldn't remember the last time I'd been hugged. It had probably been before Mother went away on her honeymoon and everything changed. I would have thought I'd recoil at physical touch now, yet the feeling of Bess's warm little body pressed up against mine was oddly comforting.

"Come on now," I said, giving her a squeeze. "It's absolutely freezing down here and you're shivering like anything. Can you take yourselves back to bed or do I need to supervise you?"

"We'll go straight back, miss," Martha promised.

"I'll be up to check on you in a moment," I said.

Once I'd heard their steps echo away down the corridor, I turned back to the box of Frozen Charlotte dolls. They lay there like little corpses in their coffin. I snatched the brown wrapping paper up off the floor to stare at the writing again – my name and address, spelled out in an uneven scrawl. Was it the same handwriting? Or was it just my mind playing tricks, making me see a resemblance that didn't exist?

Slowly I reached out and picked up one of the dolls. It lay cold and heavy in my palm. My fingers wrapped round the chilled body as I closed my eyes.

Charlotte says don't open the door, whispered that voice from my nightmare. *Charlotte says there are some horrors that burn…*

Suddenly, in the darkness of my mind, a flame flared into life and I was back at Whiteladies again. The smell of burning hair filled the air and a growing pool of blood spread across the floor towards my feet…

The Frozen Charlotte doll fell from my hand, smashing into pieces when it hit the floor. An arm here, a head there, a leg over in the corner. My heart beat its fast *thud, thud, thud* in my chest as I looked at the shattered doll and tried not to think about that last night at Whiteladies and what might have happened. I shoved the broken pieces of the china doll back into the toy chest and then closed the lid.

As quickly as I could, I replaced the key in Miss Grayson's desk and then went back up the stairs to the girls' dormitory to check all was well. There were no curtains and moonlight filtered in through the bare windows, providing just enough light to see by. Everybody seemed settled enough, including Bess and Martha who had returned to their beds, Bess with her arms wrapped round her teddy.

But when I walked over to Estella's bed, which was in the corner by the window, I saw that she was awake, clutching her thin bedsheet tightly enough to turn her knuckles white.

"Are you all right?" I whispered, crouching down by her side. "Bess said you had a nightmare."

Estella turned her head towards me. A strip of shadow fell across her bed from the window frame and I couldn't see her face properly as she spoke in a dull voice. "I dreamed there were dolls in the basement," she said. "Their china hands were knocking and their little fingers were scratching and their teeth were biting, and they wanted to get out and tear us all to pieces."

I frowned, unable to suppress a shudder, although I tried to tell myself that my reaction was simply a result of the icy temperature of the room. Still, it did seem a little odd that Estella should dream about dolls the very night a box of them arrived at the school.

"It's all right," I said. "It was only a dream." I thought of my own recurring nightmares and, seeking to reassure myself as much as Estella, I added, "Dreams can't hurt us."

"But the dolls—"

"Dolls can't hurt you, either, Estella," I told her. "Only people can."

Chapter Six

Isle of Skye – January 1910

After returning to my room, I hardly slept. The chest full of dolls played on my mind, causing a dull ache to start up behind my eyes. Several hours later, a strange blanket-like hush seemed to fill the air and, when I got up to look out of the window, I saw that it was snowing heavily, with a thick carpet already covering the ground. The moonlight reflected off the snow in a pinkish haze, making my headache even worse. By the time morning came I'd resolved to take the toy chest and throw it away but, when I went downstairs, I discovered that someone had already beaten me to the dolls.

Today was a Sunday and there would be church that morning but no formal classes. The girls had some free time after breakfast, during which Miss Grayson insisted they went outside to get some fresh air. She seemed to enforce this no matter how bad the weather might be and today was no different.

I went outside to find a small group of pupils, including Martha and Bess, wrapped up in their threadbare cloaks and hunched over something on the ground. I thought they were probably making snowmen but, as I got closer, I saw that they were playing with dolls and I stopped in my tracks. They were Frozen Charlottes.

"Where did you get those?" I asked. My breath smoked and my lips felt stiff in the freezing air.

The girls all fell silent at once and looked up at me guiltily.

"Well?" I said, when nobody spoke.

"They didn't want to be locked away in the luggage room, miss," Martha finally said. "They were lonely in there and cold."

Martha and Bess must have seen the dolls last night and decided to go back for them. I supposed that, for children who had nothing, an entire box of dolls was too much of a prize to ignore, even if they were broken and chipped. Unfortunately Miss Grayson chose just that moment to come out from her study and immediately asked about the Frozen Charlottes.

Panicking, I came out with the first lie I could think of. "Someone from the village just dropped them off," I said. "As a gift for the girls."

Miss Grayson narrowed her eyes and I could tell she didn't like this random act of kindness from a stranger but, in the absence of any sensible reason to object, she simply shook her head and pressed a key into my hand. "You may retrieve your parcel from the luggage room," she said. "I hope that you might have finally learned your lesson about time-keeping."

As soon as she was out of earshot I turned back to the girls and said, "How did you manage to get in without a key?"

Martha shrugged and said, "The door wasn't locked, miss."

I frowned. Had I forgotten to lock it behind me? I honestly couldn't remember. Either way, I thought I'd better get down there quickly, before Miss Grayson could discover anything amiss.

I left the girls to their game and hurried back downstairs to find that the door to the luggage room was indeed wide open. The toy chest stood in the middle of the floor, with the lid pushed back. It was completely empty – every doll had been removed and so had the note.

In the light of day, I suddenly noticed something I hadn't seen before and I frowned, peering closer. The inside of the lid was completely covered in scratch marks that crossed and criss-crossed each other over and over and over in angry-looking slashes.

Estella's words from last night came back to me: *Their china hands were knocking and their little fingers were scratching and their teeth were biting, and they wanted to get out...*

I shook my head. It had to be a coincidence. Squinting closer, I ran my fingertips over the marks. Could someone have shut a cat up in the box, perhaps? The scratches didn't seem quite deep enough for that, though. I saw that the sides were covered in similar marks.

It really was most odd. Perhaps some deranged person had filled the box with mice or rats? I shuddered at the thought but didn't have time to wonder about it. Miss Grayson would be expecting me at the school gates in a few minutes to accompany the girls into the village for the church service.

I gathered up the box and turned back to the door. And then stopped in surprise. All around the keyhole on the inside were dozens of marks, like scratches made by tiny claws or fingers. As if something had been trapped in here, seeking a way out. Had those marks been there last night? I didn't remember them but, in the candlelight, I probably wouldn't have seen them anyway.

Shaking my head, I left the luggage room, locking the door behind me before taking the chest up to my room. I just about had time to tie the ribbons of my black mourning bonnet under my chin before hurrying down to the school gate where the girls were already lined up waiting with Miss Grayson. I was sure she'd hoped to catch me being late again but this time I managed to deny her the pleasure.

We set off in procession with Miss Grayson leading the way, the girls following in pairs behind and me bringing up the rear. There was an odd number of girls and I noticed that Estella was walking on her own, up near the front. She often seemed to be the odd one out if the girls needed to split into pairs and she didn't appear to have any particular friends. Unfortunately what Miss Grayson had said my first morning about Estella being a compulsive liar did appear to be true to some degree – I had heard the other girls complaining about it and they seemed to avoid her where they could. No one likes to be the odd one out, though, and I had tried to make an effort to be particularly friendly towards her.

About five minutes after we set off, Henry caught up with us with Murphy. It took the best part of an hour to walk to the church in Dunvegan, which was too far for the little dog, so Henry had scooped him up, buttoning his coat round him so that only the dog's head poked free.

The clifftop had been transformed into smooth fields of white and the snow compacted beneath our boots with every step. In London the carriages and new motorcars usually turned the snow to muddy ice, so I rather enjoyed seeing this pristine country snow, even if my mind was still troubled with thoughts of the mystery package.

Henry chattered away as we walked and I did my best to respond to him but, when we were about halfway to the village, Henry said, "So do you want to tell me about it, Mim? Or should I mind my own business?"

"Tell you about what?" I asked.

"Whatever is bothering you," Henry replied.

"What makes you think anything is?"

Henry shrugged. "I can still tell when you're upset, you know," he said. "Plus I just asked you whether Miss Grayson was easing up on you a bit and you agreed with me that it was very cold weather, so I thought that perhaps you might not have been paying attention."

"I'm sorry," I sighed.

"Not at all," Henry replied. "Mother says that my ramblings are enough to bore the hind legs off an albatross."

"Isn't the saying meant to be a donkey?"

"I believe so, but nothing makes Mother more cross than being corrected over such things, as you may remember," Henry replied. "Fastest way to get your ears boxed for cheek, that. So is it Miss Grayson?" he asked. "Is she still being rather a witch?"

"Yes, but that's not the problem," I replied.

I hesitated for a moment, unsure whether I should confide in Henry or not. But then my eyes fell on the two girls directly in front of us – Violet and Olivia. They were two of the older girls, at around nine, and I saw that they were leaning over a Frozen Charlotte doll, clutched in Violet's gloved hand. The head of another doll poked out of Olivia's pocket. It seemed like its eyes were screwed up tight against the cold, its rosebud mouth pinched in distaste.

"A package arrived for me," I said. "A box of dolls."

Henry raised his eyebrows and I realized that a box of dolls didn't really sound like something to be overly concerned about.

"I think they were sent by someone ... from my past. Someone who wishes me ill."

Henry gave me an astonished look. "Why on earth would anyone wish you ill?" he asked.

He looked so genuinely puzzled by the idea that I was on the verge of telling him everything. But before I could say another word, one of the girls suddenly cried out, "No!"

I looked up in time to see Olivia give Violet a push that sent her tumbling on to her knees in the snow.

"No!" Olivia said again. "Charlotte says *you're* the bitch!"

Those two words, *Charlotte says*, hit me like a slap in the face and for a moment I was speechless. Henry hurried forwards to help Violet to her feet and I grabbed Olivia by the arm, turning her round to face me.

"Olivia!" I said sharply. "You do not speak to other girls like that!"

She was usually such a well-behaved little thing. I had never seen her act in such a way before.

"I don't know what could have got into you!" I said. "If Miss Grayson had heard you just then you would have been punished severely – probably have spent an entire day in Solitary."

I had since learned that the 'Solitary' I had seen written down in the Punishment Book was a reference to a little hut that stood in the school grounds. Particularly naughty pupils were sometimes locked in there to contemplate their wickedness. During that time, they were not allowed to see or speak to anyone, there were no toilet facilities and they were denied food. I'd heard the girls talking about Solitary with a keen sense of dread, due to the fact that Estella had become ill and almost died after an extended spell in there last summer, apparently for telling a particularly spectacular lie, although I wasn't too sure of the details. No doubt this was why she looked pale and sickly even now.

Startled by my harsh tone, Olivia burst into tears and said, "I'm sorry, miss. It's just that Charlotte said—"

"Do *not* blame your behaviour on dolls," I said. I took the Frozen Charlotte from her and put it into my own pocket. "If you can't play nicely with them then they'll be taken away. Now, apologize to Violet this instant."

Olivia turned to the other girl. "Sorry, Violet," she mumbled.

"Life's too short to squabble with friends, you two," Henry said cheerfully. He dug in his coat pocket and gave each of the girls a sticky toffee.

"How about you, Mim?" he asked, falling back into step beside me and offering me a sweet.

I took the toffee and, as our fingers touched, I felt a shiver run through me. Part of me still shrank from physical contact and yet some other part of me longed to take Henry's hand in mine.

"So this parcel, then," he said. "Why do you—?"

I shook my head. "Never mind," I said brusquely. "Forget I said anything."

We were almost at the church now and I hoped he would let the matter drop. I should not have said anything in the first place.

He was silent for a moment before brushing his fingers lightly against my sleeve. "I'm sure it's just a misunderstanding, Mim," he said. "No one could ever wish you ill. You're the best person I know."

I shook my head and pushed his hand away. "I'm sorry, Henry, but you don't really know me any more. If you did, then you wouldn't say a thing like that."

Henry tightened his grip on my sleeve to stop me on the path.

"Jemima—" he began, looking troubled.

I pulled my arm free. "Please forget I said anything. I'm sure you're quite right and the dolls were meant as a gift."

We'd arrived at the church and I walked in with the girls before Henry could say anything further. I heard him say my name and try to follow but a verger spotted Murphy and stopped him at the door. Henry must have momentarily forgotten that dogs were not allowed in the church and went to tie Murphy up outside.

Meanwhile I took my place in the pews and prepared to worship a god I no longer believed in.

No one could ever wish you ill... Henry's words echoed in my head and I dug my nails into my palms. It was a sickening thing to have someone hate you so much that they physically wished to hurt you but unfortunately it was a sensation I was all too familiar with.

I kept my eyes fixed on the lectern in front of me and tried to force my mind to remain in the present moment. If I didn't think about Whiteladies then perhaps it might be almost as if it had never happened.

Chapter Seven

Whiteladies – Eighteen months earlier

I peered out of the carriage window and marvelled at the multitude of glorious white towers and turrets that made up the eighteenth-century building in front of us. It looked more like a castle than a home. The two chestnut horses came to a stop at the end of the drive and Mother gave me one of her sudden grins.

"Ready to put on a show, darling?" she said.

I smiled back at her. "Lead the way."

We stepped out into a bright summer's day that immediately made me feel rather uncomfortable in my grey velvet outfit. Mother insisted on these gowns whenever we visited a house as mediums. Our tailored dresses and matching coats were designed to resemble the most fashionable garments from Paris although they had, in fact, been made in a London back room by Mrs Collins. Mother had picked a shade called 'ashes of roses', which she felt struck just the right tone for a séance. She'd even given up her favoured floral bonnets in order to sport a more impressive wide-brimmed hat, complete with a plume of dark ostrich feathers.

I wore a similar hat, although I longed to remove it so that I might feel the sun on my face. Before I could think of doing so, the front door swung open and a middle-aged man came striding out. He didn't look like a servant so I thought this must be Edward Redwing.

As with all her clients, Mother had done her background research the moment he contacted us, and we knew him to be one of the newest members of the Ghost Club – the prestigious paranormal research organization founded in London almost fifty years ago, and graced by the likes of writers such as Charles Dickens and Sir Arthur Conan Doyle.

We also knew that Edward Redwing had been particularly active in London's spiritualist scene ever since his six-year-old daughter, Vanessa, died in a horse-riding accident a couple of months earlier.

As the man hurried down the steps towards us, I saw that he wore a perfectly tailored grey suit the exact same shade as his eyes and carried an ornate silver-topped cane. To my surprise, he was glaring quite ferociously.

"Out!" he cried, brandishing the cane. For a shocked moment I thought he meant us, but then I realized he was gesturing at the carriage driver. "Get them out!" he said. "I'll have no horses at Whiteladies! Damn your eyes, didn't you see the sign at the gate?"

The driver hastily gathered up the reins and sent the horses trotting back down the drive. Composing himself with an obvious effort, Redwing turned to us and said, in a voice that was absolutely, almost unnervingly, calm, "I apologize for my outburst, ladies, as well as my language. I'm afraid that ever since my daughter's death, I have not been able to tolerate the sight of horses. It's ... become almost a sort of phobia, you see."

I noticed his right hand shaking slightly as he smoothed back a loose strand of hair, while his left gripped his cane so tightly that his knuckles were white. The cane was an elaborate object made from rosewood, with a solid silver topper in the shape of a vicious-looking hawk that had gleaming, blood-red rubies for eyes.

"My behaviour is inexcusable," Redwing went on. "I hope you can forgive me."

He had quite the most beautiful voice I'd ever heard – deep and mellow and somehow magnetic.

"My dear Mr Redwing, there is nothing to forgive," my mother said, taking charge of the situation. "The fault was ours entirely. And, of course, we perfectly understand how unspeakable it is to be bereaved in such a way as you have been."

"Unspeakable." Redwing murmured the word back at her, a startled look in his grey eyes. "Yes. You are right. Do you know, that is the first time anyone has used a word even remotely suitable to describe the … the magnitude of what I have lost." He shook himself and said, "Allow me to welcome you properly to Whiteladies. I am Edward Redwing, and you must be the renowned medium Elizabeth Black and this is your charming daughter. Jacqueline, was it?"

"Jemima, sir," I said, bobbing him a curtsy.

"Delighted to make your acquaintance, miss," Redwing said with a bow. "Please do come in. Tea will be served in the drawing room and then we will retire to the parlour, which has been prepared in accordance with your instructions for tonight's séance."

We followed Redwing up the steps into the entranceway of Whiteladies – a vast, white marble portrait hall dominated by an ornate double staircase that curled up and around to the first floor. A magnificent stained-glass window let in plenty of light from above and I saw that there were multiple hawks depicted in the glass – wings spread, talons extended, red eyes gleaming. Two more hawks, carved from dark, shining wood, sat atop the balustrades at the foot of the staircase. Almost every inch of wall space was taken up with portraits. And they all depicted the same person: Vanessa Redwing.

She'd been a pretty girl, with a tumble of curls as dark as her father's, blue eyes and an engaging smile. Along with the usual formal portraits, there were other paintings that showed her sitting in the garden or at play in the nursery. They were beautiful oil paintings and there had clearly been no expense spared in their commission but, even so, there was something a little disconcerting about having a dead girl gazing down at you from every angle. There weren't even any paintings of the late Mrs

Redwing, who we knew to have died in childbirth. The hall was a shrine to little Vanessa.

"This, of course, is my daughter," Redwing said, gesturing at the paintings. "The reason I invited you here. And why I want to hold a séance at Whiteladies." He looked at my mother with an almost painful expression of desperation. "Vanessa is here in the house, madam, I'm certain of it. Just yesterday I was sure I heard her singing in the garden. And last night I heard her running up and down the stairs well into the early hours. She was just outside my door. The servants have sensed her, too. She's often in the nursery, playing with her toys. The teddy bears move around in there from one day to the next." He straightened his shoulders a little and said, "I consider myself a steady sort of man, Mrs Black, and please believe me when I say I am not given to wild flights of fancy or imagining things as I wish them to be. My daughter's spirit haunts this house and nothing will convince me otherwise."

"You've come to the right person, sir," my mother assured him, easily slipping into her comforting tone. "Spirits often linger after their passing so I would not be at all surprised if your daughter is still here. With our assistance, you are sure to break through the veil that separates our world from theirs."

I hardly listened to my mother's speech. I'd heard it, in one form or another, many times before.

"Do you have something of Vanessa's?" Mother asked. "As I said in my letter, it'll make it easier for us to establish a connection with her."

"I have just the thing," Redwing said. He set his cane down against the wall and then produced a white porcelain doll from his coat pocket.

Completely white from head to toe, I immediately recognized it as a Frozen Charlotte doll. I'd had one myself when I'd been younger and remembered the tale that went with it, of a silly, vain girl named Charlotte, who froze to death because she refused to wrap up warm on a carriage ride to a ball with her fiancé. It was a freezing New Year's Eve and she was a corpse by the time the carriage arrived at its destination.

Let that be a lesson to you, Jemima, my mother had said laughingly as she gave me the doll. *Don't allow yourself to become vain and conceited or you'll end up like Charlotte here...*

I looked at the Frozen Charlotte in Redwing's hand and it struck me as appropriate that he'd chosen a dead toy as a way of communicating with his deceased daughter.

"Vanessa loved those dolls," he said. "She had a whole collection of them." He swallowed hard. "She was dreadfully shy, you see, dreadfully timid, a reserved sort of girl. I believe she enjoyed spending time with ... with horses more than she enjoyed being around people." His expression twisted suddenly as he was gripped by a fresh spasm of grief. "She said she felt most comfortable with her own horse, Blackie. That he understood her and made her feel safe. I cannot bear the irony of it!" He took a deep breath and went on. "People made her tongue-tied and awkward. So she would use the dolls to talk to guests, servants, even me sometimes. *Charlotte says she is tired and would like to go to bed. Charlotte says the thunder is too loud and hurts her ears. Charlotte says she doesn't want to go out in the rain.* That sort of thing."

Mother took the doll from Redwing to examine it, then nodded her approval before handing it back.

"You'll speak to your daughter again tonight, Mr Redwing," she said. "I'm quite sure of it."

Chapter Eight

Isle of Skye – January 1910

The service came to an end and we filed out into the churchyard. To my relief, Henry was unusually quiet as we walked back and did not bring up the subject of the dolls again. When we arrived at the school, he returned to his cottage and I followed Miss Grayson inside. I was just removing my cloak when the schoolmistress said to me carelessly, "Another parcel arrived for you yesterday, Miss Black. I asked the servants to deliver it to your room this morning."

I didn't waste time asking why on earth she'd waited until now and hadn't had it sent to my room yesterday. Instead I made straight for the stairs, desperate to know what this second parcel might contain.

When I opened the door to my room I saw that the second box was similar in size to the first and addressed to me in what looked like the same spiked handwriting. When I ripped open the brown paper,

I found that there was a letter inside.

The parcel was from Edward Redwing's solicitors, Messrs Goadsby, Grimes and Scott. The writer of this particular letter was Mr Vincent Grimes, and in it he expressed his condolences for my loss and explained that they were in the process of packing up the few items that had survived the fire at Whiteladies, including this dolls' house which was, miraculously, completely unharmed.

Relief washed over me. The solicitors must have sent the box of dolls, too, and simply neglected to include a covering letter. How foolish of me to think that Redwing had sent them. The man was dead after all and ghosts did not send post – one did not have to be a medium to know that. I picked up the brown paper and re-examined the handwriting. The penmanship was a little spiky, to be sure, but I saw now that it was quite different from Redwing's script. In my panic, I was seeing similarities where there were none.

Even so, the sight of the dolls' house sent a shiver through me. It had been Vanessa's and was an exact replica of Whiteladies itself, complete with the elegant white towers that had given the house its name. Edward Redwing had had it specially commissioned for one of Vanessa's birthdays and it was an exquisite work of art. Even the interior décor and furniture of the various rooms mirrored those of the real house.

The entire front swung open to reveal replica carpets, minute brass candlesticks and a miniature grandfather clock that actually ticked, tocked and chimed out the hours, although I noticed that it appeared to have stopped on six o'clock which, oddly, was the exact hour I heard chiming in my nightmare.

The dolls' house was installed with battery-powered electric lighting that could be controlled by switches at the back of the house. Tiny versions of the oil paintings hung in the portrait hall and the doorknobs were the same, too, including the one on the study door. It was stamped with the Redwing coat of arms, with its two hawks on either side of the shield.

I peered at that door now, thinking of my dream again. Something had happened in that room. Something terrible.

Charlotte says don't open the door…

I took the doll that I'd confiscated from Olivia out of my pocket and placed her in the living room. The Frozen Charlottes weren't really designed for a dolls' house. The fact that her limbs weren't jointed made it impossible to sit her down on the chaise longue and, when I tried to lean her against it, she simply slid to the floor and lay stiffly on the rug, her hands held up in a fixed position in front of her.

Her movement upset the nearby umbrella stand, sending Redwing's replica cane, with the silver hawk top, rolling out across the floor. Unlike the real cane, this one didn't have rubies for eyes but glass gemstones instead.

Automatically I reached out to pick it up but, when my fingers were inches away, I stopped dead. I simply could not touch it. It was the same instinctive aversion one might have to stroking a wasp.

I righted the umbrella stand and left the cane where it was on the floor. Then I shut the front of the house with a snap and immediately sat down to write a letter to the solicitors, thanking them for the Frozen Charlottes and dolls' house but requesting that they sell off everything else at auction. I had no wish to have anything that had come out of that house.

I also asked in my letter about where the toy chest with my name on it had come from. I could not remember ever seeing it before and it was an irritating unanswered question that niggled away at the back of my mind. But then I hit on what appeared to me to be an explanation. The solicitor who had sent the dolls must have seen my school address and mistakenly believed me to be an orphaned child – a pupil at the school rather than a mistress. Feeling sorry for me, they must have had the toy chest made up as an act of charity.

Feeling pleased with this explanation, I folded the letter and sealed up the envelope, just as there was a knock at my door. I went over to answer it, only to find Henry on the other side.

"You shouldn't be up here," I said, glancing down the corridor. "Miss Grayson will be most irate if she sees you."

"Miss Grayson can go to the devil," Henry said as he neatly stepped past me, into the room. "I absolutely must speak to you and it cannot wait. I have delayed this conversation for far too long already."

I closed the door and turned to face him warily. "Is something wrong?" I asked.

"Undoubtedly," Henry replied. "Something has been quite wrong since the moment you arrived here. At first I thought it was because you had been through a great ordeal with the fire. Then, if you'll forgive my self-absorption, I thought perhaps it might be because your feelings for me had changed and you didn't know how to break it to me. But now I see that it is more than that. Something has happened. Something is wrong, and I will not move from this spot until you have told me what it is and how I can help you."

With that he plopped himself down on the floor cross-legged, gazing up at me with a look of calm defiance.

"You silly fool," I said. "There is nothing wrong."

"Just this morning you said you were being sent mystery parcels by someone who wished you ill," Henry said. "That's enough to make a chap feel quite alarmed, Jemima." His eyes narrowed. "Who is it? Tell me and, whoever they are, whatever they want from you, I will pay them a visit and ensure you are never bothered by them again."

I sighed. "Henry," I said. "I know I've been a bit distant since I arrived and I'm sorry. But there really is nothing wrong. The dolls were just a misunderstanding. They were actually sent by Mr Redwing's solicitor, as was the dolls' house there." I gestured at it. "It was just my mind playing tricks on me."

"But—"

"Listen to me, please," I said. "In the last month I've lost my mother and my stepfather, and my home has burned to the ground. I like to think I'm a steady enough girl and you know I've never been prone to fits of fainting or hysterics, but it's a lot, Henry. It's an awful lot for anyone to have to cope with."

Henry was on his feet again and coming towards me. "Mim—" he began.

But I took a step back and held up a hand. "As for the things we said to each other when we were children," I said, "those were just childish fantasies. Nothing more."

Henry stopped and I saw some strange emotion pass across his face. "You no longer care for me in that way," he said. "That is what you are saying?"

I couldn't look at him. "We were only children playing at make-believe."

I fully expected Henry to bluster. To backtrack and tell me that he didn't feel that way about me, either, that this was all a misunderstanding between us.

Instead he gazed at me with those honest green eyes of his and simply said, "My dear thing, it was never a game for me. I'll have no misunderstandings between us on that account. The truth is that I have loved you from the moment I laid eyes on you. I love you still. But if my feelings aren't reciprocated then I hope I'm enough of a gentleman to accept that with good grace." He gave me a crooked smile but his eyes were sad. "We've been friends for almost our whole lives, Mim, and I hope you can still think of me as a friend now. I can be quite content with that. If everything is all right then I'm glad. And, if it isn't, then just know that you can always come to me and I will do whatever I can to help you."

In that moment I wanted nothing more than to walk over, grab him by the lapels of his shabby coat and kiss him as fiercely as I could. But what then? I still couldn't tell him the truth about what had happened to me at Whiteladies. I couldn't explain how I had come by my extensive collection of scars. So I swallowed the impulse down, opened the door of my bedroom and said, "Thank you for coming to check on me, Henry. You were always a good friend."

Chapter Nine

Whiteladies – Eighteen months earlier

The white Frozen Charlotte doll stood out starkly against the dark fabric of the séance table.

"Let us begin," my mother said.

We had taken over the parlour in order to conduct our séance. The circular walnut table in the centre had been draped with a black tablecloth; the lights in the glittering chandelier above us had been extinguished; the mirrors had been covered with shrouds, and candles had been placed on the large marble mantelpiece and throughout the room.

Once I would have felt a little thrill of excitement at this point, but not any more, for I had long since lost any belief in ghosts.

You may have the gift, Jemima, my mother had said to me many times. *It passed me by, but these things can skip a generation. Your grandmother didn't discover her ability until she was seventeen, you know. Girls of that age are more susceptible to psychic phenomena, more sensitive to the spirit world. It's the age when ghosts are most drawn to you and your abilities are strongest…*

I couldn't help thinking that, in all likelihood, my grandmother had been every bit as much of a fraud as my mother was, even if she had believed her own performance. After conducting hundreds of fake séances with never so much as a whisper of a ghost, I was now quite sure that, wherever people went after they died, they did not linger here on earth.

"I need you all to hold hands and form a circle," Mother said.

Redwing had invited some of his gentlemen occultist friends and there were eight of us altogether. Mother and I were sat opposite each other so I found myself holding hands with a Ghost Club member named Mr Jasper on one side and Edward Redwing himself on the other.

I was surprised by how cold and clammy Redwing's hand was when he folded his fingers around mine. A chill crept down my back and I resisted the urge to shiver.

"I must ask for complete silence," my mother went on. She had added some jet-black mourning jewellery to her grey dress, along with a mourning ring that she had picked up in a pawn shop. She had also powdered her face in order to make it seem even paler in the candlelight.

"Until we have successfully made contact," Mother said, "the only people who may speak are my daughter and myself. As we know, spirits are more attracted to women because of our delicate sensitivities." I inwardly rolled my eyes at this. "Spirits can be nervous about approaching the living – and men, in particular," she went on. "Any sudden loud noises may frighten them away." The candle on the table was there for the sole purpose of casting an eerie glow over Mother's face as she closed her eyes. "We pray for protection from any negative apparitions or ill-intentioned spectres and ask that only friendly spirits join us tonight." She opened her eyes and addressed the guests once again. "Do not break the circle under any circumstances or the psychic energy will be lost. And now, let us begin."

She took a deep breath. "We are here today to try to make contact with Vanessa Redwing. Vanessa, are you there? If you can hear me, please follow the sound of my voice."

I noticed the gentlemen's eyes darting around the room, no doubt looking for some sign of a ghost – perhaps a blur in a dark window pane or a faint childish giggle or shoes protruding from beneath a curtain. The flickering candlelight cast everything in jumping shadows that made it all too easy to see signs of supernatural activity. In reality, we had near-darkness during the séances in order that we might engage in table-tipping and wood-knocking more easily.

My gaze returned to the Frozen Charlotte doll, lying cold and stiff on the table, as I waited for Mother to resume the script.

"What was that?" she asked suddenly, right on cue. "Did anyone hear that noise?"

"Yes, I heard something," one gentleman promptly said with confidence. There was always one person at every séance who could see and hear absolutely everything.

There had been no noise, of course, and I knew that my mother was just acting, but the men glanced round at each other. It did not take much effort to create an unnerving atmosphere. Sitting quietly in the candlelight, waiting for spirits to appear from the unknown was enough to set people a little on edge. And until someone had sat silently in a dark room, they didn't realize quite how much noise a house could make all by itself. Doors creaked, pipes gurgled, floorboards settled, the wind rattled the windows in their frames, all without any help from a ghost. Houses talked all the time, it was just that nobody ever thought to listen.

"Yes, there is someone there," Mother went on. "Vanessa, is that you? Don't be afraid, dear. You're with friends. Please give us a sign to let us know you're here."

This was my cue to shift my leg in such a way as to rock the table, which I did automatically. Redwing's hand tightened around mine at the movement and someone on the other side of the table gasped.

"Did one of you do that?" demanded a member of the Ghost Club, staring round at everyone accusingly.

The others assured him that they had kept perfectly still the entire time.

"Quiet, please," Mother said before continuing with her performance. "Vanessa, dear, that was very good. Now, we're going to ask you some questions and I'd like you to try to answer them by knocking on the table, giving us one rap for yes and two raps for no. First of all: are you Vanessa Redwing?"

My boot had been specially adapted by Henry's mother so that it had a small wooden block concealed in the toe. Taking care not to move my upper body in any way, I kicked once against the table leg. Redwing tightened his grip on my hand even further, until it was on the verge of being painful.

"Vanessa," Mother said softly. "I'm so sorry about your terrible accident. Your father is here, dear, and wants you to know that he loves you very much." She looked at Redwing and said, "You can ask her a question if you like."

For a moment he was silent. I glanced at Redwing and saw that beads of sweat had formed at his hairline. He swallowed hard, then said hoarsely, "Are you all right?"

I moved my foot and kicked once on the table leg for yes. He asked if she was in pain and I kicked twice for no. The séance continued on in this manner for some time until, finally, Mother gave me the sign to finish.

"Vanessa has left us," she said. "The lights can be switched back on."

Over the following months, Mother and I returned to carry out several more séances at Whiteladies. We used all our usual tricks and acting ability, but none of it seemed to be sufficient to satisfy Edward Redwing that he really had spoken to his daughter.

It was, however, enough to make him take a shine to Mother for other reasons. She was quite delighted when she realized he was courting her and I was rather pleased myself. After all, professional mediumship wasn't the most reliable work and we were often left short at the end of the month. A life at Whiteladies meant luxury, status, comfort and privilege. I would miss having all of Mother's attention to myself, but she had spent seventeen years bringing me up, mostly on her own. My father had died after being knocked down by a carriage when I was only a toddler and then my grandmother had passed away eight years later. If a chance of love and companionship and comfort were offered to my mother, I certainly wouldn't do anything to spoil that.

It was a sunny afternoon in March and Redwing had arrived at our lodgings to visit about an hour previously when Mother called me downstairs. I walked into the sitting room to see them standing before the fireplace together, hand in hand, and I knew at once that the proposal had been made.

"Jemima, my dear, something quite wonderful has happened," Mother said, beaming at me with an expression of pure happiness. "Mr Redwing has asked me to marry him and I have accepted."

I offered them my genuine congratulations.

Redwing let go of my mother and walked across the room to stand in front of me. Taking both my hands in his, he leaned forwards slightly and said, "You will, of course, join us at Whiteladies, Jemima, and live with us for as long as you wish. I want you to think of the house as your home. I can assure you that every effort will be made to see to your comfort and happiness, as well as your mother's."

The words were friendly and there was nothing but sincerity in his eyes as he looked at me. Everything was going to be wonderful, I thought.

But the day my mother and Edward Redwing returned from their honeymoon, I knew immediately that something was dreadfully wrong. That a mistake had been made that could not be undone.

Chapter Ten

Isle of Skye – January 1910

When I returned to my bedroom after lunch I opened the door of the dolls' house to retrieve the Frozen Charlotte, only to find that she had moved. She was no longer in the living room where I had placed her. At first, I thought she'd disappeared altogether but then I spotted her in Edward Redwing's study. She was lying on the floor in front of the desk, covered in a curtain, like a dead body in a shroud. Only her hands were visible, sticking up straight in front of her as if she was clawing for air.

One of the girls must have been in here playing. My mind instantly went to Estella. Of all the pupils, she was the naughtiest and the only one bold enough to come into my room like that. I glanced around, half expecting to see her hiding under the bed or sneaking out of the door, but the place was empty.

I turned back to the dolls' house, picked the curtain off the Frozen Charlotte and carefully slid it back on to the tiny rail. Then I noticed that the cane had moved, too. Someone had put it on the desk in Redwing's study.

Unlike all the other rooms, the study was not quite the same as the real one. The horse's skull was missing from the wall and in its place there was a stag's head, which I assumed was what had been there when Vanessa was alive, before Redwing had taken a rifle down to the stable and put a bullet in her beloved horse's brain.

I took the Frozen Charlotte and put her in the dining room, lying her down on the rug in front of the fire. It felt wrong somehow to leave her in Redwing's study.

I didn't particularly want the dolls' house – or to be reminded of Whiteladies. It was probably worth quite a lot of money and I supposed I could have sold it, but remembering how Bess had cried over her teddy I decided to give it to the girls instead.

I left my room and was about to go downstairs when I heard a girl humming to herself in the room next door to mine. Miss Grayson insisted on calling this the toy room although, in reality, it held precious few toys. There was a morose-looking rocking horse, a broken Jack-in-the-box and a few incomplete sewing kits.

The tune the girl was humming was one my mother used to sing for me when I was little. It was the 'Fair Charlotte' ballad – the story of the vain girl who froze to death in her finery.

Such a dreadful night I never saw,
The reins I scarce can hold.
Fair Charlotte, shivering faintly said,
I am exceedingly cold...

The girls were all supposed to read from their Bibles for half an hour after lunch and I knew Miss Grayson would be cross if she found one of the pupils up here so I pushed open the toy room door and stepped inside. Bess was sitting by herself in the middle of the floor. She had her back to me and was hunched over something, slicing at it with a pair of scissors.

"Bess, what are you doing in here?" I said. "You're supposed to be downstairs with the others."

She didn't reply or turn round, but continued humming that irritating little tune and snipping away with the scissors. I wondered whether she might be making a dress for one of the Frozen Charlottes.

I recalled that was why the dolls came unclothed and remembered how my mother had given me scraps of fabric to make little dresses for my own Frozen Charlotte.

I strode past Bess and then gasped. She wasn't making a dress. She was cutting up George, her teddy bear. Stuffing spilled out on to the floor as she calmly snipped off his ear and then slashed at his face, a button eye coming loose to roll along the floorboards.

"Bess, what are you doing?" I cried.

She finally looked up at me and I saw there were tears in her eyes. "The Frozen Charlottes told me to do it," she whispered. "They don't like the other toys."

"Give me those," I said, snatching the scissors away from her. "Now go downstairs and join the others before Miss Grayson notices you're missing."

With one last look at her teddy bear, Bess left the room. I put the scissors back in the supply cupboard with the sewing kits and then bent down to gather up the scraps of bear. She had done a thorough job – George was nothing more than a sad collection of fur and fluff. There was no chance he could be repaired so I disposed of the scraps before making my way downstairs, still shaking my head over Bess's extraordinary behaviour. Just last night she'd seemed so desperate to retrieve George from the luggage room and yet hours later she was cutting him into shreds.

After checking that Bess really had joined the other girls, I made my way to Miss Grayson's study and told her that I'd received a dolls' house from my late step-father's estate, which I would like to donate to the school. I could see Miss Grayson didn't much care for the idea of the girls having such a thing – perhaps she thought it would make them spoiled – but she seemed unable to come up with an objection so the house was duly placed in the toy room.

When I went to bed later, my mind was full of Whiteladies and Redwing and the agony of not knowing what had happened that night. So I was awake around midnight to hear the quiet creak of the floorboards as someone walked past my room. Thinking one of the girls must be wandering around out there, I got up, lit a candle and stepped into the corridor.

There was indeed a girl there, wearing a long, white nightdress, with fair hair spilling down her back. Then she turned round and I saw it was Estella. Her eyes were huge in the gloom and the dark circles round them looked like bruises.

"What are you doing out of bed?" I asked her quietly. "Did you have another nightmare?"

Estella shook her head. "It's the dolls," she said. "They're whispering together in the toy room. Can't you hear them?"

"Don't be ridiculous."

"The dolls are bad," Estella insisted. "Whiskers can sense it, too. He was in there earlier, hissing at them."

"Whiskers is a silly old cat," I said. "I wouldn't pay any attention to him."

"But, miss, they *are* talking! Talking about something terrible—"

"Estella! This is no time for games. Go back to bed, please."

She gave me a black look but returned to the dormitory. Once she'd gone I paused in the corridor, listening. The school was quite silent.

I shook my head and went back to bed.

The next morning I awoke early and glanced out of the window to see that the school was still surrounded by snow, with fresh flakes falling. I thought it looked ever so pretty and was feeling in rather a good mood as I went downstairs.

As an assistant mistress, I sensed it wasn't quite my place to be in the kitchen, but I was desperate for a cup of tea and, at this time of the day, the kitchen was the only room in the entire school that would be halfway warm. Besides, I knew that Henry often spent time in there and if it was all right for the drawing master to do so then surely it would be all right for me, too. Indeed, when I walked in Henry was already there, lounging in one of the chairs by the fire, Murphy at his feet. Cassie was perched on the arm of his chair in what she clearly felt was a fetching manner. She was giggling in an over-the-top way at something Henry had said and I realized at once that she was sweet on him.

I felt a powerful flash of jealousy that took me by surprise. But what had I expected? Henry was wonderful. Of course other girls would be interested in him. I could not expect him to sit around pining for me forever. Still, he could do so much better than a giggling fool like Cassie.

After the frank conversation we'd had in my bedroom the night before, I was a little nervous about seeing Henry again but, as soon as he saw me, he grinned and beckoned me over, pushing out the other chair. Cassie narrowed her eyes as I sat down in it.

"The cottage was freezing last night," Henry said, referring to the single-storey dwelling on the grounds that he occupied. "I thought I'd come in to warm up."

Mrs String and Hannah both ignored me but Cassie got up and made a great show of fetching me a cup of tea. I would've liked to have thrown it straight back in her face. She was clearly only trying to seem kind in order to impress Henry. I'd known other girls like this in my time and the two-facedness was the thing that always vexed me the most.

"Miss Black, have you seen Whiskers?" Cassie asked, simpering a little as she pressed the teacup into my hands.

"Please," I said in my sweetest voice, forcing a smile, "do call me Jemima." Two could play at that game, after all.

"Jemima, then," Cassie said. "He's usually here first thing in the morning yowling for his milk, you see, but I haven't seen him today. And I'm ever so fond of him."

Fond enough to kick him outside the kitchen the other day? I longed to say.

"He's probably out hunting," Henry told her.

"Not in this weather," Cassie replied. "Whiskers absolutely hates the snow." She put on a worried face. "Oh dear, I wonder where he could be?"

She glanced at Henry and I resisted the urge to roll my eyes. This show of concern was obviously more for his benefit than for the cat's.

"Estella mentioned seeing him in the toy room yesterday," I said. "Perhaps he got shut in there. I'll take a look after breakfast. The girls were in and out of there looking at the dolls' house all evening."

"Dolls' house?" Henry repeated.

"The one the solicitor sent," I said. "It was no use to me so I thought the girls may as well have it."

"That was jolly decent of you, Mim," Henry exclaimed. "It looked terribly expensive. Still, it explains all the activity last night."

"Activity?" I looked at him.

"Yes, I noticed it from the cottage. Several times I saw the lights turning on and off in the toy room after bedtime."

I frowned, unsure. Had the girls been sneaking in there to play? They would have had to pass my room first and I was certain I would have heard them. There was no more time to wonder about it just then, though, because the school was waking up.

I snatched a piece of toast from a plate and ate it as I walked out. It was meanly scraped with the merest hint of butter and felt too dry in my mouth – I found myself having to force it down. I followed the girls into the hall, noticing as I did so that Estella looked unusually tired, as if she'd hardly slept at all. Perhaps she hadn't stayed in her bed after I'd sent her there, but had gone to the toy room later on?

Before I could ponder it any further, there was the sudden smash of breaking crockery. I looked over to see Felicity pick up a plate and then, very deliberately, throw it straight on the floor, where it shattered alongside the first one.

Miss Grayson was by her side in an instant, demanding an explanation. Everyone had gone quiet and I distinctly heard Felicity say that the Frozen Charlottes had told her to do it.

The schoolmistress reacted with predictable anger and Felicity received a whipped palm for her lie.

Using the commotion as an excuse to slip away, I went back upstairs and walked down the corridor. When I opened the toy-room door, I half expected Whiskers to come shooting out between my legs, meowing in loud, indignant protest, but the room was silent. I pushed the door open all the way but couldn't properly make out the interior – the sun wouldn't rise for at least another half hour. My hand found the gaslight on the wall and I heard the hiss of air as it ignited.

I saw the scissors first, the blades red and glistening on the floor at my feet. Suddenly the room was too quiet. I felt like there were a hundred pairs of eyes staring at me, willing me to look up, waiting for my reaction.

Slowly I raised my head. When I'd left the room the previous day, the dolls had been tucked away in the toy chest but now every single one of them was out. The broken ones lay in neat lines by the chest, but the complete dolls were standing with their little china feet balanced on the wooden floorboards, hands stretched out in front of them. Every one of them faced towards the door, as if they'd been waiting for someone to walk in.

But that wasn't all. The contents of the sewing kits had been emptied out across the floor. I saw a second pair of bloody scissors by the windowsill and a third by the toy chest. And the blood was not only on the scissors. It was smeared across the floorboards, too. It was on the walls. It was on the frozen windowpanes.

So one of the girls *had* been in here, playing with the dolls. There were doll-sized footprints in the blood on the floor, and tiny handprints in the blood on the walls and on the windows. When I looked more closely at the Frozen Charlottes I saw that many of them had dried blood staining their white fingers or peeling in rust-coloured flakes from their feet. I swallowed, my heart beating too hard against my ribs. Where had all that blood come from?

My eye fell on the toy chest and I noticed that the lid was closed. Being careful not to step in the blood, I walked over and opened it.

I had never been at all squeamish and the sight of blood didn't normally bother me in the least, but I couldn't help gasping.

I had found what was left of Whiskers.

For a long moment as I stared down at the dead cat I simply didn't know what to do. Should I inform Miss Grayson? Or quietly dispose of the body and clean up the blood before anyone could find out what had happened?

Children could be cruel sometimes but this was the most shocking violence. My main thought was that the girls mustn't see Whiskers. The cat was not merely dead, it had been butchered. It was the work of a deranged mind. Surely none of the girls could be capable of something like this?

"Let's play a game…"

I whirled round, expecting to see one of the girls, but the room was empty. When I hurried over to the door, however, I found Estella out in the corridor. She looked up at me, her face pale in the early morning light.

"The cat's dead, isn't it?" she said.

Slowly I nodded. "Did you come back up here after I sent you to bed last night?" I asked.

The little girl held my gaze. "I wanted to see what the dolls were doing," she said.

I rubbed a hand over my face. "Estella, this is extremely serious. Did you ... did you hurt Whiskers?"

"It wasn't me," Estella said, staring straight at me. "It was the dolls."

Chapter Eleven

Whiteladies – Six months earlier

I moved into Whiteladies the same day Mother and Mr Redwing were due back from their honeymoon in France.

As soon as I heard the crunch of motorcar wheels, I ran out to the drive. I was so looking forward to seeing my mother again. These last two weeks were the longest we'd ever been apart and I'd missed her dreadfully. I couldn't wait to hear all about her trip and fully expected her to recount every detail in her characteristic happy, excitable, chattering way. I was quite sure that I wouldn't be able to get a word in edgeways for at least the first hour or so.

I opened the front door just as Redwing was helping my mother out of the motorcar and, the moment I saw her, my smile froze. Redwing looked his trim, handsome self but Mother was like a completely different person. She had lost weight for one thing – her familiar, comfortable plumpness had been replaced by a pale gauntness. There were dark hollows under her eyes and a strained look around her mouth that suggested she hadn't slept in days. But worse than all that was the dull, lifeless look in her eyes. I'd never seen my mother like this before, ever.

"Mother, what has happened?" I asked, hurrying to her side at once.

"Your mother fell ill in Paris," Redwing replied for her.

"Ill? But what—?"

"It's nothing to concern yourself with, my dear," Redwing said. "Just a passing fever, I expect."

I was deeply distressed by Mother's lack of response but tried to hide my worry as I said, "I've had the servants prepare tea in the drawing room—"

"I think it best that your mother rests in her room for a while before dinner." Redwing cut me off firmly. "We don't want her overtiring herself."

And, with that, he walked her to the entrance, supporting her up the front steps like she was an invalid.

I'd never once known my mother to be properly unwell. Even on the odd occasion when she'd had a cold, she didn't lose her cheerfulness and typically bounced back within days. As she walked past me with hardly a glance, I felt the cold touch of fear deep in my gut.

I followed them inside, hoping to accompany Mother to her room so I could speak to her on her own.

"Perhaps you might go down to the kitchen and give instruction for a pot of tea to be sent to your mother's room?" Redwing said to me smoothly at the foot of the staircase.

"Oh. But I thought I might go up and help her unpack and get changed into—"

"The maids will see to all that," Redwing replied. "I told you that you would be well taken care of at Whiteladies."

I glanced at Mother but she was looking at the floor rather than at us. I could not bear it. Why did she not speak up for herself? Why did she not tell Redwing to stop fussing, and that she did not want to rest, and that she and I had so much to catch up on, and we must sit and gossip together in front of the fire? She was right there, and yet she felt miles and miles away from me.

"But I would like to—" I began.

"I'm afraid I must insist," Redwing said, lowering his voice. "It's been a long journey, Jemima, and your mother needs a little peace and quiet."

I opened my mouth to argue, then Redwing smiled and the words died in my throat before I could utter them. It was a ghastly smile that lacked all human sympathy. His grey eyes were like ice and I noticed that his long fingers gripped my mother tightly by the wrist. Standing so close to him, the overpowering smell of Macassar oil was almost unbearable. This moment felt like a test of sorts, a benchmark for how things were to be, and it was a test I failed abysmally.

"Very well." I forced the words out through trembling lips. "I'll … I'll go and speak to the cook."

"Good girl," Redwing replied.

As I watched them disappear up the stairs together my feeling of dread grew stronger and stronger. I did not see Mother for the rest of that afternoon. The master bedroom she was to share with Redwing was down the corridor from my own room and the door remained locked.

I was determined to see her, however, so when Redwing announced that Mother was going to take a light supper in her bedroom, I lingered on the stairs, watching out for the maid. Redwing had said he was going to have dinner in his study so I hoped he'd be out of the way for long enough.

Shortly after, the maid appeared with Mother's tray and I spoke to her with an air of authority, telling her I would take it myself. She seemed a little unsure but I didn't leave her much choice and she went back down the stairs without argument.

I walked over to the master bedroom and knocked firmly on the door. This time, Mother answered it.

"Oh, Jemima," she said, the first words she'd actually spoken to me directly since she'd arrived home. She glanced up and down the corridor. "I was expecting the maid."

"I thought I'd bring this myself," I said, making my best attempt to sound cheerful. "I've hardly seen you since you got back."

I bustled in with the tray before she could stop me. Mother's bedroom at home had been full of frills and doilies and pink lace. This room, by contrast, was all polished wood and silver edges, with an imposing four-poster bed and heavy red drapes.

A fire burned in the grate and I put the tray down

on a table in front of it before settling myself in one of the two wing-backed chairs. For a moment Mother looked unsure about what to do, but then she closed the door and walked slowly over to take the other chair.

"Are you feeling any better?" I asked.

She blinked at me. "I'm quite well, thank you. Simply a little overtired from the journey."

These were almost the exact words Redwing had used earlier and I was certain that he had told her to say this.

"You look dreadful," I said, for she looked no better than she had earlier. "Is it Redwing? Has he—?"

"Mr Redwing is a devoted husband," Mother replied in that same dull tone. "I am very happy."

"Mother, you're frightening me! Won't you please tell me what's wrong? Whatever it is, there must be something I can do to help."

"Please don't be silly, Jemima, I don't need your help." As she spoke, she reached towards the tray for one of the teacups, causing her sleeve to pull back and expose her wrist. There were dark, angry bruises there, and when I grabbed her hand and yanked her sleeve up to her elbow, I saw that they extended all the way along her forearm.

"Oh my God," I breathed.

"I slipped getting on to the boat at Calais," Mother said, shaking me off and pulling her sleeve back down. "Mr Redwing saved me from falling."

I recalled the sight of his fingers tightly gripping her wrist downstairs and was struck by the dawning realization that perhaps things were even worse than I had feared.

"You should go back to your own room, Jemima," Mother said. "Mr Redwing won't like it if he finds you here."

"You're afraid of him, aren't you?" I said.

"Don't be silly. I am quite content. And you will be, too, once you get used to things."

I left her. I was too upset to think properly, too shocked at the burden that had suddenly dropped upon my shoulders. Mother had always been the cheerful, happy one. I'd never had to worry about her before and now I honestly did not know what to do. I'd never felt so alone in my life.

As the weeks passed, things only got worse. Our days followed the same pattern. Redwing kept

Mother awake in his study half the night in his various attempts to make contact with Vanessa. He would not allow me to participate in these sessions as he said my presence would be too distracting. He and Mother would disappear in there, the door would close and lock, and I wouldn't see them again for hours. Often they finished so late that I wouldn't even hear them come upstairs. Whether through misery, sheer exhaustion, or a combination of the two, Mother had taken to staying in bed for much of the day. She seemed a shell of her former self.

Then one day, as she reached for her water glass at dinner time, I saw a small burn mark on her wrist. It was coming up in angry-looking blisters and was perfectly round in shape. I knew at once that it was a cigarette burn. Redwing smoked profusely and carried with him a silver cigarette case with the Redwing coat of arms engraved upon it. I'd since learned that the red-eyed hawk was the Redwing family emblem and the fierce bird appeared frequently throughout Whiteladies. I had to make a great effort to keep my expression neutral so that she wouldn't realize I'd noticed.

Personally I found the scent of Redwing's slim little cigarettes unpleasant and overpowering. To my surprise, he always asked if we minded before lighting one but, of course, Mother and I always said we did not. It seemed the most absurd lunacy to maintain gentlemanly etiquette over his smoking habits when he treated Mother monstrously behind closed doors.

The evening I saw the cigarette burn on Mother's wrist, she excused herself early, saying she didn't feel well. I followed her upstairs soon afterwards. When I paused outside her door I could hear her crying quietly in her bedroom. I raised my hand to knock, then lowered it again. She would only insist that everything was fine. So I returned to my own room, where I sat and went over it all until my head ached with the strain of trying to find a way out.

Downstairs I heard the grandfather clock strike the hours for midnight. As the last chime faded away, I stood up and crossed the room to the door. I went out into the corridor and slowly walked to the top of the stairs. Gripping the banister, I peered over into the shadows. From here I could hear the low tick of the grandfather clock but nothing else.

The house was silent, as if everybody was asleep, although I hadn't heard Redwing come to bed.

I hesitated at the top of the stairs for a moment. Part of me wanted to return to the safety of my room, pretend none of this was happening. But then I recalled the sight of that cigarette burn and anger flared up inside me once again. I could not stand by and do nothing. I simply had to confront Edward Redwing about his atrocious treatment of my mother.

I put my hand firmly on the banister and stepped on to the first stair.

Chapter Twelve

Isle of Skye – January 1910

I scolded Estella for making up stories about the Frozen Charlottes, then told her to go and find Henry and ask him to come to the toy room, before going on to the classroom. Fortunately he arrived straight away and I told him what had happened. He took in the bloodied state of the room and visibly paled when he saw Whiskers.

"Good God," he said softly. He glanced at me then and said, "Are you all right? Do you need to sit down? Here, have this chair."

"Oh Henry, stop fussing, I'm not going to faint," I said impatiently. "I need you to help me deal with this. The cat must be taken away and disposed of before the girls see it. Estella knows it's dead so you'd better tell Cassie that the cat got shut in here and died – but perhaps we could say that it ate some rat poison or something?" I ran my hands through my hair. "And then ... and then I don't know. Should we inform Miss Grayson or just clean this up ourselves?"

Henry gazed at the room for a moment. "Don't say anything to Miss Grayson," he said at last. "She'll put Estella in Solitary again. Her health isn't good and it's freezing outside. Perhaps we can talk to her and try to get to the bottom of why she did it."

"We don't know for sure that it was Estella," I pointed out.

Henry gave me a startled look. "Who else would it be?" he said. "Besides, didn't you say you saw her out of bed last night and then back here this morning?"

"Yes, but it just seems so extreme," I said. "Why on earth would she do such a thing?"

Henry sighed. "Estella is a very troubled little girl," he said, "but Miss Grayson isn't the type to make allowances. I'll tell you all about it later, Mim, but you'd better go to class or you'll be late. I'll deal with this." He gestured at the room. "Come and find me during morning break."

It was almost time for lessons to start and I was secretly grateful to have an excuse to leave Henry to clear up the mess. I made my way downstairs, arriving just as Miss Grayson rang the bell for the start of class.

142

The hours seemed to drag by. I kept a close eye on Estella but she was unusually quiet and didn't misbehave in any way whatsoever. She kept her head down over her desk, focusing on her lessons with a fierce concentration and not making eye contact with anyone.

At break time I went to look for Henry, searching all over the place before finally finding him in the kitchen. He had his arms wrapped round Cassie, who was crying quietly, her face pressed against his shoulder. Henry had obviously told her about Whiskers. I noticed a distinct lack of actual tears, for all the noise she was making with those sobs. Resentment rose up in me at once. It was a ferocious feeling, an emotion with claws, and I was astonished at the intensity of it. It seemed especially ridiculous given that Cassie was barely more than a child and yet, the feeling was so painful that I could almost have doubled over where I stood.

I did no such thing, of course, but remained rigidly upright, through pride as much as anything. Henry saw me over Cassie's shoulder and gave me a helpless look. I had no choice but to leave them to it and return to the icy schoolyard, where I was just in time to break up a squabble between Alice and Georgia. Alice was in floods of tears because, she said, Georgia had called her a bad word.

"It wasn't me!" Georgia protested indignantly. "It was the Frozen Charlottes!"

"For heaven's sake!" I exclaimed. "If I hear one more of you blame your behaviour on the dolls I'm going to quite lose my temper."

The bell rang for class and everyone filed back into the school. After lunch, the girls poured back out to play in the snow and I tracked down Henry outside. As the only man about the place, I knew that he sometimes did odd jobs in the grounds and when I found him he was on his knees, repairing part of the wire cage of the chicken coop. Fortunately it was a safe-enough distance away from everyone that we were able to talk openly.

"Did you … get rid of Whiskers?" I asked.

Henry glanced up and nodded. "I cleaned up the blood in the toy room, too," he said.

"Thank you. So, tell me about Estella. I find it

difficult to believe that a little girl could have done something so violent."

Henry sighed. "Someone did it, old thing," he said. "It's not as if the dolls could be responsible, is it?"

I thought of what Estella had said about them but said nothing.

"Estella isn't like the rest of the girls here," Henry went on. "The others all come from impoverished backgrounds, or even the streets, but Estella's parents were – are – very wealthy."

"If her parents are wealthy then couldn't they have sent her to a nicer school than this?"

"Of course," Henry replied. "But, you see, they simply choose not to. They don't care about her."

"How can they not care about their own daughter?" I asked.

Henry hammered the last nail in the chicken coop then straightened up, brushing the dirt off his hands. "There was an accident," he said. "Her brother died. Estella was there."

"How did it happen?" I asked.

"They were ice skating," Henry said, his breath smoking before him in the cold. "But the ice was too thin and her brother, I think his name was John, fell through and got trapped beneath."

"That's hardly Estella's fault," I said, already feeling indignant on her behalf. "She's only a child – there's nothing she could have done."

"The problem wasn't that he fell through the ice," Henry said. "The problem was that Estella didn't fetch help."

"She was probably terrified," I said. "Perhaps she froze and didn't know what to do."

Henry shook his head. "She went back to the house, you see," he said. "And when her mother asked her where John was, she said that he was in his bedroom."

I frowned. "Perhaps she thought she'd get in trouble if she told the truth?"

Henry gave an unhappy shrug. "Who knows what was going on in her mind, Mim? But the fact is that if she'd fetched help then John might have been saved. As it was, they didn't find him until hours later and, by that time, he'd long since drowned. It seems like Estella's compulsive lying began around then and she also started having these terrible fits where she would destroy everything she could get her hands on, throwing vases and plates and suchlike. They had to keep confining her to her room. On one occasion it seems she threw her pet budgie against the wall and, well, cracked his skull open. Her parents didn't know what to do with her any more. So they sent her here."

"How do you know all this about her?" I asked.

"Miss Grayson has said things from time to time," Henry said. "And Cassie saw a letter from her parents lying on Miss Grayson's desk once. I think Cassie is a little spooked by Estella, to be honest. She even told me once that she thought Estella might have pushed her brother through the ice on purpose."

"Cassie shouldn't have been poking about in private letters," I said, more sharply than I'd meant to. "Or allow her imagination to get the better of her."

Henry sighed. "Estella is a lost, unhappy little soul," he said. "But she doesn't make things any easier for herself. She's always misbehaving and getting punished for something or other. Just last summer she made up some wild ghost story about the servants' staircase and now the other girls are terrified to go near it. She even managed to frighten

Cassie and Hannah. Perhaps Estella does it for attention." He gave me a troubled look. "But this business with Whiskers is … it's unlike anything she's done here before."

"I'll keep an eye on her," I said. "If we tell Miss Grayson then she'll probably flog her or something, and I don't think that's going to help."

"I agree with you," Henry said. He gave me a sudden smile. "If there's a way to help Estella then we'll work it out between us, I'm sure."

I got another chance to speak with Henry straight after the lunch break when the girls had their drawing lesson. Henry said the snowy weather was too beautiful to waste, and had them bundle up in their cloaks and boots to work outside for a little while. He told them each to pick something to draw – an iced spider web or a frosty window or whatever else they liked. They were to make a rough sketch and then complete their drawings from the comparative warmth of the classroom.

As the girls worked, I wandered around overseeing them for a bit and then noticed Estella sitting on the low brick wall that surrounded the vegetable patch, staring up at the second floor of the school. I went over and crouched down by her side. Her drawing pad lay blank and untouched on her lap.

"Are you going to draw the school?" I asked.

She shook her head.

"You're looking at it very intently," I pressed.

Estella turned her gaze on me. "There was a Frozen Charlotte doll," she said. "Just now. At the window."

"Which window?"

"It was at the toy room window first," she said, staring up at the school again. "Then it went away from there and then it was suddenly in the dormitory window and then your bedroom window, miss. It's running around up there, I think, peering out from all the different rooms."

"Estella," I said in my gentlest voice, "dolls don't move around on their own."

She looked back at me. "But how else could it appear at the windows?" she asked. "We're all out here."

I glanced up at the school and, just for the merest fraction of a moment, it seemed like a little white

149

blur appeared on the inside of my bedroom window and then jerked back.

I rubbed my eyes and looked again but the window was dark and empty. There was nothing there. I shook my head firmly. That white blur had probably been a snowflake – the snow was coming down again heavily now.

As I turned away, Estella said, "I suppose it could be Miss Grayson playing with the dolls. She does that sometimes after everyone else has gone to sleep. One time I went upstairs to the toy room in the middle of the night and she was rocking back and forth on the rocking horse."

"I find that very hard to believe, Estella."

Looking back at the school, she said, "Another time, she'd placed all the teddy bears around a blanket and they were having a picnic. She was talking to them and the bears were talking back to her in squeaky voices she put on herself. That's why she confiscates all the toys. Because she wants to play with them."

I leaned a little closer to her. "Estella, look at me," I said. When she met my gaze I continued, "Tell me honestly. Is that really true?"

Estella was silent for a long moment. "If I say it's not true then I'm calling myself a liar," she said. "And if I say it's true then you'll call me a liar anyway."

"Let's get inside, girls," Henry was calling. "Before we're lost in a blizzard."

I sighed. "Come on," I said to Estella. "Let's think of something nice to draw."

Stamping the snow from our boots, we piled into the empty classroom. A little fire burned in the fireplace, barely more than a single coal smouldering sullenly. The girls took their seats at the individual desks and started work on their drawings. I went to put some more coal on the fire but found the coal shuttle had been locked. What a horrid old harpy Miss Grayson was. She was such a penny-pincher that I even wondered whether perhaps she scraped a little off the top for her own pleasure. Although what on earth she might spend her money on I had no idea.

Fortunately Miss Grayson had little interest in drawing lessons. She thought it rather a waste of the girls' time, since it was only ladies from better families who had the leisure for such things in their adult life. Making pretty sketches was beyond the remit of housemaids. The girls enjoyed the class, though – particularly Martha, who was a very talented artist, especially since Henry allowed her to use her left hand.

Towards the end of the lesson I walked around the desks to see what the girls had drawn. Most had chosen things they'd seen in the garden. Estella's drawing, however, was different – a very basic sketch with straight, slashed lines. It showed a lake with a floating stick figure lying horizontally beneath the surface. On the far bank stood another stick man. In the foreground of the drawing was a stick-figure girl, gazing towards the person on the bank.

"Would you like to tell me about your drawing?" I asked, crouching down beside her.

"That's my brother, John, under the ice." She pointed at the horizontal figure. "And that's John at the side of the lake. After he'd drowned. Talking to me."

I glanced at her but she didn't return my look. Her concentration was on the drawing as she energetically scribbled in the outline of dark, looming trees surrounding the lake.

After the lesson, I made my way to Miss Grayson's study and knocked on the door. When she called for me to enter, I opened the door and stepped inside. I had been in there before when I had taken the key to the luggage room but I hadn't had the chance to properly examine it on that occasion. It was a plain enough room, with a desk and dark wooden cabinets lining the walls. These were closed and locked, and I couldn't help wondering what they might contain.

Miss Grayson was sitting at her desk. When she looked up at me, her mouth was as pinched and serious as always, and I simply could not imagine her running around the schoolhouse playing with dolls while we'd all been engaged outside. Estella was, after all, a compulsive liar. It was how she'd ended up at the school in the first place.

"Yes?" the schoolmistress said. "Can I help you with something, Miss Black?"

"I wondered if I might have the key to the toy room?" I said.

"For what purpose?"

"It's just that Henry mentioned seeing the light go on and off in there a few times last night," I said. "I think the girls might have been in there playing with the dolls' house. I thought that if the room was kept locked then they wouldn't be tempted to wander about when they ought to be in bed."

I'd hoped that my puritanical approach might be the best way of achieving my aims and, indeed, Miss Grayson looked almost approving as she said, "Very sound. Yes, you may take the key. In fact, take the dormitory key as well. And if they insist on running about the place after lights out then I suggest you lock them in. They'll learn soon enough."

She took two keys from the drawer of her desk, put them on to the same ring and handed it over to me.

Chapter Thirteen

Whiteladies – Six months earlier

Determined to speak to Redwing, I made my way down the stairs, searching out light switches and flicking them on as I went. I was not yet properly familiar with Whiteladies, and the house felt strange and still and too quiet in the darkness. The grandfather clock in the entrance hall gave its slow, low *tick tock* as I walked past, into a corridor that branched off from the main entrance. I was fairly sure this led to Redwing's study and saw that one of the doors had a thin strip of light shining out from underneath it.

I paused outside, hesitating, wondering whether I should go inside or not. When I put my ear to the door I couldn't hear any noise from within. Making up my mind, I raised my hand and knocked.

Redwing's mellow voice called at once for me to enter. I took a deep breath, grasped the handle and turned it.

The door swung open to reveal Redwing's study, a room I had not yet been into. It was a dark, wood-panelled, elegant space with a lot of deep red leather, glowing paraffin lamps and wing-backed armchairs. The walls were lined with bookshelves and the remains of a fire smouldered in the grate. A big walnut desk dominated the room and this was covered in a large pile of pristine white paper, a box of Frozen Charlotte dolls positioned nearby. Edward Redwing was sitting in the chair behind the desk, a pen held loosely in his hand, the nib slowly releasing an ink spot on to the white paper.

It looked like he'd been running his hands through his hair – dark strands of it had come loose from their Macassar oil slick, falling down around his face.

"Is something wrong, Jemima?" he asked, staring at me with bloodshot eyes.

My gaze fell on the umbrella stand behind his desk, in which sat his rosewood cane. The expression on the hawk's face was horribly cruel and those ruby eyes seemed to glare at me.

"I–I'd like to talk to you, please."

I immediately hated myself for the stammer, as well as the 'please'.

Redwing blinked slowly, then said, "It's very late. I'm astonished that you are still up. Can't it wait until morning?"

I almost wavered and returned to bed then, but forced myself to gather together the scraps of my courage. "Actually, no," I said. "It cannot wait another moment, sir."

"Well," Redwing said, laying down his pen. "That does sound serious." A slight smile hovered at the edge of his mouth and I could tell he thought he was indulging a child as he gestured towards the chair on the other side of the desk and said, "You'd better sit down."

I wanted to insist on standing but didn't know how to do it without sounding churlish, so I took the chair, perching right on the edge. My eyes kept sliding back to the hawk cane propped in the corner. I longed to turn it to face the wall so those ruby-red eyes would stop looking at me.

"Were you ... writing a letter?" I asked, gesturing at the sheaf of blank paper.

I had no interest at all in Redwing's correspondence but merely asked the question to buy myself some time.

Redwing glanced at the paper and said, "I thought I would try a spot of automatic writing but I'm afraid that, so far, my efforts have not been particularly productive."

"Automatic writing?"

"I first heard about it at the Ghost Club," Redwing said, leaning back in his chair. "It involves putting oneself into a trance and then inviting spirits to use you as a vessel to communicate." He looked down at the papers. "I thought I might reach Vanessa this way but so far I have not been successful, as you can see."

I frowned. "But … is that not dangerous? My grandmother always said you should never invite spirits to take over your body. Anything could be waiting and listening – not just ghosts but ghouls and dark spirits. Even demons, which are the most dangerous of—"

Redwing waved a hand. "Your mother expressed the same concern. But a man's mind is far stronger than a female one and I am in control at all times." He leaned forwards slightly and picked up the pen, tapping it lightly against the paper. "Now," he said. "I know you didn't come down here past midnight to discuss the practice of automatic writing with me. What's troubling you?"

He sounded so calm and reasonable that it was hard to believe he could do the things I was about to accuse him of, but I had seen the bruises and the cigarette burns with my own eyes.

I felt physically sick with nerves but there was no putting it off any longer. I swallowed hard and unstuck my tongue from the roof of my mouth. My heart was beating so fast that it made me short of breath and, when I spoke, the words came out in a sort of strangled gasp that was far from the cool, authoritative tone I'd been aiming for. "Mr Redwing, I have come to … ask you … to p-please s-stop … abusing … my mother."

There was absolute silence as Redwing gazed at me, an unreadable expression in his eyes.

Blood rang in my ears.

My breathing sounded too loud in the room.

The air was too warm.

The hawk's eyes were too red.

Redwing put down the pen again. "Abusing her?" he finally said. It seemed to me that there was a small gleam of surprised pleasure deep in his eyes, as if this conversation was not one that he had expected but yet somehow relished.

"It cannot go on, sir," I said desperately. "It simply cannot. She will become ill."

"Jemima," he said, "I am not obliged to discuss my marriage with you, or anyone, for that matter, but I will try to be as patient as I can with this wild accusation. Have I not provided both you and your mother with a beautiful home? Is there not food on the table? Books to read, chocolates to eat, dresses to wear? Pray tell me in which area you feel me to be amiss?"

I gripped the arms of my chair. "I have seen the bruises on my mother's arms," I said. "They appear there regularly. And today I saw a cigarette burn as well." Anger finally gave me the power to free my tongue. "I don't know whether these are the result of mistreatment in the bedroom, or something obscene that goes on when the two of you are locked away here for hours on end. I don't know and I don't care. I am simply telling you it must stop."

Redwing's lips thinned into a straight line. "That is quite enough," he said in a low voice. "How dare you speak to me of matters of the bedroom? You are too young to understand such things, and no decent girl or woman would ever broach such a topic with a gentleman."

I could feel the blood flooding my face in a deep flush. Fear pulsed through me but I recalled that earlier occasion, after they had returned from their honeymoon, when I had bowed to his strength. I thought of the bruises I'd seen on Mother's wrists and arms, the dull, hopeless look in her eyes, and it seemed to me that I must not make the same mistake again and let myself be cowed into silence by a bully. I must stand up to this man. I must be strong for my mother as well as myself.

"No decent gentleman would treat his wife as you do, sir," I said, my voice remaining steady for the first time. "A real gentleman would never stoop to—"

But that was as far as I got before Redwing erupted from his chair so fast that it fell backwards. I shrank away but he grabbed me by the hair and dragged me to my feet. I cried out in shock as much as in pain – no one had ever laid a hand on me before. Instinctively I clutched at his arm with both hands, trying to loosen his hold, but his grip might as well have been an iron vice for all the power I had to break it. He was larger and taller and stronger than me, and was easily able to stride across the room, pulling me with him, my feet scrabbling along the wooden floorboards.

I thought he was heading towards the door at first and imagined that perhaps he meant to throw me out of his house altogether. A cold fear touched my heart at the thought, for I had nowhere else to go and I couldn't possibly leave Mother here. But instead Redwing stopped before the opposite wall, yanking my hair back in order to raise my head.

I found myself staring up at a skull. The entire wall was covered in hunting trophies, but this one wasn't a deer, or a rabbit, or a pheasant. It was a horse. With a single bullet hole right in the centre of its forehead.

"This devilish beast took my daughter from me," Redwing said quietly in my ear, his breath warm against my neck. "And ever since that day I've regretted shooting it in the head."

"I-I'm sure Vanessa would have understood that you w-were overwrought," I stammered, but Redwing cut me off with a cold laugh.

"No, my dear, you misunderstand me," he said. "My regret does not stem from guilt. It is simply that an execution was more than that horse deserved. I ought to have flayed the skin from it strip by strip. I should have gouged out its eyes, sawn off its tongue, ripped out its teeth, hammered its hooves into jelly. No punishment would have been terrible enough for what that animal took from me, and if I could go back in time and prolong its suffering, I would."

He finally let go of my hair and gripped me by the shoulders, his fingers digging into my flesh as he turned me round to face him. I could smell his breath, sour on my face, as he said, "I will speak to Vanessa again, do you understand? If it's the last thing I ever do, I will speak to my daughter. And I don't mean a couple of knocks on a table – I mean actually speak to her and have her speak back."

"But ... but how?" I gasped. "How do you possibly expect to do that?"

"Trance mediumship," he said. "The medium goes into a trance and then welcomes spirits to communicate through them. Your mother is one of the most renowned mediums in London and I have mastered no small amount of skill as a mesmerist, and yet so far we have not made contact with a single spirit. But if we carry on for long enough then we must break through eventually. We must." He took a deep breath. "You made me lose my temper, damn you, which is something that very rarely happens. But if you get in my way, Jemima, you will regret it, I promise."

Redwing leaned even closer. We were almost nose to nose and for a sickening moment I thought he was going to kiss me. But then he moved his lips to my ear and said, in a hushed voice, "Do. You. Understand?"

"Yes," I said through gritted teeth. "Yes, I understand."

"Good." Redwing let go of me abruptly and returned to his desk.

A thought came to me then and I hated the idea of it, but I saw that it was the only way to help my mother.

"I understand," I said again. "And I think you should use me instead."

"You?" Redwing sat back down in his chair. "You're just a girl. You lack your mother's experience."

"Experience isn't the most important thing when it comes to being a medium," I said. "Mother has told me many times that adolescent girls are more susceptible to psychic phenomena and more sensitive to the spirit world. It's the age when ghosts are most drawn to us and our abilities are strongest. After that, they get gradually weaker and weaker."

Redwing drew his silver cigarette case from his pocket and extracted one of the slim cigarettes. "Do you mind?" he asked, indicating with it.

After what had just taken place, I couldn't tell whether or not he was mocking me with the nicety, so I just shook my head.

Redwing lit the cigarette and a plume of smoke drifted slowly towards me.

"Why would you offer to do this?" he finally asked. "Why do you care about contacting Vanessa?"

"I don't," I told him. "I just want to spare my mother."

"Well," Redwing said, leaning back in his chair. "I have heard other members of the Ghost Club suggest that adolescent girls make for more powerful mediums. Given the lack of progress with your mother, it does not hurt to try, I suppose."

"When would you like to begin?" I asked, despising him.

"Right now, if you're agreeable," he said. He pointed at an armchair beside the fire. "You will sit there," he said. "You will hold this doll." He picked a Frozen Charlotte out of the box on the desk. "And you will do exactly as I say."

I took the cold little doll from him and sat on the armchair he had indicated. Redwing picked up his cane and pulled up another chair, positioning it so close that our knees almost touched. He leaned forwards slightly, placing the cane between his knees with a solid thump on the floor.

I had no expectation that this would work but I intended to do as I was instructed and give it my very best effort. It was quite clear that putting on a show wasn't enough. My grandmother had firmly believed it was possible to speak to the dead and perhaps she had been right. Perhaps my age really did increase my chances of success. If I could help Redwing make contact with his daughter then maybe this awful madness that had clearly taken hold of him since her death might abate and he would return to some sort of sanity.

"Look at the hawk's ruby eyes," Redwing instructed. "Concentrate all your focus on them. And follow the sound of my voice. You will empty your mind of all conscious thought. You will be a blank slate, ready and willing to be written upon. You will relinquish control and give yourself up to any spirits who may be nearby, inviting them in, welcoming them to settle into your skin and use your tongue as if it were their own…"

Chapter Fourteen

Isle of Skye – January 1910

I tried several times throughout the rest of that day to talk to Estella about Whiskers but she had obviously made up her mind to say nothing more on the subject.

"I already told you what happened," she said. "And you don't believe me. So what's the point?" She looked perfectly wretched as she turned away from me.

For the first time, I wondered whether she might actually believe the lies she told. Perhaps seeing her brother drown like that had made her a little deranged. I knew well enough that the mind was a delicate thing that could be broken apart if sufficient pressure was applied to it.

When I returned to my bedroom after dinner that evening, I was startled by the sight of a Frozen Charlotte doll on my pillow. I recalled the white blur at my window I thought I'd seen with Estella but pushed the thought away. One of the girls must have left her here. I would have to start locking my door.

I picked up the Frozen Charlotte and went along the corridor to the toy room. I hadn't been back there since I'd discovered Whiskers earlier and now I walked in with slight trepidation.

Henry had done a good job of clearing up. When I switched on the gaslight, I couldn't see any blood on the floorboards or the walls. The toy chest, too, was completely clean. Strangely, though, he hadn't put the dolls back in the chest, as I'd expected, but had lined them up on the windowsill. They were all pressed against the glass with their curly heads facing away from me, china fingers resting on the frosted window as if they were gazing out at something in the grounds.

I placed the doll from my room in the toy chest and then wandered over to the window, glanced out and found myself staring straight into the eyes of a hawk – a ferocious beast of a bird with gleaming red eyes. I jerked back, seeing that cane of Redwing's, but then I looked again at the window, just as the bird spread its magnificent two-metre wingspan and

169

took off into the night, leaving the Frozen Charlottes staring silently after it.

I told myself it was simply a sea eagle and nothing to do with Redwing. Then I scooped up the Frozen Charlottes and placed them in the toy chest before snapping the lid closed. The front of the dolls' house had been left open so I closed that, too, before locking the door securely behind me and returning to my bedroom.

My sleep that night was disturbed by visions of red-eyed hawks flying at me with talons outstretched, determined to pluck my eyeballs right out of my skull. I woke sweating and shivering, just in time to hear a faint *tap, tap, tap* through the wall on the far side of my bedroom. It was, without doubt, coming from the toy room.

Still half tangled up in the terrible hawk dream, I scrambled out of bed, wincing at the cold, shoved my feet into my slippers and lit a candle. The tapping started up again and I couldn't understand it. I had locked the room myself only hours ago. Could there be another key that one of the girls had managed to get hold of?

I hurried from my room and pushed down on the handle of the toy-room door but, to my surprise, it was still firmly locked. Perhaps one of the girls had been hiding in there earlier and I had locked her in?

Fumbling with the key, I unlocked the door. It swung open to reveal a room in darkness except for one bright spot of light. It was coming from the dolls' house and I immediately knew which light had been turned on. It was, of course, the light to Edward Redwing's study.

I switched on the gas lamp and glanced quickly around the room, but there was nothing amiss. The toy chest remained closed and, when I opened it, the Frozen Charlotte dolls were exactly as I had left them. Clearly there were no girls in here. Perhaps I had still been half asleep and dreaming when I thought I heard those taps through the wall. Or perhaps it had simply been mice in the walls. Now that poor Whiskers was gone, the school's mouse problem was likely to get worse.

And yet I did not remember there being a light

switched on in the dolls' house. I walked over to it and pulled open the front but all the rooms looked just as they should have.

I switched off the light and closed the house. The light must have been on before. I hadn't noticed it, that was all. I straightened back up, walked out and locked the toy-room door behind me.

Chapter Fifteen

Whiteladies – Six months earlier

Redwing snapped his fingers and I blinked and tried to speak, only for blood to dribble out between my lips, running over my chin and dripping on to the Frozen Charlotte doll cupped in my hand. Confused, I wiped my mouth with my fingers, swallowing blood without meaning to. My mouth tasted of metal, my tongue throbbed, my throat was dry. My head was pounding and my thoughts were all tangled up in some dark fog. It was hard to think, hard to remember where I was or what was happening.

It felt like we had only just begun the trance session and yet, to my surprise, sunlight streamed in through the windows. Could it actually have worked?

"You did well, Jemima," Redwing said from the other side of the room. I looked up and saw that he was standing before the window with his back to me, gazing out towards the grounds.

"Why … why is my tongue bleeding?" I asked, my mouth still slick and hot with blood.

Redwing did not turn round. "You bit it during the trance. That can happen."

"Did it work?" I asked, setting the Frozen Charlotte down on the nearby table. "Did you speak to Vanessa?"

From what I could recall, I had given it my best effort, had not resisted Redwing in any way.

"You did well," Redwing said again, finally turning to face me. He looked tired but there was some light burning in his eyes. A sort of triumph that I hadn't seen before. "I suggest you get some sleep," he said pleasantly. "We will resume our session again tonight."

Still in a haze I tried to stand up, only for the room to swim around me and the floor to tilt beneath my feet. I reached out to steady myself on the back of Redwing's armchair and that was when I noticed my sleeves had been pushed back and there were cigarette burns, three of them, on my right arm.

"What are these?" I asked.

"It is how I establish if you really are in a deep trance state," Redwing said, moving over

174

to his desk. "When one is deep in trance, one becomes impervious to pain."

"Surely just one burn would have been enough to establish that?" I asked.

Redwing lifted the corner of his mouth in an ugly smirk. "It pays to be thorough," he said. "And I take mesmerism very seriously, my dear."

In that moment I saw that he enjoyed inflicting pain, that he relished having the opportunity to punish me.

With an effort, I gathered my wits and walked towards the door without saying another word. Out in the hall the grandfather clock seemed to tick too loudly as I walked past it and the stairs stretched on forever. It felt like an eternity before I reached my bedroom, where I could finally close and lock the door.

With my back to the wall I slid down to the floor. My breathing was fast and shallow in my chest, and I had to concentrate hard on slowing it down. Had Redwing told the truth when he said I'd bitten my own tongue? What had really happened in his study during those long hours I could not remember?

I put my head in my hands. When I'd offered to take my mother's place, I hadn't really thought the trance was likely to work, let alone that I would be able to remember nothing afterwards.

My head throbbed with the most appalling headache and I felt exhausted, so I drew the curtains across the windows and reeled to bed, where I immediately fell into a deep, dreamless sleep.

Chapter Sixteen

Isle of Skye – January 1910

I returned to bed only to be woken an hour later by the loud, relentless ringing of a bell from somewhere downstairs. It was the one Miss Grayson used to mark the start of class – the large brass bell that sat on her desk at the front of the room.

On and on and on it went.

Someone was down there in the middle of the night, ringing the bell loudly enough to wake the dead. I scrambled out of bed, thrust my feet into my slippers and snatched up my dressing gown. My eye fell on my bedside table and I noticed that the key to the toy room was missing. I was sure I had put it there before. Throwing on my dressing gown to cover up my scarred arms, I hurried out on to the landing, just as the doors to the dormitory opened and the girls peered out, looking alarmed.

"What's happening, miss?" Olivia asked. "Who's ringing the bell?"

"I don't know," I replied.

"Estella isn't in her bed, Miss Black," Martha piped up. "She isn't in the dormitory at all."

The girls exchanged looks. They clearly thought it was Estella who was downstairs, making that noise.

Miss Grayson came out of her own room just then, her leather tawse clutched in her hand. Even though it was the middle of the night and she was dressed, like the rest of us, in a nightgown and slippers, her hair was still arranged in that elaborate pompadour bun. There was no way she would have had time to do that in those short moments. I finally realized that Miss Grayson must wear a wig. In her haste, she had put it on a little crookedly and I distinctly heard one of the girls snigger.

"What is the meaning of this?" she said, glaring at us. "Who is downstairs ringing the bell?"

"I have no idea," I replied. Hoping to protect Estella I said, "I'll see to it, Miss Grayson."

But the schoolmistress was not to be dissuaded. "Is anyone missing?" she demanded. "Whichever girl it is will be punished severely."

And then she was striding towards the staircase, switching on the gaslights as she went.

"Go back to bed," I whispered to the girls, before hurrying after the schoolmistress.

We made our way down the stairs. I was shivering with cold but Miss Grayson was so furious that I think she hardly felt it. The bell continued to ring as we went down to the ground floor. As we approached the classroom, I saw that no strip of light shone from beneath the door. Someone was ringing the bell in the pitch-black.

Miss Grayson threw open the door and there was a dreadful clanging noise as the bell fell to the ground and rolled along the wooden boards. Miss Grayson quickly found the gaslight, which hissed into life, illuminating the room in a sickly, yellow glow.

I took in the scene and gasped. Estella wasn't there. In the moments it took to turn on the light, she must have slipped out through the back door into the corridor that looped round to the servants' stairs. This confirmed in my mind that it had been Estella who'd been here. As Henry had told me, the other girls all avoided the servants' stairs.

But the classroom wasn't empty.

It was filled with Frozen Charlotte dolls.

They were lined up on the desks, balanced upright on their small white feet, all staring directly towards the blackboard. I had wiped it down myself earlier but it wasn't blank any longer. Someone had written the same sentence across it in chalk, over and over again, in uneven, childish writing:

Miss Grayson is a bald, beastly bitch.
Miss Grayson is a bald, beastly bitch.
Miss Grayson is a bald, beastly bitch.

I glanced at the schoolmistress, wondering how on earth she was going to react. She was staring at the board in silence but had gone completely white, and I noticed her lips were quivering.

"I'll wipe it off," I said.

"Leave it," Miss Grayson said, before I could take a step.

"But—"

"Leave. It!" she hissed.

I stopped, just as the back door opened and Cassie poked her head round it.

"What's wrong?" she asked. "We heard a bell ringing."

"It's just one of the students misbehaving, Cassie," Miss Grayson said. "Nothing to concern yourself with.

Please go back to bed."

The maid cast one last dubious look at us and the dolls scattered everywhere before turning away and closing the door behind her.

"Fetch the girls," Miss Grayson said.

"But ... but it's the middle of the night—" I began.

"I won't ask you a second time, Miss Black."

I had no choice but to go back upstairs and fetch them. They were still awake anyway, waiting to find out what was going on. I saw at once that Estella had rejoined the others.

I ushered them down to the classroom. Most of the girls didn't own dressing gowns or slippers and stood shivering in their nightdresses and bare feet. Miss Grayson was before the blackboard and I heard some of the girls gasp when they saw what had been written there.

The schoolmistress suddenly gestured at the board with her tawse. The movement was so fast that several of the girls jumped.

"Who," she said in a dangerously low voice, "is responsible for this outrage?"

The girls stared back at her. Nobody said a word. The silence in the room was almost deafening.

"I will give you one more chance to tell me who is responsible," Miss Grayson said. "If anyone knows who did this, speak up now."

The silence stretched on as the girls wrapped their skinny arms round themselves and shivered.

Finally Estella spoke. "Perhaps it was the Frozen Charlotte dolls, miss. They move around after dark. And they know things—"

"Estella, your lies get wilder by the day!" the schoolmistress exclaimed. She snatched up one of the Frozen Charlottes from a nearby desk. "If you think anyone is going to believe that this tiny doll was somehow able to pick up a piece of chalk and write on a board, as well as ring an extremely heavy bell, then you are quite deluded."

Estella folded her arms across her chest. "Perhaps they told someone else to do it," she said. "Perhaps they managed to persuade someone to—"

Miss Grayson pointed the tawse at Estella. "Not one more word out of you!" she snarled. "Not another word! I will not have human wickedness blamed on dolls. I will not!" She let the crop fall to her side and then reached up to pat at her hair. "As you can all see," she said, "I am very far

182

from bald. So whoever wrote this is both insolent and a liar. Since you refuse to tell me who the culprit is, I have no choice but to punish you all." Her eyes narrowed into slits. "There will be no breakfast served tomorrow. Instead I expect you all to present yourselves here for your punishment at seven o'clock sharp. Anyone who arrives late will be flogged. Now, get back to your room."

As the girls filed out, Miss Grayson finally picked up the duster and began wiping away the words. In an effort to help, I started to collect up the dolls but Miss Grayson snapped at me to leave them.

"They will be put to use as part of tomorrow's punishment," she said. "And we'll see how fond of the things the girls are after that. Speaking of which, I thought you were supposed to be locking the toy room at night, Miss Black?"

"I'm very sorry, Miss Grayson, but I did lock the room," I said. "The key was gone when I woke up. Someone must have crept in and taken it while I was asleep."

"Well, why didn't you say so before?" the schoolmistress demanded, turning away from the now clean board. "If we find the key then we identify the culprit!"

To my dismay, she insisted on searching the dormitory. The girls watched silently from the edge of the room as their space was turned upside down. Miss Grayson went at it like a crazy person, especially when it came to Estella's bed and her small collection of belongings.

"Perhaps it wasn't one of the girls at all," I said, once Miss Grayson had finally admitted defeat and joined me out in the corridor. "Perhaps it was one of the maids?"

Miss Grayson chewed her lip furiously. "I'm sure it was Estella," she said. "But it pays to be thorough."

I walked with her down to the servants' quarters where Cassie and Hannah were roused in turn. Hannah accepted the search in silence and Cassie sulked quietly, but there was still no sign of the key.

"What about Dolores?" I asked. "Aren't you going to search her room, too?"

"I have searched her room," Miss Grayson replied. "Cassie sleeps in it now."

"Then where does Dolores sleep?" I asked, confused.

Miss Grayson stopped abruptly at the foot of the stairs and turned round to face me. "How do you know about Dolores?" she demanded. "Has Estella been talking about her again?"

"No. I met her on my first day."

Miss Grayson stared at me. Her nostrils flared. "I beg your pardon?"

"We passed each other right here on the servants' staircase," I said, gesturing towards it. "She was dusting the—"

Miss Grayson slapped me hard across the face. "You wicked girl!" she cried. "How dare you lie to me so brazenly?"

"I'm not lying!" I gasped, one hand pressed to my stinging cheek.

"You could not possibly have met Dolores because the stupid girl fell down this staircase and broke her neck. She died two years ago!"

Chapter Seventeen

Isle of Skye – January 1910

I rose early the next morning and went down to the classroom before everyone else, opening the door and peering in cautiously. Part of me feared that more writing might have appeared on the board or that the dolls might be in different positions from those they'd been left in. But the Frozen Charlottes were still on the desks and everything seemed to be in order.

I walked quickly over to Miss Grayson's desk and took the Punishment Book from the top drawer, flipping over the pages until I found the one I was looking for. The entry for Estella last summer when she had spent almost three days in Solitary. I ran my finger across the line, looking for the crime she had committed, but there was only a single word written there: *lying*.

I closed the book and replaced it in the desk just as Miss Grayson walked in, carrying a basket full of sewing kits.

"Distribute one of these on each desk," she ordered.

I did as she'd asked and the girls filed in soon after.

"You will each find a Frozen Charlotte on your desk," Miss Grayson said. "Along with some sewing materials. Today we will put your fascination with these toys to some useful purpose." She walked slowly up and down in front of the blackboard, her eyes gleaming. "When you leave this school," she said, "you will be expected to make yourselves useful as servants and maids. Needlework is likely to be an important skill for you all, which is why we have weekly lessons here. Today we shall spend the entire day perfecting our needlework. We will not break for meals and there will be no playtime. Food and leisure are luxuries that must be earned." She stopped in front of her desk and said, "By five o'clock this evening, you will each have sewn fifty dresses for your doll."

"Fifty!" I exclaimed.

Miss Grayson gave me an icy look. "Fifty," she repeated. "Anyone who doesn't have fifty finished dresses at the end of the day will be flogged. You have

187

ten hours. That is plenty of time, providing you stay focused on your task and work hard."

Estella put her hand up.

"Yes, Estella?"

"I haven't got a Frozen Charlotte doll," she said. "I've got a Frozen Charlie."

I saw she was right. Her doll was the male figure I remembered from the luggage room.

"So you have," Miss Grayson said softly. "Well then, you had better sew suits instead."

"Suits take longer than dresses," Estella replied.

"Then I suggest you begin at once."

Estella lifted her chin slightly but said nothing. I was quite sure that Miss Grayson had given her the Frozen Charlie deliberately. She wanted Estella to fail.

The girls hurried to snatch up scraps of fabric and lace, threading needles with an air of urgency.

"Miss Black," the schoolmistress said, turning to me.

"Yes, Miss Grayson?"

"Please take away the girls' thimbles. We will not be using those today. Thimbles encourage carelessness."

"Very well," I said miserably.

"After that," Miss Grayson said, "I suggest you get started on your own dresses straight away."

"I'm sorry?"

"I hope you did not expect to escape punishment after last night's outrageous lie," she said. "You will join the girls in their task."

I bit my tongue. Once all the thimbles were collected, I picked up one of the dolls from Miss Grayson's desk, fetched a sewing kit and took my seat at a spare desk at the back of the room.

The rest of that day was pure torture. Although the dresses were tiny, they were fiddly, and creating fifty of them was no small task. The girls worked in frenzied silence. Miss Grayson did not keep the fire going and the room got steadily colder. My fingers turned blue and numb. Working so fast, without thimbles, it was impossible not to regularly prick yourself. After the first hour, there wasn't a single desk that did not have a spot of blood on it somewhere.

By lunchtime I had made twenty-four dresses but my fingers throbbed and my insides felt scraped out with hunger. When I glanced at the other desks

I saw that most of the other girls were managing to work quickly enough. Estella in particular was clearly extremely skilled at needlework, for she had quite a pile of neat little suits at her elbow. One or two of the others appeared to be struggling, though, including Bess, who was crying quietly as she bent over her doll.

Finally Bess put up her hand and asked Miss Grayson in a timid voice whether she might be allowed to go to the lavatory.

"That is entirely up to you, Bess," Miss Grayson replied without looking up. "If you think you can spare the time to go all the way upstairs for a lavatory break, by all means you may leave."

Bess put her hand back down and carried on working, looking wretched. She fidgeted around in her seat for the next hour before finally getting up and running to the lavatory. She returned to her seat less than five minutes later but I could see that she was behind on her dresses. Unless she sped up, she wasn't going to finish on time.

As the hours drew on it only got harder and harder, and our fingers became cold and sore and stiff. By the time it got to four o'clock, we all had blood trickling down our wrists. It felt like a nightmare that simply would not end. Several of the girls were crying but no one dared stop working for fear of not meeting the target and getting a flogging as a result.

I completed my fiftieth dress with about twenty minutes to spare. When I looked up I saw that almost all the girls had finished or were about to – all except Bess, who was sobbing more loudly now as she desperately tried to complete her last dresses. She wasn't going to make it in time. I could see that at once.

But then, to my astonishment, Estella reached over and slid several dresses on to Bess's desk. Bess stared at them for a moment before quickly putting them into her own pile. She glanced over at Estella, who was already starting work on her next suit. She must have noticed Bess was falling behind and stopped her own work to help. It was an act she paid for, however, when five o'clock arrived and Miss Grayson ordered everyone to put down their needles.

The schoolmistress walked around, checking the work that had been done, apparently unmoved by everyone's raw, bleeding fingers. Finally she returned to the front of the classroom.

"Estella," she said softly. "How many suits have you produced?"

"Forty-eight."

"How many were you asked to make?"

"Fifty."

"And why have you not done as you were asked?"

Estella stared straight at the teacher. "I wasn't fast enough, miss."

"You are the only girl here who has failed to produce fifty outfits. The only girl here too lazy to apply herself and work hard."

I noticed Bess staring down anxiously at her own pile of dresses and although I longed to say that Estella had made some of them I knew I couldn't without getting both girls in trouble. It was so dreadfully unfair. Suits were a lot more complicated and Estella had done marvellously well to make so many. But it was obvious that Miss Grayson was not going to be fair.

"Miss Black," she said. "Kindly write Estella's name in the Punishment Book and record that her penalty for idleness is to be twelve lashings of the tawse."

Feeling physically sick, I made my way to the front of the class and did as the schoolmistress had asked. I lay down the pen as Miss Grayson beckoned Estella to the front of the room and the words burst out of me. "Miss Grayson, may I say something in Estella's defence?"

"You may not," the schoolmistress snapped. "And if you utter one more word, Miss Black, I will double the number of lashes she receives."

Seething, I could do nothing but stand and watch as Miss Grayson instructed Estella to lay her hands flat on the desk, with her back facing towards her. Miss Grayson then picked up her tawse, raised it high over her head and thrashed Estella as hard as she could. It was a vicious whipping that split the shirt on the girl's back, and caused blood to well up with each stroke. There was total silence in the room except for the sound of that dreadful lashing, which seemed to go on for an eternity.

Tears ran silently down Estella's face but she didn't utter so much as a whimper and I admired her greatly for that. Sweat spotted Miss Grayson's face and stained her shirt beneath the arms by the time it was finally over.

"I trust that a lesson has been learned here today," Miss Grayson said. "You will go straight to bed without dinner. I suggest you all reflect on your dishonesty in order that another day like this does not occur."

The girls filed out in a subdued fashion, Estella leaving last, walking slowly and stiffly, wincing with every step.

I set about collecting the dolls, beginning with Estella's Frozen Charlie. I couldn't help starting at the sight of his suits. They were all grey and, although I knew it could only be a coincidence, the thought rose in my mind that Edward Redwing always wore grey suits.

When I passed by Bess's desk I saw that the top dress, one that Estella had made for her, had been cut from a striking cornflower blue fabric, almost the same shade as the dress I had been wearing the night Whiteladies burned to the ground…

"The same goes for you, Miss Black," Miss Grayson said from her desk, interrupting my thoughts. "Once you've collected up the dolls, please put them on my desk and then go directly to your bedroom. I do not want to see you again until tomorrow."

I took a basket from the cupboard, gathered the dolls and put them on Miss Grayson's desk, then turned and walked from the room without a word. I went straight to my bedroom but only paused long enough to collect my cloak before creeping back down the servants' stairs. I half expected to see Dolores there with her duster but the staircase was empty. I slipped out without being seen and made my way to Henry's cottage.

He opened the door at my knock, Murphy hopping around his feet in excitement.

"Jemima!" he exclaimed, beaming at me.

"I can't stay," I said at once. "Miss Grayson has sent me to my room and will be furious if she finds I'm gone. There's something I need to ask you. Something that can't wait until tomorrow."

"What is it?" Henry asked, immediately serious.

"You mentioned that Estella almost died last year after Miss Grayson put her in Solitary for several days?"

"That's right," Henry replied. "It was August and there was a heatwave. It was all hushed up, of course. Miss Grayson doesn't want any negative publicity for the school."

"Do you know what Estella did to get put in there in the first place? I looked in the Punishment Book and it said she was punished for lying, but it doesn't say what the lie was. Do you happen to know?"

"I do," Henry replied. "In fact, you and I have spoken about it before. The girls were all very upset about it at the time and so were the maids. You see, there used to be a girl who worked here called Dolores. She fell down the servants' stairs and died a couple of years ago."

"Yes, Miss Grayson told me."

"Well, last summer, Estella told everyone that she had seen Dolores, that she'd even spoken to her, on the servants' staircase. It caused a terrible furore at the time. That's why Estella got put in Solitary." He gave me another close look. "But why does any of that matter now, Mim?"

I hadn't meant to tell him but, somehow, the words spilled out of me anyway. "I've seen Dolores, too," I said. "I saw her on my first day at the school. She was on the servants' staircase, dusting the banister. She seemed surprised when I spoke to her and I thought perhaps it was because no one had told her I was coming, but now I think it must have been because she didn't expect me to be able to see her."

Henry grasped my arm gently. "But, Mim, old thing," he said, "you don't believe in ghosts. You've told me so many times. All those séances you held with your mother were completely fake, weren't they?"

I rubbed at my temples with my hand. Henry knew the truth about our séances well enough. After all, his mother had designed my special shoes with the concealed wooden block herself.

"I know," I said, "but I did see Dolores, Henry, and I spoke with her, too—"

"Jemima! What the devil has happened to your hands?" Henry exclaimed.

I dropped my hand and looked at my bloodied fingers.

"Oh," I said. "That was Miss Grayson's punishment for the girls and me. We've been sewing all day. There was an incident last night with the dolls—"

"Come inside for a moment," Henry said, gently tugging me over the threshold.

I found myself standing in a cosy little kitchen with a wooden table in the centre of the room and

Murphy now warming himself in front of a fire.

"Sit down at the table, Mim," Henry said.

"But Miss Grayson—"

"If she finds out then I'll tell her I kidnapped you. It'll be my fault entirely."

I didn't have the energy to argue with him, so I pulled out a chair and sat down. Murphy struggled to his feet and hopped straight over to me, flopping down and laying his scruffy head on my feet. It was a relief to stroke his ears and allow my mind to go blank for a moment.

"I suppose Miss Grayson withheld meals today, too?" Henry said. "I hear that's a favourite punishment of hers."

"That's right," I replied. "She was in a terribly bad mood with us all."

A few minutes later, Henry placed a cup of tea and a plate of toast in front of me, before setting down a bowl of soapy warm water and settling himself on the floor beside me. "Can you manage all right with one hand, if I clean the other?" he asked.

"I can. Thank you."

Henry took one of my hands and carefully rinsed away the blood, gently cleaning the many pricks and cuts, while I set upon the tea and toast. I hadn't realized quite how ravenous I was until that moment. As I was enjoying the food, though, I felt a deep throb of guilt for the girls who'd gone to bed hungry back at the school, especially Estella.

Henry didn't speak, for which I was grateful, but bent over my hand in silent concentration. Gazing down at his chestnut curls, I felt an almost overpowering surge of affection for him. He really was quite the most kind, decent, wonderful person I had ever met. But something had broken in me back at Whiteladies and I was no longer the person Henry had once loved.

Finally he finished with my hands and threw away the bowl of bloody water before pulling out a chair across from me.

"I suppose you think I've absolutely lost my mind," I said, putting down my empty cup.

"Not a bit of it," Henry replied. To my surprise, he reached over and took my hand in his. "If you tell me you saw Dolores at the school then, of course, I believe you. It does mean that Estella isn't the liar everyone believes her to be, though."

"Yes," I said. "I need to speak to her." I looked back at him. "Henry, thank you for everything but now I really must go." I stood up.

Henry moved past me to open the front door. As I walked by he said, "Just remember I'm here. If you ever want to tell me about it."

I looked at him but his gaze was fixed on his feet rather than me. I touched his arm briefly, then stepped out into the freezing evening. I'd already been gone longer than I'd meant to and I clutched my cloak tightly about me as I hurried across the grounds.

When I was only a few metres away, I glanced up just in time to see a light suddenly switch on. Even before counting the windows, I knew which room it was shining from. Someone was up in the toy room again, with the dolls.

I quickened my pace back towards the school.

Chapter Eighteen

Isle of Skye – January 1910

I quietly let myself into the schoolhouse and made my way directly to the toy room. The door was slightly ajar, light spilling out into the corridor. When I pushed it open and stepped in, I half expected Estella or one of the other girls to be there, but the room was empty. Miss Grayson must have brought up the basket of dolls, for I saw it placed just inside the room, the Frozen Charlottes laid out in their new outfits.

My eyes went straight to the dolls' house version of Whiteladies and, once again, I saw that there was a single light on. The light inside Edward Redwing's study.

Charlotte says something bad happened in that room...

Unbuttoning my cloak, I walked over and pulled open the front of the house. Immediately I saw that someone had placed three dolls inside, grouped together in the wood-panelled room. Firstly there was the Frozen Charlie Estella had been making suits for earlier. Secondly the Frozen Charlotte in the cornflower blue dress I'd noticed on Bess's desk. And finally a Frozen Charlotte in a pale green tea gown with an empire waistline and a flowery porcelain bonnet attached to her head. I couldn't help thinking that Mother had owned several bonnets like this, as well as a Lucile dress Redwing had bought on their honeymoon that was almost the exact same shade of green.

The doll wearing the bonnet lay on the floor behind the desk, with just her feet poking out the other side. The Frozen Charlotte in the cornflower blue gown had been awkwardly placed in the armchair beside the fire, just where I had always sat during Redwing's trance sessions. And the Frozen Charlie was standing behind this chair. He'd been propped up in such a way that he leaned forward slightly, looming over the Frozen Charlotte, the tiny hawk cane cradled in the crook of his arm. Just the sight of the little scene made a shiver run through me.

It could only be a coincidence. No one here at the school knew anything about what had happened at Whiteladies.

Hastily I snatched up the dolls, ignoring the cane that rolled across the floor. I took them over to the basket by the door where, to my surprise, I saw the toy-room key, glinting dully in among all those pale limbs.

I placed the dolls in the basket before picking out the key and then closing and locking the door behind me. It was not yet seven o'clock and I thought the girls would probably still be awake. I walked down the corridor to their dormitory, wishing that I had some food or drink to bring them. I'd thought I'd been doing an act of kindness by giving them the Frozen Charlottes and the dolls' house but it seemed like the toys had caused nothing but trouble ever since they'd arrived. Perhaps I should have thrown them out the moment I received them.

When I opened the door and peered into the dormitory, I saw that almost all of the girls were in their beds. No doubt they were trying to keep warm. With no fire, the room was bitterly cold, and going hungry was only likely to make them feel even colder.

There was just one girl who wasn't in bed and that was Estella. She was standing gazing out of the window. I knew at once it was her because she hadn't changed out of her shirt, which was bloody and ripped.

"She's out there," Estella said, without turning round. "She's looking up at the schoolhouse."

"Who is?" Martha asked, sitting up in bed.

"One of the Frozen Charlottes," Estella said. "She must have got outside somehow."

"The dolls are magic," Bess said from her bed.

"The dolls are murder," Estella responded. "They want to do terrible, awful things to us. They want to see us bleed and burn and rot in hell."

"They do not!" Bess exclaimed. "They told me they wanted to be my friends – my best friends!" She started to cry.

"Why do you always have to spoil everything, Estella?" Martha demanded. "Why can't you just be normal?"

"It doesn't matter anyway," Estella said. "The Frozen Charlottes will slaughter us all if they can. Every last one of us."

Bess cried even harder.

"Shut up!" Martha cried. "God, Estella, you're such a freak!"

"Martha, that's enough!" I said, stepping into the room.

She fell silent at once, clearly startled by my presence.

"Bess, please stop crying. The dolls can't hurt you," I said. "Estella, come with me for a moment."

She turned from the window and then walked slowly over. "What have I done wrong now?" she asked, giving me a defiant look.

"Nothing," I replied. "Just follow me, please."

We left the dormitory and I led the way down the corridor to the bathroom, ushering Estella inside and then closing and locking the door behind us.

"We need to get you out of that shirt and wash the blood off your back," I said. "I'd like to help if you'll let me."

Estella gave an angry shrug, which I took as permission. In the hour or so since she'd been flogged, the blood had congealed and dried, sticking the shirt to her skin. I tried my best to be gentle, but there was no way of removing the shirt without re-opening the wounds, which immediately started to bleed again.

"I'm sorry," I said, as Estella flinched.

She didn't reply and I silently set about sponging away the blood, wincing at the sight of those angry red slashes.

"I saw what you did for Bess today," I said.

"I don't know what you mean," Estella replied.

"It's all right, I won't tell anyone. I thought it was a very kind thing to do."

Estella said nothing. I rinsed out the sponge, watching the water turn pink in the basin.

"Estella, I need to tell you something," I said. "I've seen Dolores, too. She was on the servants' stairs on my first morning here."

Estella looked up sharply, meeting my gaze in the mirror that hung on the opposite wall.

She looked doubtful, so I said, "I swear to you I'm telling the truth. I really did see her." I proceeded to describe her appearance.

"She's often there," Estella said. "Dusting on the staircase. Humming. Sometimes I think she forgets that she's dead. And she gets stuck in a loop. Going round and round and round. Over and over again."

"Tell me about what happened when your brother died," I said quietly. "And, Estella, I promise I'll believe you this time."

"He fell through the ice," Estella said in a quiet voice. "I lay by the hole and stuck my arm into the water and waved it around but he never grabbed hold of my hand. He never grabbed hold of it. Then suddenly he was standing there on the other side of the lake. Talking to me. He told me not to worry and that he was all right." She frowned. "I couldn't understand why he wasn't wet. It was like he'd never fallen through the ice at all. He disappeared into the trees before I could ask him and, when I got back to the house, he was in his bedroom. I could hear him talking to himself in there. John always used to talk to himself."

"Only he wasn't in his bedroom at all, was he?" I said.

"No," Estella almost whispered. "John drowned in the lake when he fell through the ice. He was already dead when he spoke to me. No one believed that I had really seen him."

Holding her arms, I gently turned her round to face me so I could look her straight in the eye. "I believe you," I said. "I believe that you saw him and that you saw Dolores."

Estella looked at me in silence before, finally, she

said, "If you believe me about that, then do you believe me about the Frozen Charlotte dolls, too? Do you believe that they're the ones who killed Whiskers?"

I gazed at her. "Estella, I don't know what to think. I've never believed in ghosts my whole life. But since I arrived at this school, I'm not so sure. Dolls that move about on their own, though? That … I mean, that's just madness."

"They're evil," Estella said. "You should get rid of them."

"I can't."

"Why not?"

"Because if what you say is true, if the dolls really are haunted somehow, then I think they might know the answer to something I want to know. Something I need to know."

I saw that closed door in my mind's eye once again.

Charlotte says something bad happened in that room…

"You should get rid of the dolls," Estella said again. "Before something really terrible happens."

"I'll keep them locked in the toy room," I said. "I have the key and I won't let it out of my sight this time. It'll be all right, I promise."

Estella simply shook her head at me. "You'll see," she said. "Everyone will see in the end."

I fetched a nightdress for her to change into and then sent her to bed. When I got back to my room, I pressed my fingers against my aching temples, trying to make sense of it all. Could it be that the dolls were haunted, or was I simply allowing myself to get pulled into the disturbed tales of a small girl? My mind was in a whirl and I felt exhausted after the long and difficult day.

I tucked the key into the pocket of my nightdress before climbing into bed, where I was immediately dragged down into sleep.

Several hours later, I was woken by a scream.

Not a cry, or a moan, or a whimper.

An ear-splitting, bloodcurdling, hair-raising scream of agony and terror.

And it was coming from the girls' dormitory.

Chapter Nineteen

Whiteladies — One month earlier

My trance sessions with Redwing became a nightly occurrence. Each time he would have me hold a Frozen Charlotte doll and stare into the red eyes of that devilish hawk, and then his mellow voice would lead me to some dark place where I lost all sense of self. I could never remember anything of what had happened during the sessions. Often, when he snapped me out of it, I would have new cuts or burns or bruises. On one occasion, my clothes were even ripped in several places.

"It was necessary to restrain you," Redwing said, when I asked him about it. "You became over-excited."

The sessions made me feel strange and tired and unlike myself. Mother still mostly kept to her room, but she soon found out that I had taken her place and was wretched about it, fairly begging me to tell Redwing I no longer wished to participate.

"It's too late for that, Mother," I told her. "He won't allow me to stop now, even if I ask. I know he won't."

I still nurtured the faint hope that, eventually, Redwing would be satisfied and the trance sessions would stop. But it was a hope that grew smaller with each passing day. What had I got myself into and how on earth could I make it stop?

I occasionally thought of suggesting to Mother that we run away, but we had surrendered our tenancy of the townhouse after the wedding and we had no money between us, nowhere to go, no shelter in which to hide. Besides which, the law wouldn't look kindly on a deserting wife, and I was sure that Redwing would use his wealth and power to track us down eventually.

One afternoon I was sitting in my bedroom, wearing my favourite cornflower-blue dress, staring into the mirror and wondering what on earth I could do to make my lot in life bearable. Then, without making any conscious decision, I found myself walking downstairs to Redwing's study. The room was empty so I set to work going through his desk, rifling through his private papers. I don't know quite what I expected to find. Something to blackmail him with perhaps – some way out of this dreadful nightmare.

The bottom drawer was locked but I forced it open with a letter opener, not caring that Redwing would know I'd been there. I found the drawer stuffed full of paper – sheets and sheets of it, all covered in writing. I grabbed a fistful and saw that every sheet was covered in an erratic, slashed scrawl, spreading all over the page in the most terrible mess, liberally stained with ink spots and splashes. It seemed that Redwing had made rapid progress with his automatic writing. There had been no attempt to write neatly or in lines. Some of it was, in fact, completely illegible. But there was the odd word that stood out starkly upon the page.

Devil…

Hell…

Blood…

Murder…

Kill…

Kill…

Kill…

And there were other words, too. Language so unspeakably vile that my face went hot at the sight of them.

"God in heaven!" I muttered.

"Did you find what you were looking for?"

I looked up to see Redwing standing in the doorway watching me, an unreadable expression on his face.

"This is … obscene," I said. "All of this is … it's unnatural and wicked." I closed my fists around the paper, screwing it up into balls and dropping them on the floor. "I thought you only wanted to speak to Vanessa?"

"Other voices are stronger than hers," Redwing replied. "But, if we just persist, a professional medium like you is eventually bound to—"

"I'm not a professional medium, you fool!" I cried. "I'm a professional fraudster! An actress, a performance artist, an illusionist! The same is true for Mother!"

And then, without pausing to think about the wisdom of it, I proceeded to detail every single trick Mother and I had ever used. I explained exactly how we deceived our clients, making them believe we had spoken to their loved ones; I told him that we were actors playing a part and that neither one of us had ever glimpsed a single ghost, not even so much as a shadow in a mirror. I suppose some small part of me hoped that, if he knew we were fakes, perhaps those awful trance sessions might stop.

Throughout my tirade, Redwing simply gazed at me, his expression neutral. By the time I finally ran out of words, I was breathing hard.

For a moment there was just the sound of my panting.

Then Redwing said quietly, "You have deceived me, is that what you're saying? That I have been tricked into a sham of a marriage by a pair of clever bitches whose only aim was to get their hands on my money and my estate?"

"It wasn't the only aim," I said hopelessly, already regretting what I'd done. "Mother would have been a good wife and I would have been a good stepdaughter to you if you had only permitted us to—"

"I see how it is perfectly," Redwing cut me off. "Your mother practised an elaborate deception, worming her way into my home on the pretence of being able to help me establish contact with my dead daughter and yet somehow I am the one who is to blame. In your own mind, I think you honestly believe that I am the villain."

Tears began to roll down my cheeks. I simply didn't know what to say or do any more. Everything I tried just seemed to make the situation worse.

Redwing crossed the room in a few strides and suddenly his hand was round my throat, squeezing hard enough to cut off the air and choke me.

"Don't waste your crocodile tears on me, my dear," he said softly. "They will do you no good. And if you think your little confession is going to excuse you from future trance sessions then you are quite wrong. We will not stop. We will never stop until I have made contact with Vanessa."

He released his hold and I sucked in air in a painful gasp, my throat burning, my heart filled with the most poisonous hatred for him.

"Speaking of which," Redwing said, turning away from me and picking up his hawk-topped cane. "It is almost time to begin. Take your seat, please, Jemima."

Still crying, still despising him, I sat down in my usual chair by the fire and our last session began.

Just a few hours later, I found myself standing in the gardens with the servants, watching Whiteladies burn to the ground, with no memory of how I'd got there or what had happened since I fell into the trance some hours before.

Chapter Twenty

Isle of Skye – January 1910

The scream was the most terrible sound I'd ever heard. I was out of bed, my bare feet smarting on the freezing boards, before I even understood what was happening. It was not just one girl screaming now, but several of them.

My first confused thought was that some madman had broken into the school. Some Jack the Ripper lunatic intent on slaughtering us all with a carving knife. I ran to the door, out into the corridor and straight to the dormitory.

One of the girls had already switched on the gaslight and a shocking scene lay before me.

There was no frenzied serial killer but there was blood. It was on the bedsheets, splattered in big smears across the white pillow; it was on the floorboards and it was on Martha's nightgown, running in twin trails down her face – straight from the two needles that pierced each of her eyes, pinning them closed.

Nausea churned in my stomach at the sight. Martha was slumped on the floor by her bed, making an anguished moaning sound. A few girls were clustered around her, although no one seemed to want to touch her. The remaining girls were in their beds, gripping their bedsheets. And Estella was standing silent and motionless on the other side of the room, a sewing kit hanging from her hand.

Miss Grayson burst in. I couldn't believe that she'd paused to put on her wig. There was a time and a place for vanity, and this surely was not it.

"Everyone be silent!" she yelled. "What is the meaning of this?"

"Martha's hurt," I said, striding through the girls to kneel down on the floor next to her. The moment I said her name and touched her shoulder, she threw her arms round my neck and clung to me. Her entire body was trembling and she was practically choking on her sobs.

"What happened?" Miss Grayson rasped out.

"There was a Frozen Charlotte doll!" Martha gasped. "I woke up and … it was there … on the bed … looking at me. She had needles in her hands and I thought … I thought she wanted me to make another

218

dress for her. But then … when I … when I … b-b-blinked … she … she stabbed me with them!"

"That is nonsense!" Miss Grayson said in a hoarse voice. "Utter nonsense! Girls! Speak up! Someone must have seen what happened."

"It was Estella!" Bess cried, pointing at the other girl. "She had an argument with Martha tonight and then she attacked her!"

Everyone looked at Estella.

"I didn't do it," she whispered. "It wasn't me. It was the doll." She looked down at the sewing kit in her hand. "I tried to stop her but it was too late. It was too late."

Miss Grayson flew at her, grabbing the girl by her collar and practically dragging her from the room.

"Wait here," the schoolmistress said to me over her shoulder. "And, whatever you do, don't let Martha remove those needles!"

I pulled a blanket from the nearby bed and wrapped Martha up in it, trying to keep her warm as best I could, although I knew well enough it was more than cold that made her tremble. Her hand kept coming up to claw at her eyes and I had to grab her wrists in the end.

"Martha, dear, I'm sorry, but you mustn't," I said. "You might make it worse. Miss Grayson will send for the physician and he will know what to do."

Miss Grayson returned soon enough, without Estella, and informed us that Henry had been sent on a horse to Dunvegan to fetch the physician. In the meantime, we would just have to wait. Miss Grayson sat herself down in a chair as far away from everyone as she could. She didn't speak to Martha or attempt to touch her or reassure her in any way. I didn't know what to say, either, so I simply held the trembling girl tight and hoped that the physical contact was somehow reassuring.

We seemed to wait an age in that room. Time stretched on and on. The girls cried and shivered in their beds. Martha clung to me, her breathing too loud and too fast.

Finally there was the sound of carriage wheels on the drive outside and, a moment later, men's boots upon the stairs. Henry burst into the room, closely followed by the physician – a tall, thin man with an overly waxed moustache.

Martha was bundled away from me and taken downstairs by the physician and Miss Grayson.

I wanted to go with them but Miss Grayson had instructed me to remain upstairs. Henry and I were left with the task of calming the girls and persuading them to go to sleep. It wasn't as difficult as I'd anticipated. The girls were frightened and upset but they were also exhausted. Soon enough they were tucked back in, and Henry and I tiptoed out into the corridor.

He immediately grabbed my hand, hurried us both into my bedroom and closed the door behind us. I expected him to bombard me with questions about what had happened to Martha but instead, the moment the door closed, he turned round and stared at me.

And that was when I realized. In my haste to get to the girls, I hadn't paused to put on my dressing gown. I hadn't covered up my arms. My scars were displayed for all the world to see. I wrapped my hands round myself but, of course, it was too late for that now.

Henry drew a deep breath. "Tell me who did this to you, Jemima," he said. "Tell me at once."

"Henry, really, it doesn't matter any more," I tried.

"Doesn't matter?" he replied, his voice low and harsh. "Doesn't matter? How can you say that? It matters tremendously, in fact, because I am going to murder whoever's responsible."

"Don't talk nonsense," I said. "Even if you wanted to do something foolish, you can't. Edward Redwing is responsible and he's gone, as you know. Burned to death in the fire at Whiteladies."

Henry ran both hands through his hair. "But why in God's name?" he said. "Why would any man act in such a manner?"

"He was out of his mind," I said softly.

As I said the words I could feel, once again, those fingers pressing into my neck, smell burning flesh as the red-hot tip of a cigarette was pressed against my skin and held there, hear Redwing's mellow voice whisper in my ear, breathe in that dreadful scent of Macassar oil. I saw the fixed gaze of the Frozen Charlotte doll staring back at me, dead hands outstretched, while the hawk's eyes burned their hot, ruby stare straight into my soul...

"Oh Henry, he was just completely out of his mind!"

Perhaps it was the shock of what had happened to Martha, or the lateness of the hour, or the pressure of having kept everything to myself for so long, or a combination of all of these things, but before I could stop myself, I started to cry.

Henry crossed the room, gathered me up in his arms and held me tight against his chest, stroking my hair.

"I've got you, Mim," he murmured in my ear. "I've got you. I've got you."

When there were no tears left, I found myself grabbing his arm and begging him to stay.

"Please, Henry," I said. "I can't face being here on my own tonight, I really can't. Please say you'll stay?"

"My darling girl," he replied, "I'll be here with you for as long as you want me."

I couldn't help but give a raw sob of relief. Despite the outrageous impropriety, we slept in the same bed that night. Miss Grayson was unlikely to come bursting into my bedroom in the middle of the night but in that moment I wouldn't even have cared if she'd discovered us and thrown me out. In fact, I would have been glad to leave this awful school.

The heat from Henry's body warmed my back as he wrapped his arms round me and tucked his chin against my shoulder. I clutched his hand, holding it tight, and that's how we fell asleep.

It was the first time in an age that I had felt warm and safe and loved.

Chapter Twenty-One

Isle of Skye – January 1910

The intimacy of having been wrapped up with Henry all night, coupled with the fact that he now knew the truth about my time at Whiteladies, made me feel terribly embarrassed the next morning. He didn't behave any differently towards me, although I noticed a faint blush on his cheeks and I think we were both a little shocked at how rashly we had behaved.

When Henry returned to his cottage to feed Murphy, I went straight to the toy room. The door was still locked, and when I opened it and stepped inside, there was nothing amiss. The dolls lay innocently in their basket; the Whiteladies house was exactly as I had left it.

The Frozen Charlottes had been in a locked room all night. How could they possibly be responsible for what had happened to Martha?

I went downstairs and found Miss Grayson

in her study. The large cabinet behind her was unlocked and I saw for the first time what was inside. Shelf after shelf was filled with dolls, but they weren't like the Frozen Charlottes. These were bigger, with elaborate lace dresses, pretty painted features and long, flowing hair. There must have been thirty dolls there, all gazing out at me with their glass eyes. Their hair was all different styles and colours, from red ringlets to elaborate blond chignons.

Miss Grayson was seated at her desk with a brunette doll sat before her. To my astonishment, she was calmly and methodically brushing the doll's hair. I cleared my throat, and the schoolmistress stopped brushing and glanced up. She looked like she hadn't slept all night. There were dark shadows beneath her eyes and her wig was crooked on her head.

"What do you want?" she asked in a flat voice.

"Martha—" I began.

"Is blind," Miss Grayson said shortly. "The physician cleaned and bandaged her eyes, but she'll never see again."

I didn't know what to say. Absurdly I found

myself thinking of what a talented artist she had been – those beautiful drawings she had created during Henry's art classes.

"I have already sent Hannah to inform the police," Miss Grayson said. "They should be here any moment to collect Estella."

"But we don't know that it *was* Estella—" I began.

"Of course it was Estella, you stupid girl!" Miss Grayson snapped. "You saw her with the sewing kit in her hand! We know she argued with Martha last night. She is a wicked child."

"Where is Martha now?" I asked.

"Resting in bed," Miss Grayson replied. "In the sick room where she can have some peace and quiet."

"Have her family been informed?"

"A telegram will be sent as soon as the post office opens."

"And what about Estella?"

"She's in Solitary."

"Solitary?" I repeated, aghast. "My God, you can't be serious! It's freezing outside!"

"I'm quite aware of that, Miss Black." Miss Grayson looked up and fixed me with a glare.

"I must ask you to please stop bothering me with these endless questions. Estella is none of your concern. None of the girls are. Now, as you can see, I am currently occupied here, so please go and tend to your duties."

I left her to her dolls. As I made my way to the cloakroom, I couldn't help remembering what Estella had said about Miss Grayson confiscating the toys so she could play with them herself. Suddenly it didn't seem quite so unlikely, although I never would have thought the old shrew would be the type to play with dolls.

I threw on my cloak and boots and hurried out to the little hut on the edge of the grounds. It was a ramshackle thing, the roof covered in snow and the wooden door fastened shut with a padlock.

I banged on the door with my fist. "Estella!" I called. "Are you all right?"

To my dismay, there was no answer. I peered through a gap in one of the boards and saw a small, bare room with only chinks of light shining through the gaps. There was nothing inside except for a metal bucket in one corner. And there was Estella, curled up in the middle of the floor with her back to me, wearing nothing but her thin nightdress. The wounds on her back from yesterday's flogging must have re-opened because the white material was bloodstained.

"Oh my God!" I said under my breath. I looked around, searching for help, but there was no one nearby and Henry's cottage was on the other side of the school. I was torn, wanting to run and fetch him but hating the thought of leaving Estella lying on the frozen floorboards like that.

I threw my shoulder against the wooden door with all the force I could. It made a groaning sound and a few pieces splintered off but it remained locked tight. I peered through the gap in the planks again, expecting to see Estella where she'd been before, but there was no sign of her. For a moment I thought the shed was empty, that she had managed to get out somehow.

Then I saw her standing motionless in the corner of the shed, facing the wall, talking to someone who wasn't there.

"Let's play a game," she was saying, over and over again. "Let's play a game, let's play a game, let's play a game..."

A second voice seemed to come from the shed – a thin, high-pitched tone that must have been put on by Estella herself, for there was no one else in there.

"Yes, yes, yes! Let's play the fingernails game!"

Estella groaned, a low moaning sound in the back of her throat. "We already played that game," she said with a dry sob. "I don't want to play that game any more!"

"Estella!" I called through the gap. "Who are you talking to?"

She remained facing the wall with her head bent, her long hair hanging down in curtains past her face. But although Estella stayed motionless, a Frozen Charlotte doll suddenly popped up over her shoulder, its little china head pointed towards me, its painted eyes seeming to stare straight into mine.

There was a high-pitched giggle and I knew it must have come from Estella, but it seemed as if it had come from the doll.

"Hello, Mother! Do you want to play a game? The first one to bite off all their fingernails wins! Ready, set, go!"

At that moment a police motorcar pulled into the drive. Frantically I waved it down and before long two burly constables were tackling the door. They quickly forced it open and I pushed past them to get to Estella, gripping her shivering shoulders and turning her round to face me. She clutched the Frozen Charlotte in a bloody hand and I gasped as I saw that every single one of her fingernails was gone. They looked as if they'd been ripped off and the blood smears on Estella's chin, coupled with what she'd just said, made me realize she must have bitten them off herself. When I looked down I saw that the bloody fingernails lay on the floor around us. Blood ran down Estella's fingers, and I winced at the sight of the delicate, pink, exposed skin where her nails had been.

"God, Estella, what have you done?"

She gazed at me with a lifeless look in her eyes. "The Frozen Charlottes get inside your head," she said. "They make you do things. Things you don't want to do. Things you can't take back. Things you'll go to hell and burn for."

"Can you bring the girl out, please, miss?" one of the constables called from the doorway.

Ignoring him, I crouched down and said, "Estella, did you hurt Martha last night?"

231

She shook her head. "It was Charlotte," she said, holding up the bloody doll. Its ugly little face seemed to pout at me. "I tried to stop her but I wasn't fast enough." She gazed at the doll. "One minute she was lying on the floor, in the corner of the room. The next second she had flashed across to Martha's bed with the needles. Just a white blur. There was nothing I could do. Nothing anyone could do."

"But … but even if what you're saying is possible, why would the dolls do something like that?" I said desperately.

"Why don't you ask them?" Estella replied. "They're not shy. If you talk to them, they'll probably talk right back. Only you might not like what they have to say."

Fed up with waiting, one of the policemen was squeezing himself into the shed. Estella pressed the doll into my hand. "Lock her away," she whispered. "Somewhere safe."

The next thing I knew, Estella was being bundled up by the police and taken, bleeding and shivering, into the kitchen.

"What is the meaning of this?" Miss Grayson

demanded when she walked in a few moments later. "Who authorized this girl to be removed from Solitary? I gave strict instructions that the police were to be shown to my study the moment they arrived."

"Madam, it is freezing outside," one of the officers replied. "Had this child stayed out much longer, she certainly would have died."

"The girl maliciously blinded another student during the night!" Miss Grayson said. "What else could I have done? She has a deranged mind and is a danger to us all!"

"Yes, we received your report that a girl had been blinded," the second police officer said. "And then we arrive to find another girl, bleeding and half frozen to death, locked in a shed." He turned his gaze directly on to Miss Grayson. "What the devil," he said, "is going on at this school?"

The physician returned, this time to see to Estella. I could tell that Miss Grayson resented the expense but she didn't have much choice with the police there. Once he had gone the constables questioned Martha,

Estella and Miss Grayson herself – something the schoolmistress was most put out about. She was even more vexed when they refused to arrest Estella without any evidence against her. Martha's family had sent a telegram to say her father was still in debtors' prison and her aunt said she already had too many mouths of her own to feed. Estella's parents had also been contacted and their brief reply simply stated that they would pay for any medical attention their daughter might require but that she must remain at the school.

Martha still occupied the sick room and as Miss Grayson didn't want the two girls together, Estella was put in a cot bed before the fire in her study. The schoolmistress gave instructions that Cassie and Hannah were to take it in turns sitting with Martha but that nobody was to go near Estella.

"The girl is dangerous," she said. "She's likely to attack us if she's given half the chance."

I hated them all. Simply hated them. Estella was a sad, lonely little girl who had received no warmth or kindness or understanding at this school. Even now, when she lay in bed shivering and barely conscious, half-frozen, with a whipped back and missing fingernails, they still insisted on treating her like a savage animal.

"I thought there was something funny about her," I heard Cassie whisper to Hannah once Miss Grayson had left. "She's always given me the creeps, especially after what she said about Dolores. Weird little freak."

"She belongs in an asylum," Hannah replied. "It's not right having her here. It's not right."

"Perhaps you should seek employment elsewhere if you're so uncomfortable here," I snapped at them. Then, unable to resist, I added, "Besides which, Estella is not at all mad, she is just uncommonly sensitive to the spirit world."

"And what would you know about that?" Cassie sneered, not bothering with any pretence of friendliness towards me now that Henry wasn't here to witness it.

"Plenty. My mother was a medium," I replied. "I grew up conducting séances with her. Ask Henry if you don't believe me. And Dolores is still here at the school. I've seen her." I pointed a finger at Hannah. "Mostly she follows you around as you're going about your chores. I've often seen her standing behind you, peering over your shoulder, sniffing at the poor job you're doing."

Hannah gave a squeak of alarm and scuttled off.

"That was a mean thing to say," Cassie said in a self-righteous tone.

"Don't you dare play high and mighty with me," I said. "You didn't seem to care much about kindness when you were gossiping about Estella or nosing at private letters sent by her parents, or kicking the cat one moment and acting worried about him the next. Girls like you, who pretend to be all sweet and lovely but are actually poisonous, are even worse than the obviously nasty ones. Well, I'm not falling for it! I see you for what you truly are."

Cassie scowled at me and then turned and left the room. As she went, I distinctly heard her mutter an insult that would have made most girls blush. After she'd gone, I stood there, breathing hard. I knew what it was like to be an outsider and it seemed to me that no one at this school had made the slightest effort to make Estella's life any easier. I was determined to help her, even if no one else would. Estella's life could be turned around – I was sure of it. It did not have to be a doomed, tragic tale from start to finish. I would not allow it.

The bell had rung for first lessons, but I ignored it and went to Miss Grayson's study instead, pulling up a chair and sitting down by Estella's bedside. If Miss Grayson wanted to dock my wages for ignoring her instructions and missing class, then so be it. Estella was asleep but I sat with her anyway, holding her hand, and watching the rise and fall of her thin chest. The physician had said that she should recover as long as she was kept warm but listening to the rattling sound she made with each breath made me anxious.

The schoolmistress appeared after an hour had passed by, her mouth forming itself into that straight, thin line I'd grown to dread.

"Miss Black," she said. "I thought I might find you here. Perhaps you would be so good as to do your job and take the girls for their cookery class?"

"I don't think Estella should be left alone," I said. "She needs someone to watch over her."

Miss Grayson gave a great sigh. "I have correspondence to see to," she said. "I will be here." She sniffed. "It's probably a good idea to keep watch over her at any rate. In case she decides to go on the rampage again, with a carving knife or some such."

I stood up reluctantly. "I'll take the cookery class, then."

With one last glance at Estella, I left the study and made my way to the kitchen. The girls were lined up in front of the worktops when I arrived and were, unsurprisingly, terribly subdued. A few of them asked after Martha but nobody, I noticed, wanted to know how Estella was.

"Come on now," I said briskly. "We must get on with the lesson. We'll be making toast sandwiches today."

A few of the girls groaned and I couldn't blame them. The dry, flavourless sandwiches were not a favourite of anyone's. They were one of the most economical recipes in Mrs Beeton's book and consisted of a thin, dry piece of toast, sandwiched between two pieces of buttered bread. It did not make for a satisfying meal, by any means.

"But," I said, "instead of butter you may take anything you like from the confiscated shelf and use that in your sandwich instead. We could even make some chocolate spread."

This definitely cheered them up. Miss Grayson was very much against the girls having sweet treats of any kind. Sugar was bad for their teeth, she said, and made them unruly, excitable and lazy. On the odd occasion when one of the girls received an edible gift from their families, it was almost always confiscated and placed on the forbidden top shelf.

I knew I'd certainly get into trouble for allowing the girls to loot it but right then I didn't care. They hurried over and I passed down chocolate, biscuits and various other treats. There was a jar of peanuts on the shelf, too, but given that Estella mustn't have nuts under any circumstances, it seemed to me that the jar shouldn't have been in the cupboard at all. I threw it straight in the bin.

After all the awfulness of the last few days, it was pleasant to be able to forget about everything that was happening for a while and concentrate instead on doing something normal. Soon enough, the kitchen was filled with the scent of toast and melted chocolate. The girls plastered the chocolate spread thickly on to their bread and I let them put on as much as they wanted. At the end of the lesson they had their toast sandwiches for elevenses and everyone was a little more cheerful than they had been at the start.

I let the girls go for their morning break a few minutes early and stayed behind to clean up the kitchen. And that was when I discovered the jar of nuts, now empty, standing on the work surface. I stared at it for a moment, flabbergasted. I'd thrown it away – I knew I had. And yet, when I strode over to the bin, I saw that there was no jar in there now. One of the girls must have taken it out at some point when my back was turned.

I felt a flash of worry but then reasoned that the girls had gobbled up their sandwiches quickly enough, and Estella was closeted away in Miss Grayson's study. I was still annoyed with myself for not noticing sooner, though, as I shoved the jar deep into the bottom of the waste bin.

I glanced out of the window a few times as I finished tidying and saw the girls outside in their cloaks, but they weren't playing as they normally would. Instead they were huddled together in miserable-looking groups, or wandering about, kicking up clumps of snow.

Ten minutes or so later the kitchen was tidy and

I went straight to Miss Grayson's study, eager to see Estella. I hoped that, by now, she might have woken up and we could talk, and I could reassure her that everything was going to be all right.

But when I pressed down on the handle of Miss Grayson's study, I found to my surprise that the door was locked. Frowning, I knocked hard on the wood.

"Who is it?" Miss Grayson's voice called from inside.

"It's Miss Black," I replied. "I've come to see how Estella is."

"I have had to lock the door," the schoolmistress called back.

"Yes, I can see that," I replied. "Why is it locked? Is something wrong?"

There was such a long pause that I was almost about to knock again when, finally, I heard the click of the key in the lock and Miss Grayson opened the door a crack, to peer out at me with her watery blue eyes.

"I have some bad news, I'm afraid," she said in a flat tone.

I felt my heart speed up in my chest. "About Estella? Is she all right?"

"No," Miss Grayson replied. "She is not all right. In fact, she's dead. She—"

I didn't wait to hear any more but pushed past her into the room.

I didn't believe it. I wouldn't believe it.

And yet, as soon as I saw her, I knew it was true. In every aspect, death announced itself in a terrible, universal, undeniable language.

She lay on the little cot by the fire, just as I had left her. Her hands clutched fistfuls of the bedsheets in what looked like an iron-tight grip. The sheets around her feet and legs were all messed up, as if she'd been thrashing about, but now she was completely motionless.

Her eyes were open, glassy and unseeing, staring straight up at the ceiling. And, most horribly of all, her mouth was stretched wide, almost far enough to unhinge the jaw, as if she had been desperately trying to suck in air or scream. Her face was a frozen mask of terror.

Chapter Twenty-Two

I heard myself give a strangled sob as I ran over to the bed. Estella's skin was still warm when I wrapped my arms round her. Hugging her small body to my chest, I was unable to stop the tears that ran freely down my face.

"I stepped out for a moment," Miss Grayson said in that same flat voice behind me. "And when I came back, I found this."

I looked up and saw that the schoolmistress held a chocolate-spread sandwich on a plate.

"One of the girls must have brought it for Estella," Miss Grayson went on. She put the plate down on a nearby table and I saw that it had a single, neat bite taken from it. "One mouthful is all it would have taken," she said. "The physician was quite clear about that when she had her funny turn before. Whoever brought it for her must have forgotten." She gave me a chilly look. "It is a great pity that you were not paying more attention during the cookery lesson. I did tell you how serious the consequences would be if this was to happen."

"I … I threw the nuts away," I said. "But then the empty jar was on the work surface. One of the girls must have taken them from the bin…"

I trailed off. I knew that all Miss Grayson would hear was excuses and perhaps she was right. It had just never occurred to me that one of the girls would take the nuts and add them to the spread.

My mind felt like it was filled with fog. Had any of the girls taken their sandwiches with them? I thought they'd all eaten them before they left but it would have been easy enough for someone to slip the sandwich into their pocket without me noticing. Which girls had I seen outside while I'd been clearing up? Had there been someone missing? It was impossible to remember.

And yet I couldn't shake the feeling that Estella's death was no mere accident. There was something more to this, I was sure of it.

Estella's body was collected a short while later. The girls piled on to the steps and watched as the plain wooden coffin was loaded on to the back of the undertaker's carriage. There was absolute silence, save for the horses occasionally snorting in the icy air or stamping their hooves on the frozen gravel.

The police officers returned to the school and spoke to everyone individually, including me. No one admitted to taking the sandwich to Estella. All of the girls said they had eaten their toast sandwiches themselves and that they hadn't seen Estella since the night before.

However, the police seemed to agree with Miss Grayson's theory that one of the girls must have been responsible and was now simply too upset, or afraid, to admit it. It was, they concurred, a most tragic accident.

Lessons for the rest of that day were cancelled. As soon as the police left, I went back to my bedroom and cried until my eyes were red and sore. I could hardly believe that Estella was really gone. I couldn't stop seeing that awful expression on her face. She had known what was happening to her, had seen death coming. I felt like I absolutely had to do something but I didn't know what.

Sitting at my dressing table, staring into my mirror in despair, I suddenly noticed that a letter had been placed there for me. One of the maids must have brought it up. I couldn't have cared less about any letter at that moment and only tore the envelope open as a means of temporarily distracting myself from the horror of what had happened. It was from the solicitor.

Dear Miss Black,

Thank you for your correspondence. We are glad that you received the dolls' house safely and note your request that no further objects from the Redwing estate be sent to you.

However, we are confused by your mention of dolls and a toy chest. I can confirm that no such item has been sent to you from this office. Thus far, the only asset to have been salvaged from the fire at Whiteladies is the dolls' house.

I therefore suggest you make enquiries into this matter elsewhere.

Yours sincerely,

Theodore Goadsby

Messrs Goadsby, Grimes and Scott

I let the letter fall from my hand. Then, remembering the doll in my pocket, I took it out and placed it on the dressing table. Its white body was still stained with Estella's blood.

Let's play the fingernails game...

I remembered how the doll had popped up over Estella's shoulder.

Hello, Mother! Do you want to play?

Then Estella's voice was there in my mind:

If you talk to them, they'll probably talk back...

I picked up the Frozen Charlotte and held it at eye level. "Are you alive?" I said. "Can you understand what I'm saying? Can you speak to me?"

The doll stared back, its painted eyes as blank and unseeing as Estella's had been.

I peered closer, trying to see some spark of life. "Did you shove needles into Martha's eyes?" I asked softly. "Was it you?"

The doll didn't reply.

And yet...

There was something about its expression, something about the pursed look of its mouth, that made me feel perhaps it really was about to say something. Surely there was a twist to its lips that hadn't been there before? I could almost have sworn that its expression had changed slightly.

"You can talk, can't you?" I pressed. "This silence is just a new game, isn't it?"

I kept my eyes fixed on it. It was about to move, or speak, I was sure of it...

Then a sudden knock made me jump. The doll fell from my hand, landing with a thump on the table. I ran my hands through my hair in frustration before crossing the room and answering the door.

Henry stood on the other side. He looked pale and miserable, just like everyone else at the school. He wore a cloak and I saw he carried mine over his arm.

"Come on," he said. "Let's get out of this horrid place for a while."

I was glad to leave. The unnatural silence felt suffocating and I suddenly longed to be outside in the fresh air. I paused just long enough to shove the Frozen Charlotte doll into my pocket. I still didn't know what to believe when it came to the dolls but I wasn't about to leave one lying around unattended.

Our boots crunched on the snow as we walked out of the gates and along the coastal path towards

Neist Point. It felt like the most natural thing in the world when Henry took my hand in his. To begin with we walked in silence, the sea pounding against the rocks below providing a constant background roar, the tang of salt strong in the air.

Once we had put some distance between us and the school, I started to talk. I told Henry about the dolls and all that had happened since I'd arrived at the school. The girls saying that the Frozen Charlottes moved around at night, the writing that had appeared on the blackboard, the bell ringing, the marks on the inside of the toy chest as if tiny fingers really had scratched and scrabbled, desperate to get out…

We'd reached Neist Point now and stopped there, looking out over the cliff at the vast expanse of sea. I took the Frozen Charlotte from my pocket and stared down at it in my gloved hand.

"God, I just don't know what to think," I said. "I feel like I'm going mad."

Gently Henry took the doll from me and then, without a word, he drew back his arm and threw it, as far as he could, out over the clifftop. I watched as the little body sailed in a high arc, cutting a path through the snowflakes that had started to fall before dropping down into the sea, where it was immediately swallowed by the grey water.

Then he put his hands on my arms and turned me round to face him.

"Why don't we just leave it all behind?" he said. "Whiteladies and that villain, Redwing, are all in the past. This school can be, too. I have a little money put away. We can just go. We'll go anywhere you want."

"But, Henry—" I began.

"I know I'm an odd sort of chap but I would do my very best to make you happy, Mim," he said. "We could build a good life together, I know we could."

I longed to throw my arms round him and agree to his suggestion. To simply walk away from Dunvegan School for Girls and never look back. And yet...

"I can't," I said.

"Why not, in heaven's name?" Henry said. He ran his hand through his windswept hair in an impatient gesture. "You needn't think there'd be anything improper about it. We could just live as friends, if that's what you want. If we moved to a new place we could tell everyone we were brother and sister, and there'd be no scandal then. We could find a little cottage to rent, just you, me and Murphy—"

"Henry." I cut him off firmly. "Please listen to me. I don't think you could behave improperly if you tried and that is not my concern. Furthermore, I love you to distraction and nothing would make me happier than to go away with you."

Henry's eyes widened at this and he opened his mouth to reply, so I pressed on before he could do so.

"But I can't just walk away," I said. "I can't. Not until I find out what the devil is going on with these wretched Frozen Charlotte dolls. I must know, Henry. If I am ever to have another peaceful moment or unbroken night's sleep. And I can't leave the school unless I'm sure the girls are going to be all right."

For a long moment Henry stared at me. "Did I mishear you, Mim, or did you really just say that you love me to distraction?"

I couldn't help a small smile. "You are very distracting at times, Henry."

Before I could go on, he put his hands round my waist and lifted me up, whirling me in a circle through the snowflakes.

"Put me down, you ridiculous fellow!" I said. Part of me wanted to laugh and be happy, but it wasn't the time for that yet. Estella was dead. There were things that needed to be done.

Henry obediently set me down on my feet.

"We will find the answers to your questions," he said. "I don't know how yet, Mim, but we will. And then—"

"Then we will be married and gloriously happy and all of this will be nothing but a distant memory long behind us," I said.

Henry beamed at me and one of his hands curled tenderly round the back of my neck. "Gosh, I love you," he said. "May I kiss you now?"

In response, I gripped the front of his cloak and pulled his head down to mine. His lips were warm, his hands were gentle and it was my first ever kiss, with the boy I loved, surrounded by snowflakes on the clifftop. A sweet, perfect moment as if we were standing inside a snow globe and the rest of the world simply didn't exist. But it could not go on forever.

We were both breathless by the time we pulled apart and Henry gazed down at me with a foolish grin on his face.

"I know," he said, before I could speak. "I know full well that I have a foolish grin on my face and I really don't care. I hope to grin foolishly for the rest of my days, in fact." He wrapped his arms round me and held me tight for a moment. "You've made me the happiest chap in the world," he said. "You really have."

I kissed him on the cheek then took a step back. "I love you, too, Henry. I hope we can leave this horrible place soon."

But before I could do that I knew I had to go right back to the very beginning, to where this had first started – at Whiteladies.

Chapter Twenty-Three

Isle of Skye – January 1910

As soon as the girls had settled for the night and the school had gone to sleep, I crept down the corridor to the toy room.

Once again, there was a light on inside the dolls' house and, as I locked the door behind me, I was sure I heard a muffled giggle coming from the miniature version of Whiteladies. I switched on the gaslights and saw that most of the Frozen Charlotte dolls lay in the basket by the door, right where they'd been left. But I knew they wouldn't all be there and, sure enough, when I swung open the front of the dolls' house, there were three dolls inside Redwing's study.

They were in almost exactly the same position as last time. The bonneted doll lay on the floor behind the desk. The doll in the cornflower-blue dress was sitting in the wing-backed chair by the fire. And the Frozen Charlie doll was standing behind it, the hawk cane propped in the crook of his arm.

The dolls were there that night at Whiteladies. They saw what happened. And I thought that perhaps, somehow, they'd been trying to tell me. Estella had said that if I talked to them then they'd probably talk back. Well, here I was. Ready to talk. Ready to listen.

Taking a deep breath, I kneeled down on the floor in front of the dolls' house.

"All right," I said. "I'm here and I'm listening. If you have something you want to say, then you'd better say it now."

Silence. Nothing but silence for long, long minutes.

Then the idea came to me all at once and I leaned forwards slowly, peering in at the stubbornly silent, motionless dolls.

"I know," I whispered. "Why don't we play a game?"

Even though I was looking for it, even though I was half expecting it, part of me still didn't really believe that the dolls were supernatural in any way. And so, when the Frozen Charlotte in the blue dress turned her head to look at me, I let out a yelp and jerked back.

I was half pleased and half terrified as I peered at the dolls' house. "Well?" I said after a moment, when my heart no longer hammered quite so hard. "Do you want to play a game?"

"*The fingernails game?*" said the doll in the blue dress, her painted lips moving rapidly.

"No," I said, shuddering at the memory of Estella's ruined fingers. "Definitely not that game."

"*The stick-a-needle-in-your-eye game?*" said the doll lying on the floor.

The Frozen Charlie didn't speak but what followed was a disturbing back-and-forth between the two Frozen Charlottes.

"*The eat-your-face game?*"

"*The séance game?*"

"*The rip-off-all-your-skin game?*"

"*The stab-a-knife-into-your-heart game?*"

"*I know! I know! We should play the tear-apart-the-cat game!*"

"*Oh, that's my favourite, my favourite!*"

"*We just need a cat! Is there another cat?*"

"*There's got to be a cat here somewhere!*"

"*Here, kitty, kitty, kitty!*"

"*Impossible to play the tear-apart-the-cat game without a cat!*"

"*Ha ha! Cat! Gutted cat!*"

"Shut up! Shut up!" I cried, pressing my hands to my head, unable to bear it another moment longer.

"*Sorry, Mother,*" the doll in the blue dress said in a small, subdued voice.

"Why on earth are you calling me that?" I demanded.

"*You let us out,*" the Frozen Charlotte replied. "*So we're yours. Yours!*"

"*Yours forever!*"

"Well," I said weakly. "All right then. If you belong to me then I think I should get to pick the game. And I know exactly which one we should play."

"*What is it?*"

I took a deep breath. "Let's play the Whiteladies game."

The doll in the blue dress squealed. "*Oh yes, yes! Such horror! Such violence! Such wickedness!*"

"*Hee, hee, hee!*"

And then, with a pop, the gaslights went out and darkness spilled into the room.

The only source of light came from the lamp in Redwing's study. And then I saw what Estella had meant about the dolls moving fast because all of

257

a sudden the Frozen Charlotte in the bonnet, the one that reminded me so much of my mother's, was no longer lying on the floor behind the desk but standing in the corridor outside the study door. The Frozen Charlie was standing in front of the seated Frozen Charlotte doll, placing the hawk cane directly in front of her.

I watched as the bonneted doll went into the study, walking in odd, jerky movements as if some unseen child's hand was guiding her. The Frozen Charlie twirled slowly round towards her in the same way. For a moment they faced each other. Then the bonneted doll spoke, her voice high-pitched and overly dramatic like a bad actress at the theatre. *"You can't keep using my daughter like this, Edward! I won't let you!"*

The Frozen Charlie didn't speak but waved his cane at her in a threatening manner.

"No, I don't care what happens to me!" the Frozen Charlotte cried. *"I won't let you hurt my daughter!"*

With startling speed, the Frozen Charlotte shot across the room towards the Frozen Charlie. A strange tussle ensued between them, the two dolls dancing in the air around each other. The doll in the blue dress remained motionless in her seat all the while, staring blankly ahead.

Then the bonneted Frozen Charlotte was on the floor and the Frozen Charlie loomed over her, raising his cane high above his head. I watched as, with a terrible inevitability, he drew the cane down upon her, over and over and over again, until her little porcelain head had been entirely smashed in.

I closed my eyes, heard the crunch of bone and the squelch of brain matter; saw blood running out in a slowly growing pool...

Suddenly I was there, right there at Whiteladies, deeply held in a trance, unable to move or speak or do anything at all, as Edward Redwing dragged my mother across the room, flinging her down on the floor behind his desk.

From my position I could only see her feet, ankles and lower legs as Redwing raised his cane above his head. My mother's legs jerked violently when he brought it down for the first time. As the cane came down again and again, those legs kicked and struggled – fiercely at first, then growing weaker until they no longer moved at all. The cane kept coming down, though, the sounds it made becoming wetter and wetter. Redwing exerted such physical effort that his shirt split across his back.

When he finally turned to face me, blood splatters ran up his white shirt and even stained his face. His hair had fallen loose and he ran a hand over his head to smooth it back into place.

"Now," he said, taking a deep breath. "Where were we?"

When I opened my eyes, the Frozen Charlie doll was standing before me, holding out the cane. The sight of that red-eyed hawk filled me with dread but I knew I had to take it if I was to remember it all. Slowly I reached out my hand and closed my fingers round the little stick.

And the rest of what happened that night burst in, like a blow to the head.

Chapter Twenty-Four

Whiteladies – One month earlier

"Now," Redwing said, smoothing back his hair. "Where were we?"

The hawk cane was covered in blood. It ran in clotted streams down the silver and over the rosewood, dripping on to the carpet, filling the air with the scent of iron. The room was quiet but inside my head there was a scream that went on and on. I'd been silently screaming the entire time I'd watched the rise and fall of that cane, seen my mother's legs eventually stop kicking, twitch feebly and then lie still. I had been completely unable to break out of the trance in time to save her.

Pouring all of my mental willpower into the effort to break free, I finally managed to stand up from the chair, still half in a daze.

"You can't stand up!" Redwing said. "You're in a trance!"

My lips were slow and clumsy, my tongue wouldn't work properly, but I still managed to force out two words: "You … monster."

Redwing laughed and without a word crossed over to his desk, walking past my mother's dead body to yank open the bottom drawer and pull out the papers I'd discovered earlier that very evening – the reams of writing from beyond the grave. I found myself stumbling towards him like a sleepwalker.

"I fear you were labouring under a misconception earlier, my dear," he said. "You believed that all this depravity was the result of my automatic writing when, in fact, these are the words you have written yourself while you've been in a trance."

I stared at him, trembling, not wanting to believe it.

He smiled at me. "All those weeks and months of effort on my part and I was never able to contact so much as a single spirit," he said. "Your mother experienced a similar lack of success. But the first time you went into a trance, the devils and demons all flocked to you like you were the strongest magnet on the planet. Yes," he said, shaking the papers at me and breathing hard now. "Yes, everything I say is true and you know it. It is not I who has the dark soul, madam, it is you! And if you can speak to devils, then you can speak to my daughter, damn you!" He thrust the cane in my face and I felt the malevolent influence of his voice ensnare my mind like a net. "Try again!" he hissed.

Despite all the rage boiling up inside me, I couldn't stop myself from obeying his order. Perhaps it was because I had already gone willingly into a trance earlier and now, even as I struggled to break free of it, Redwing's words seemed to have a peculiarly powerful influence over my physical body, while the real me stared out from behind my eyes, screaming for this to stop.

"We are here to make contact with Vanessa Redwing." I heard myself say almost the exact same words my mother had spoken, a lifetime ago, at that very first séance at Whiteladies. "I open myself up to the realm of the spirits. Vanessa, are you there? If you can hear me, please follow the sound of my voice."

Only it wasn't Vanessa Redwing that answered my call. I could sense, somehow, that all the anger and grief building up inside me was like the sweetest nectar to the black thing that drew near and then was suddenly there, inside my head. It was ancient and dark and twisted and warped, and it was black and it was evil and it was dangerous and it was terrible but, most of all, it was bored. And it wanted to play.

Redwing must have sensed the change. Perhaps he saw it in my face, perhaps there was a kind of devilish madness there, staring back at him. Either way, he suddenly stepped back from me with an uncertain expression.

"Don't be frightened yet," I heard myself say quietly, and I couldn't quite tell whether it was me talking or the unnatural dark thing inside of me. "I'll tell you when it's time to be frightened."

And then the demon, or the dark spirit, or whatever it was, rushed down my arm with a flash of pain so intense it was like the skin was being flayed from the bone. Then it passed out through my fingers and went into the Frozen Charlotte doll I still clutched tightly in my hand.

"*Hello, Mother!*" it cried. "*Do you want to play a game?*"

The doll seemed to leap from my grasp, straight to

the desk, where it snatched up the letter opener and used it to smash the glass of the paraffin lamp.

The fire roared into life much faster than it should have, as if some supernatural force were fanning the flames. Redwing staggered back, away from the heat, raising his arms to protect his face, choking on the sudden smoke. Out in the hall, the grandfather clock pealed out six brooding chimes.

And I didn't hesitate to take my chance. I lunged towards the desk, seized the letter opener and plunged it with all my strength into Redwing's chest. It was more difficult than I had expected – clothes and skin offered significant resistance – but all my anguish was in the movement and I felt the blade cut through his shirt, pierce through skin and scrape over bone.

Redwing made a little grunting noise and then lifted his head, staring me straight in the eye with a look of pure surprise.

"No," he gasped, coughing up blood that marked my face.

"Yes!" I snarled.

He tried to push me away but the strength was draining out of him already and I pulled the letter opener free to plunge it back into his chest a second time. And then a third and a fourth. In fact, I eventually lost count. Redwing ended up crumpled on the floor at my feet, and I gripped the letter opener in a hot, slippery hand and allowed myself a small smile of satisfaction.

"Now," I said, wiping the blade on my cornflower skirts, "it is time to be frightened."

"Let's play the burn-down-the-house game!" cried a chorus of voices.

I turned in their direction and saw that all the dolls were moving about now, in strange, jerky little gestures as if someone else were in control of them. While I'd been occupied with murder, the Frozen Charlottes had been spreading the fire, tossing books and papers on to the flames.

Already the fire was quite the inferno. The flames reached up to lick the ceiling, peeled the wallpaper away and bubbled the paint on the windowpanes. The smoke seemed to reach its charred fingers straight into my lungs.

"We need to leave," I gasped. Without thinking, I snatched the nearest Frozen Charlotte, dumped her into the box and scooped it up. I suppose I didn't want to leave them to burn in the house. They were the reason I'd finally been able to break free of the trance and hurt Redwing, after all.

As I made my way across the room, coughing the entire time, the remaining dolls raced towards me – little blurs of white coming from all directions as they piled, one on top of the other, into the box, giggling the entire time.

"What fun! What fun!" one of them cried.

When I reached the door, I turned back and took one final look at my mother's legs protruding from behind the desk. I didn't want to leave her there but nor could I bear to see whatever bloody pulp remained of her head. I simply couldn't. I turned my back on the scene and, with the box tucked under one arm, went straight down the corridor to the nearest bathroom, where, still half in a daze, I washed the blood from my hands before making my way out of the house.

A few minutes later I was standing in the gardens with the servants, watching the flames dance through the windows as Whiteladies blackened.

"The poor thing's in shock," I heard Amy, one of the maids, say. "She saved those ugly Frozen

Charlotte dolls for some reason. I'll take them, dear.
You sit down over here."

I found the box of dolls being removed from my
grasp. The cold, clear air seemed to cut through the
murky fog that had filled my mind and I breathed
it in deeply. The last few hours felt like a dream
and I could no longer remember why it had seemed
important to remove the dolls or what had just
happened.

I only knew that I had survived. That I was
still alive.

Chapter Twenty-Five

Isle of Skye – January–February 1910

The shock of the memory returning was physically painful. For a moment I was right back there. I could smell the smoke that was choking me, could feel the warm blood, slick and slippery between my fingertips.

"Oh God!" I said.

I'm a murderer! I didn't say the words aloud but perhaps they were ringing loudly enough in my head that the Frozen Charlottes heard them anyway.

"*He started it!*" one of the dolls piped up. "*He started the game with his cane!*"

"*Ha ha! That rhymes!*"

"*He started the game with his cane!*" the first doll sang out again. "*And then it was tag, tag, tag, you're it! Atishoo, atishoo, we all fall down dead!*"

Devils are like chameleons, you know, Grandma had once told me. *They shape themselves to fit whatever identity is presented to them.*

I hadn't understood what she meant and so she'd reminded me of the painting she'd mentioned before – the one of the old woman in the wedding dress.

The demon possessed that painting and became trapped inside it, she'd said. *And so it took for itself the identity of a bitter, twisted old bride. It wept and wailed, and it hated all men with a passion. That devil had come straight from hell so, of course, it had never been left at the altar. But it put on the first mask that it found and it played the part.*

I stared at the little dolls before me. Was that what had happened to the Frozen Charlottes? A devil had possessed them and now it was childish and playful, but in a way that was twisted and evil and warped. When Vanessa had been alive, she had used the dolls to make innocent comments about the thunder being too loud, but now that the dolls had voices of their own they only wanted to talk of murder.

"I left you behind!" I cried, clenching my fists. "How did you get here?"

"*Oh, Mother, we knew you didn't mean to leave us!*" the Frozen Charlotte said, its little head twisting back and forth. "*Amy took us home for her daughter to play with, but she was a wimpy-wimp and too afraid to play the blood games. And we missed you, Mother! So we whispered to Amy at night and told her to ask the lawyer men where you were."*

"Then we made her order a glorious toy chest to send us in."

"With your name on it because we belong to you!"

"We'll always belong to you, Mother."

"Always."

"Oh! Oh, what are you doing?"

The last doll cried out as I snatched it up and shoved it into the toy chest, before collecting up the others, who giggled as I piled them in.

"It's a new game, I think," one of them said. *"Yes, we're going to play a game!"*

I snapped the lid of the toy chest shut, picked it up and made my way back through the silent school, and out into the freezing grounds, where the snow glittered in the moonlight. I took the most direct route to the clifftop edge and hurled the toy chest over the side, watching it drop into the ocean. Perhaps the little dots of white I saw down there were Frozen Charlotte dolls floating out to sea after the toy chest had broken open. Then again, perhaps they were merely flecks of foam and the dolls were already sinking to the bottom inside their chest.

As I stared down at the sea, I felt an inner shiver of revulsion at myself and my overriding thought was that Henry must never find out about what I had done. He was decent and kind and good, and I was a monster. I couldn't bear the thought of him looking at me with disgust, as he surely must if he ever learned the truth. I felt a raw flash of animal panic at the thought. I couldn't lose Henry – I just couldn't. Redwing and my mother were both dead. I was the only one left who knew what had really happened and it was a secret I would take to my grave.

"To my grave," I muttered, staring down at the dark ocean.

The dolls had clearly been possessed by one of those demons my grandmother had warned me about. But it didn't matter any more. The Frozen Charlottes were gone. I so wanted to believe I had all the answers I needed, and yet … I still couldn't quite accept that Estella's death was the simple, tragic accident it had appeared to be. How had the sandwich got there? There was some other missing piece to the puzzle that had not yet slotted into place. I glanced back at the school, hunched against the night sky. Much as I wished it were otherwise, it was not yet time to go.

After a few days, the physician said Martha was well enough to join the others in their lessons – although she could no longer read, or write, or draw, or do anything much at all. She could only sit there in silence at the back of the classroom, letting out the occasional moan, which Miss Grayson would promptly reprimand her for.

The schoolmistress had been in a particularly bad mood ever since she'd found out that the Frozen Charlottes were missing. Indeed she showed far more emotion over their disappearance than she had over Estella's death. I was glad when my monthly day off arrived and Henry insisted on taking me to the Fairy Pools. We had to leave the school early to make the most of the daylight but it was worth the journey. Nestled at the foot of the craggy Black Cuillin mountains there was an incredible collection of waterfalls and clear, icy pools of green and blue water.

"Good heavens," I breathed, when we reached the first pool. "It's … it's magical."

Henry flashed me a smile. "I thought you'd like them," he said. "You know, the first time I ever came here, I thought I saw a fairy."

I glanced at him to see if he was joking but he appeared to be in earnest.

"It was right there." He pointed to the other side of the pool. "Just for a moment, before it disappeared behind some heather."

He gave me a quick, almost embarrassed, smile as if he felt suddenly foolish for bringing up fairies at all.

"Then again, perhaps it was only a trick of the light," he said.

I looked back at the spot where he'd pointed. If there really was such a thing as fairies, then Henry seemed exactly the type of person who might see one. It was only dark souls like me who attracted devils and heard cursed dolls whispering in the night.

It occurred to me then, quite forcefully, that I simply wasn't fit to be Henry's wife. He ought to marry a sweet, gentle girl – the sort who'd wear flowers in her hair and dance barefoot and glimpse fairies flitting between roses. That girl was not me. And yet, I was not selfless enough to give up Henry. I wanted him more than I had ever wanted anything.

"I threw the Frozen Charlotte dolls in the sea," I told him as we made our way up the path to the next pool, a waterfall cascading into it in perfect, pearly white bubbles.

Henry exhaled and then said in a relieved tone, "That seems like a good idea, Mim. Whether they really were haunted or not, they weren't doing any good here."

We walked on in silence for a few more minutes before Henry said, "Does that mean we can leave now?"

"Not yet," I replied, though I had to force the words out. "I feel like there is something more to Estella's death. I don't think we know the whole truth."

Henry sighed beside me. "Darling girl," he said, "do you think, perhaps, you only want there to be something more because then you wouldn't need to feel guilty yourself?"

I stiffened instantly. "What are you saying?" I demanded.

"Well…" Henry looked desperately uncomfortable. "I mean, the nuts were brought out during your class, weren't they? So perhaps you feel that—"

"Do *you* think I am to blame?" I asked, stopping abruptly on the path.

"Of course not!" Henry replied at once. "Of course I don't think that and you shouldn't, either." He shook his head. "Look, I didn't mean to upset you. Let's not talk about the school any more today."

We continued on but all the magic suddenly seemed to have been sucked from the outing. Could Henry be right? Was I hoping for some alternative explanation for Estella's death so that I wouldn't be at fault?

Although we feigned cheerfulness, I'm sure we were both feeling the strain by the time we set off back to the school. It was late afternoon when we returned and I went inside only to find that Miss Grayson was having the entire school searched, in case one of the girls had taken the Frozen Charlotte dolls and hidden them somewhere.

"It's the kind of behaviour I would have expected

from Estella," Miss Grayson said. "It's almost as if she's still here, causing mischief."

Perhaps it was this remark that started the rumours. The girls took to saying Estella was still there in the school. Olivia said she'd heard movement from the toy room and suggested that perhaps Estella was trying to find the dolls, too. One time when the girls piled out for their break, Felicity came rushing back in to say that she'd seen Estella's face at the dormitory window, staring out, just like she had the night Martha was blinded.

A few days after the visit to the Fairy Pools, Miss Grayson was taking the class for their embroidery lesson and I was sitting on my usual stool at the front of the room when suddenly I became aware that my hands were wet.

I looked down, confused, and to my horror saw that my fingers were dripping blood. It ran, slick and slippery, in warm, scarlet lines down my hands. I cried out before I could stop myself, staring, appalled, at the gory evidence of my sin.

Murderer!

Murderer!

Murderer!

The word pealed, over and over again, inside my mind. When the Frozen Charlotte doll upset the paraffin lamp I could have run for help. I could have gone to the servants. I could have fetched the police and reported what Redwing had done to my mother. He would have been locked safely away in prison. But, no. I'd been too angry for that. Too bloodthirsty. And only murder would do.

Don't be frightened yet...

It is not I who has the dark soul, madam...

I'll tell you when it's time to be frightened...

It is you...

Now...

Where were we?

"Miss Black!" Miss Grayson's shrill voice cut through my thoughts and I looked up to see the whole class staring at me. I gazed down at my hands only to find that they looked perfectly ordinary. I ran one hand over the other, just to be sure, but they were quite dry.

The schoolmistress was positively glaring as she

took me by the arm and hurried me from the room. "Continue with your work, girls," she called over her shoulder. "In silence, please."

Miss Grayson ushered me into her study. "Are you ill?" she demanded, the moment the door was closed.

I realized I was shaking and knew that Miss Grayson must have felt this when she touched my arm. I drew a deep breath to try to steady my nerves but this only had the effect of making me feel lightheaded.

"No," I managed. "I'm quite well."

Miss Grayson folded her arms over her chest. "You are aware, I suppose, that you shrieked out in the middle of the class for no apparent reason and then stood rubbing at your hands and generally behaving most oddly?"

"I apologize," I said. "I ... I did not sleep very well last night and—"

"My dear Miss Black," Miss Grayson said, turning away from me towards her desk. "I do not believe I have ever met anyone more proficient in the art of excuses than you. We are *all* suffering from a lack of sleep. We are *all* in shock over Estella's tragic death. And yet you are the only person who is falling apart and having hysterics." She sat down behind her desk and pulled open a drawer.

I could feel a dull ache starting up behind my eyes. If I closed them I could still feel the blood on my skin, hear the wet squelching sound of my mother being beaten to death on the floor, smell the vile scent of Macassar oil mixed with tobacco heavy upon the air. I didn't feel up to battling with Miss Grayson at this particular moment.

I opened my eyes. "Please endeavour to be fair to me, if you can," I said. "It was nothing more than a minor incident; I have apologized for any disruption, and now I'm quite composed and ready to return to class."

Miss Grayson took some writing paper from her desk, slammed the drawer shut and walked over to me. There wasn't an ounce of warmth or pity in her eyes as she gazed at me.

"You are physically shaking, miss," she said. "Which suggests to me that you have not composed yourself at all." One corner of her mouth twisted with distaste. "I suppose in your old life, before you became penniless, you had male suitors fawning all over you and rushing to your aid every time a fainting fit or shaking spell occurred."

"That is not—"

"Well, I'm afraid I cannot offer the same service." The schoolmistress pressed the paper into my hand. "It must be apparent, even to you, that you are not suited to this work," she said. "I will accept your resignation on my desk the moment you care to submit it."

I wanted nothing more than to resign – to leave with Henry and never look back. But I could not, would not, go until I'd reassured myself that Estella's death had been nothing more than an accident.

I thrust the paper back at the schoolmistress. "If you think you can bully me into resigning," I said, "then you are sadly mistaken. I will leave this school when it suits me to leave and not a moment before."

Miss Grayson gave me such a glare that I really thought for a moment she might actually slap me. But before she could do or say anything, there was a knock at the door.

"For heaven's sake, what is it *now*?" the schoolmistress cried.

The door opened and Cassie peered in. "Sorry,

ma'am, but the photographer's here," she said.

"What photographer?" Miss Grayson snapped.

"He said he was asked to come," Cassie said, looking uncertain. "I told him he wasn't expected but he said he was booked weeks ago and that—"

"Yes, yes," Miss Grayson said abruptly, nodding her head, causing her pompadour to wobble. "Yes, the photographer. Well, don't just stand there, you foolish girl! Tell him to set up on the front steps."

The girls were ushered from the classroom and told to line up outside the front entrance, with the school in the background. They did as they were told, shivering in their coats. Miss Grayson grabbed Martha's hand and positioned the poor girl next to her, at the edge of the front row.

"Please stay where you are, Miss Black," Miss Grayson said, despite the fact that I'd made no move to join them. "I don't think the photograph needs to be graced by your presence."

I stood and watched as the photographer set up his camera and gave everyone directions. No one smiled. The bulb went off with a pop and a flash and then the photographer was packing up his things and taking his leave.

When I finally returned to my room that evening, I was so exhausted that I simply wanted to fall into bed fully clothed and never move from there again. I could not seem to rid myself of this damned headache and I felt tired right down to my bones. When someone knocked on my door I groaned aloud.

I got up from the bed and opened the door, expecting to see Miss Grayson come to chastize me some more or perhaps Henry sneaking in to see me. But instead I found Bess, shivering in her nightdress, tears running down her cheeks.

"Oh, Bess, what's wrong?" I said, crouching down to her level.

"I … I have a secret," she whispered. "And I want to tell you what it is but Charlotte says I shouldn't."

I couldn't help shuddering at those two words: *Charlotte says…*

"But … the dolls are all gone," I said.

"This one isn't." Bess reached into her nightdress pocket and produced a Frozen Charlotte doll with a broken arm and little gold shoes. "She wasn't with the others; she was in my pocket."

My heart sank at the sight of it.

"Are there any more in the school?" I asked.

"I don't think so."

"Come inside for a moment," I said, ushering her into the room and closing the door. "Now listen. No one else can hear us in here. Whatever your secret is you can trust me with it, I promise."

Bess lifted her eyes to mine. "I did something," she said. "Something wicked."

There was so much anguish in her expression that I instinctively reached out to wrap my hands round her skinny arms.

"It's all right," I said. "You can tell me."

"Miss Black," Bess replied, "I lied to that policeman. I was scared and Charlotte said not to tell, but I think I should have."

"Tell him what?" I asked.

"That it was me," Bess said. She gave a little sob. "I killed Estella."

Chapter Twenty-Six

Isle of Skye – February 1910

"You'd better tell me everything," I said, leading Bess over to the chair by the fire.

"Estella h-helped me," she stammered. "With the d-d-dresses. And because of that she got flogged instead of m-me. It was my fault. When we made the toast sandwiches, Charlotte said I should take mine to Estella to say thank you."

"And you forgot she couldn't eat nuts?"

Bess burst into tears then, proper sobs that racked her small frame. I was quite concerned that someone would hear her and come to find out what the noise was about. I hugged her and tried to comfort her as best I could. It was several minutes before she'd calmed enough to speak again.

"I didn't forget," she said. "I remembered she couldn't eat them. But Charlotte said it would be all right. She told me to take the nuts out of the bin to make the sandwich more tasty." She held up the little china doll, gazing at it miserably. "She said it was a good idea and, somehow, she made me think it was a good idea, too. She got inside my head and made me feel all mixed up and confused. So I took the sandwich to Estella. Miss Grayson wasn't there and Estella was asleep so I left it by her bed. She must have seen it there when she woke up and … and…"

She dissolved into tears once again.

"It's all right," I said. I took the doll from her and slipped it into my pocket. "It's all right, Bess."

I held her for half an hour or so and then, when she'd finally settled a little, I turned her to face me and said, "I want you to listen to me now because this is important. There's something wrong with the Frozen Charlottes. Something dark and evil got inside them, and this makes them want to do bad things and persuade other people to do bad things, too. It's their fault Estella died, not yours. It's not your fault, Bess. You were right not to say anything to the policeman. In fact, you shouldn't ever tell anyone else what you've told me. And whenever you feel sad about what happened to Estella, you just have to remind yourself that it was the dolls that really did it. Can you do that for me?"

Although she still looked wretched, Bess nodded.

"Good girl," I said. "Now, it's very late. You should go back to bed and try to get some sleep."

Once Bess had gone, I sat down on the edge of the bed and took out the Frozen Charlotte. I stared down at the doll in my lap, hoping it was the only one I'd missed. Although what Bess had just told me was horrifying, in a way I was relieved. At least now I knew the truth and I hoped that, in some small way, I may have helped Bess to carry the guilt that would doubtless be with her for the rest of her life.

"Do you want to play a game?" a little voice piped up.

I closed my eyes briefly. Then I reached down and snapped the doll's head off in one abrupt movement. "No," I said. "I don't."

I threw the broken doll into the fire and watched the glazed paint bubble away on the porcelain pieces, which cracked into smaller and smaller shards until there was nothing left but dust.

As the last specks fizzled away, I stood up, intending to go to bed. But before I could even turn away from the fire, there was a small, dark *pop* deep within the coals. I paused and leaned down a little, peering into the embers. The next second, a blurred shadow came racing out of the hearth towards me, hitting me full in the face.

I reeled back but the shadow seemed to attach itself to me. Suddenly I could feel dark, crooked fingers reaching up through my nostrils and in through my ears and straight between my lips, groping their way into my mouth, right down into the back of my throat. I spluttered and gagged and choked, and crashed forwards on to my knees. I thought for a moment that I was going to die right then and there.

Summoning up every once of my strength, I fought back against the thing, pushing it away with my mind until it seeped out of me and retreated back to the fireplace, disappearing up the chimney in a cloud of foul-smelling smoke. I was left gasping for air with a rotten taste in my mouth and an ache in my chest and a pain my heart.

Too late, my grandmother's words about the possessed painting came back to me: *They thought they should just toss it straight on to the fire, but luckily I was there to stop them. Otherwise they would have released that devil and who knows where we would have been then!*

Slowly I got back to my feet, feeling as wobbly and fragile as an old woman; as insubstantial as a doll made from paper. I glanced back at the fireplace but there was nothing left of the doll or whatever dark force had been inside it. I could only assume that it had escaped through the chimney and was now out there, loose in the world, because of me.

I turned away and went to bed. Miss Grayson would get her wish. My resignation letter would be on her desk first thing in the morning. The dolls were evil, there was no denying that, but the last one had just been destroyed. Everything could go back to normal here at the school, leaving me free to go away with Henry.

Finally – *finally* – I had the chance to be happy and it was one I intended to grab with both hands.

†††

I opened my eyes and found myself back at Whiteladies. The house was on fire, and smelled of ash and ruin. At the bottom of the stairs I could hear the wet crunch of my mother being beaten to death with Redwing's cane.

I made my way down to the ground floor, even though I knew that it must be too late to help her. Far too late. The sound alone told me that. The shatter of bone and the squelch of brain matter was not a noise you could associate with any living thing.

As I stepped down from the last stair, I heard the clip-clop of hooves and then, out of the darkness, rippling from the shadows, loomed a huge black horse. I knew it was Blackie, Vanessa's beloved steed, by the fact that he had a bullet hole in the centre of his forehead. Dark blood ran down the side of his face and splattered over the tiled floor with each step.

The phantom horse gave no indication of being aware of me as he passed and headed up to the first floor. The curved staircase was not designed for horses, and his hooves slipped and scrabbled over the tiles. Perhaps the sound of murder had unsettled him. It was enough to unsettle anyone.

I realized then that the sound had stopped and I turned round quickly, only to find myself face to face with Edward Redwing. A trail of blood trickled from the side of his mouth but he grinned at me in a demented sort of way before closing his hands round my throat.

"Well," he whispered, "where were we?"

His fingers squeezed tighter and tighter but all I could focus on was the sound of a bell ringing ... over and over again.

"Who's ringing that infernal bell?" Redwing said. He glared at me. "Is it you?"

I tried to shake my head but his hands were wrapped too tightly round my throat. He was going to choke me to death. I couldn't control my panic as I tried and failed to suck in air.

"*Stop that!*" a tiny voice said from the floor.

Suddenly Redwing's grip was gone as he dropped his hands with a curse and looked down. A Frozen Charlotte doll was standing there, having just plunged a letter opener into Redwing's ankle.

"*You don't hurt Mother!*" the doll said. "*No one hurts Mother!*"

"God!" Redwing cried, clutching at his head. "Would you stop ringing that damned bell?"

But the bell just kept on ringing. On and on and on...

I jerked upright in my bed, my head still full of the nightmare. For a moment I thought I felt Blackie beside me, heard him shuffle his hooves and snort into my hair. I rubbed at my temples, trying to clear my mind, trying to think. Then I heard voices calling out in the corridor and realized that the bell wasn't a leftover echo from my dream at all but that it really was ringing downstairs somewhere.

I quickly pulled on my dressing gown and hurried into the corridor, where the girls were gathered anxiously at the top of the stairs, peering over the banisters into the shadows below.

"We're all up here," Felicity said as I approached. "So who's ringing the bell downstairs?"

"Perhaps it's Miss Grayson," Olivia suggested. "I heard her wailing in her bedroom earlier. I think she's gone mad."

I did a quick sweep of the girls and saw that Felicity was right. They were all there – even Martha, who had moved back into the dormitory with the others. I saw that Bess was holding her hand to guide her way.

"Perhaps it's Estella," Bess said in a small voice.

"Estella is dead!" Martha said shrilly. "She's dead! Dead, dead, dead!"

I tried to quiet them. "There must be some explanation," I said. "Stay here. I'll go and find out what's happening."

I made my way down the dark staircase, feeling a strange sense of déjà vu. I almost expected a slaughtered horse to pass by me at any second. As I walked down, switching on gaslights as I went, the bell continued to ring. Only it wasn't coming from the classroom as I'd expected but from Miss Grayson's study. It was still ringing when I was right outside the door. I pushed it open.

The bell stopped the moment my hand found the light switch. Just like before, there was a loud clanging noise as it fell to the floor and rolled along the wooden boards. My mouth fell open as I took in the state of the room.

All the cabinet doors had been flung open and Miss Grayson's dolls had been removed. They lay scattered around – on the floor and on the desk and on the chairs. Every single one had its hair cut, shorn off at the scalp so that only bristles and spikes remained. But the cut hair hadn't simply been left on the floor, it had been fashioned into tiny wigs. They were lined up neatly on Miss Grayson's desk – wigs of all different colours, each one a perfect pompadour just like the one the schoolmistress herself wore. Even though I couldn't recall any of the dolls I'd seen having grey hair, quite a few of them were grey.

Having seen the girls' attempts at making dolls' clothes, I doubted any of them were talented enough to produce these wigs. In fact, there was only one person who sprang to mind.

"Estella?" I said quietly to the empty room. "Are you there?"

There was no answer. Nothing at all. I knew the girls upstairs would be waiting fearfully, so I turned round, intending to return to them when suddenly there was a scraping sound, followed by the peal of a bell. Someone was ringing it again, right behind me.

I stood frozen, a thrill of fear making my heart beat too fast. Slowly I turned back round. I saw the bell at once, suspended in mid-air, swinging back and forth so that it rang out loudly, only there was no one holding it. It seemed to move all by itself. As I stared around, trying to work out what was happening, my eye fell on the mirror that hung over the fireplace and I gasped.

Estella was there in the reflection. She had her back to me, facing the corner of the room, but I could tell it was her because of her white-blond hair, as well as the fact that she was wearing the same outfit she'd died in, the white nightgown marked with bloodstains from the flogging. Her head was bent forwards at the neck, her shoulders hunched, and she was completely motionless except for her right arm, which rang the bell with more and more force, eventually raising her arm so high that it reached right over her shoulder.

"Estella!" I cried, desperate to stop the frantic, discordant ringing of the bell. "Estella, stop!"

But she carried on, jerking her arm up and down in a weird, lurching movement. I could see her in the room now as well as in the mirror. I was scared of Estella in that moment, despite the fact that it was surely ridiculous to be frightened. This was not an abusive stepfather or a demonic presence, it was only the ghost of a lost little girl.

I had no business being afraid of her, especially after what I had already faced.

I forced myself to walk across the room, the bell sounding louder with each step. Finally I was right behind Estella, close enough to see that the bloodstains on her nightgown were spreading slowly down the white fabric.

"Estella," I said again, reaching my hand out towards her shoulder.

She looked so solid that I thought I'd be able to touch her but instead my fingers passed straight through, as if she consisted of nothing but smoke. I still felt her, though. Where they touched her, my fingers felt as if they'd been plunged into freezing water, and the pain of it shot right up my arm and into my shoulder as I snatched my hand back.

Estella must have felt my touch, too, because at last she turned round.

When I saw her face, I clamped both hands over my mouth and forced down the almost uncontrollable urge to scream louder than I'd ever screamed before in my life.

Chapter Twenty-Seven

Isle of Skye – February 1910

Estella's face was fixed in the same awful expression I'd seen when she lay on her deathbed.

Her mouth was open wide enough to unhinge the jaw; her eyes bulged and it looked as if the blood vessels in them had burst. She appeared terrified and wild and insane all at the same time. Her spare hand suddenly clawed at her throat and it seemed as if she was trying to speak, but only a thin rasping sound escaped.

I wanted to help her but I had no idea what to do. Her eyes darted manically around the room. She gagged and her mouth, if possible, opened wider still. She reached into the back of her throat and slowly dragged out a long piece of grey hair. In fact, it was more than just a piece – it was an entire wig! It was damp and matted and tangled with dozens and dozens of tiny white dolls' hands. I watched in horror as Estella dropped it on the floor and then, with a wordless shriek, threw the bell with startling force at the mirror.

I ducked instinctively and the mirror smashed on impact, the pieces falling down in a shower of sparkling glass. When I looked back up, Estella was gone.

I groaned in the sudden stillness of the schoolroom. The girls had been right all along – Estella's spirit really was haunting the school. And she'd been trying to speak, trying to tell me something. If I went away now then I'd be abandoning her to eternal torment, just like people had been abandoning her her entire life.

There was nothing else to do that night but to return upstairs, although my legs were trembling so badly that they almost wouldn't carry me. When I finally reached the first floor, it took some time to persuade the girls to go back to bed. Once they were settled, I went to Miss Grayson's bedroom and knocked on the door, intending to inform her of the destruction downstairs. Really, it seemed most odd that she hadn't come out yet. She must surely have heard the bell, after all, and I would have expected her to come storming out with her tawse.

There was no answer to my knock, so I called through the wood. "Miss Grayson?"

"Go away," came the muffled response.

"I need to talk to you," I said. "There's been a disturbance—"

"I do not care," the schoolmistress replied.

She sounded odd and I remembered what Olivia had said about hearing her wailing earlier.

"Are you all right?" I asked. I pressed down on the door handle but it was locked. "Miss Grayson?"

"I am indisposed, Miss Black," the schoolmistress replied. "But I do not require your assistance. Whatever has happened, I must ask you to deal with it yourself."

Shaking my head, I walked back down the corridor to my own room. Needless to say, I didn't sleep for the rest of that night.

Over the next few days, things became increasingly strange. For a start, Miss Grayson was gone by the time I woke up the next morning, which meant she must have left before dawn. Nobody had seen her go but Henry said one of the horses had been saddled up and taken. The schoolmistress had left a scribbled note under my door, which simply said she had business to attend to on the mainland, that she hoped to be back soon and that I would have to take charge of the lessons in the meantime.

It seemed mad that she would just take off in such a way but I had more pressing matters to worry about. It was perfectly apparent to everyone that the school was haunted. And not haunted in a quiet, peaceful, bemusing way, like Dolores haunted the servants' staircase. No, this was a wild, furious, out-of-control sort of haunting. It was a haunting that raged.

Objects moved by themselves. Bells rang. Desks tipped over. Lights switched on and off. Books fell from shelves. A chair even flew across the room and almost hit one of the girls in the face. I recalled what my grandmother had once told me about spirits: *Most of them are harmless enough but it's the poltergeists you have to watch out for. A ghost may not be able to hurt you but a plate flying at your head certainly will.*

The handprints were the thing I noticed first. They appeared on every mirror in the school. In all the haste and panic, we had not obeyed the usual mourning custom of covering the mirrors with black shrouds when Estella died. My grandmother had told me it was an important practice in order to prevent a spirit from getting trapped behind the glass after leaving the body.

Stopping beside a mirror that hung in the corridor on my way to join the girls for lunch, I peered into it. There were dozens of child's handprints marking it, as if someone had pressed their palms against the glass over and over again. Yet, when I rubbed at the surface with the sleeve of my dress, the handprints didn't wipe away. It was almost as if they had come from inside the mirror. I thought of how I had seen Estella behind the glass of the mirror in Miss Grayson's study and shuddered.

Still, there were no disturbances that night and the next day Miss Grayson arrived back at the school wearing what was quite obviously a new wig. It was a different shade of grey and arranged in a bun rather than a pompadour. I remembered how there had been grey wigs among the tiny ones on Miss Grayson's desk and it occurred to me that it wasn't just the dolls' hair that had been used. Miss Grayson's own wig must have been taken as well. That would explain why she hadn't wanted to open the door to me that night and why she had fled the school the next morning. Whatever state her real hair was in, it was obviously bad enough that she couldn't bear to be seen without a wig.

I'd seen her approach from a window and walked out to meet her on the steps of the school.

"What happened?" I asked. "We had no idea where you'd gone, or—"

"I left a note explaining I needed to take a short leave of absence," the schoolmistress replied. "The rest is none of your concern."

I sighed. "Well, we had an incident here the night you left," I said. "I'm afraid someone got into your study. I've sorted everything out as best I can but the dolls are all ruined—"

"I beg your pardon?" Miss Grayson stared at me, her nostrils flaring alarmingly.

"Their hair was all cut off," I said. "And they—"

That was as far as I got before Miss Grayson pushed past me, marching to her study. I had put the dolls back in their cabinets but, with their spiky, bald heads, they looked more grotesque than anything.

At the sight of them, Miss Grayson lost her composure entirely. She stormed around the room, collecting up the dolls and throwing them into a sack. When I tried to ask if there was anything I might do to help, she snarled at me to get out of her way.

I left her to it and, as she seemed to have no intention of taking the reading class, I went to the classroom and began the lesson myself.

The smell of smoke alerted us to the fire. I wasn't sure where it was coming from at first, so I ushered the girls straight outside. Once we were in the grounds we found the fire immediately.

Miss Grayson had gathered all the toys remaining in the school, including the confiscated ones from the toy room, her own vandalized dolls and the priceless Whiteladies dolls' house, and she had set fire to the lot.

"Now are you happy, you vile brats?" she practically shrieked at the girls. "You see it works both ways! If my possessions are to be destroyed then so are yours! Perhaps I have been too lenient with you and this is the result. From now on you will occupy yourselves with more industrious, worthwhile tasks. There shall be no more playing with toys in this school ever again!"

She strode back inside, still trembling with anger. Many of the girls burst into tears at the sight of their few precious toys in flames. The schoolmistress must have doused the pile in alcohol for it to blaze like that, the flames spitting and crackling against the snow, which melted in an ever-widening patch.

I watched the miniature Whiteladies burn just like the real one had, hating Miss Grayson for casually destroying such a valuable thing. At the very least, it could have been sold to keep the school in coal for a while. Soon enough, there was just a blackened circle of charred remains, surrounded by snow.

"Come on," I said to the sobbing girls. "What's done is done. Crying won't bring back the toys."

I felt terrible for them but there was nothing I could do to change what had happened. I simply ushered them into the school hall, where the maids were putting out lunch. I had no appetite myself so I made my way upstairs to my room instead.

I'd hoped to lie down and rest a while but as I passed by the mirror a pale hand reached right out of the glass and small fingers wrapped tightly round my wrist.

Chapter Twenty-Eight

Isle of Skye – February 1910

I pulled away with a cry. The hand remained stretching out of the mirror, reaching for me, fingers flexing and straining and grasping. I could see nothing else in the glass – only that small child's hand coming out of it. I forced myself to breathe slowly. It was Estella's hand. I could tell because the fingernails were gone – only soft, bloody nail beds in their place.

I took a deep breath, trying to calm myself as I slowly walked back towards the mirror. Then, before I could change my mind, I took Estella's hand in mine, holding on to her tightly. Immediately the arm pulled me forwards and I let it happen. I felt the cold surface of the glass give way beneath my touch as I passed right through and found myself on the other side of the mirror, trapped behind the glass with Estella.

She stood there holding my hand and staring up at me with that same unhinged expression

I had seen before, her mouth gaping wide in a silent scream. Only this time, I forced myself not to recoil from her. If I was to learn what had happened and find some way to help Estella, then this was surely my only option.

I glanced back out through the mirror and saw my bedroom beyond it, and myself still standing there on the other side, my hand pressed against the glass, staring blankly straight ahead.

Inside the mirror was a sort of shadow version of my bedroom. The colours were muted, and everything seemed grey and vague around the edges, like it was all made from smoke. But I could just make out the shapes of my bed and the window, which seemed to have nothing but white emptiness beyond it.

I turned to the little ghost girl at my side. "It's all right," I said, tightening my grip slightly. "Don't be frightened. I'm here with you. Can you tell me what happened?"

Estella tried to speak but, just like before, she started to choke. I could see a mass of hair and dolls' hands blocking the back of her throat.

"All right, all right," I said hastily, not wanting to

see a repeat of what had happened last time. "Could you write it down instead?"

I gazed around, searching for paper and ink, but I could already see that it would be no good. Although I could touch Estella herself, the objects on the other side of the mirror didn't seem to have any substance. Even if we found paper, I wasn't sure Estella would be able to write on it. She seemed to have an idea, however, because she suddenly gripped my hand and started tugging me towards the door. I followed her and soon we were out in the corridor, moving through the shadow school.

Just like my bedroom, the rooms seemed fuzzy, like a drawing that hadn't been properly finished. As we moved down the corridor and through the rooms, I kept catching glimpses of the real school through the mirrors, only there didn't seem to be any consistency of time or place. Sometimes the school beyond the mirror would appear like the one I was familiar with but, at others, it seemed like I was looking into a version of the school as it had been in the past. The girls I glimpsed had the ribbons, ringlets and pinafores of bygone years and, on one occasion, I was sure I glimpsed

Dolores, gossiping with another maid.

When we passed through the main hall, on the other side of the mirror I saw a dark-haired boy with a scarred hand. He was about Henry's age and playing a Baby Grand piano. The sound came out faint and muffled through the glass but I could still hear it was beautiful. He wore very odd clothes – I had never seen anything like them before and couldn't think what time period they might be from.

I didn't have time to puzzle over it because Estella tugged me forwards insistently until finally we found ourselves behind the mirror in Miss Grayson's study. This one was clearly looking out at just a few days earlier because I could see Estella there, lying in the little bed by the fire.

I glanced questioningly at the ghost beside me and had to suppress a shudder of horror at the sight of that wide-open mouth, which seemed even more stuffed with porcelain white hands and wiry grey hair than it had been before. Estella lifted her arm and pointed towards the mirror, so I turned my gaze back to the study beyond the glass.

The door opened and I saw Bess walk in with the chocolate-spread sandwich. Just like she'd told me, she went across the room and, on seeing Estella was asleep, set it down by her bed. Then she turned and left the room. A few moments later, Miss Grayson walked in. She spotted the sandwich at once, scowled and strode over to snatch it up. No doubt she disapproved of Estella being given such a treat in the first place. I'm sure she had every intention of throwing it away immediately.

But then she paused. Perhaps she caught the scent of peanuts or saw them in the spread but, all of a sudden, she lifted the sandwich to her nose, taking a long, slow sniff. I saw her eyes flicker from the sandwich to Estella and back again. And in that moment I saw in her face that she knew. She knew that the sandwich was pure poison to Estella.

Suddenly Estella stirred in her bed and sat up, rubbing her eyes. Looking around, her gaze fell on Miss Grayson and she cringed, perhaps expecting some reprimand or punishment.

Instead, without a word, Miss Grayson held out the sandwich to her. I saw Estella hesitate, perhaps sensing a trick of some kind. But Miss Grayson remained standing there, offering the sandwich. When Estella glanced at the schoolmistress again,

Miss Grayson nodded and said something. Like with the piano music, the words were muffled and I couldn't make out their meaning, but I heard the reassuring tone and the next moment Estella had taken the sandwich.

She kept her eyes on Miss Grayson as she raised it to her mouth and the schoolmistress stared right back. A small smile tugged at Miss Grayson's lips and I saw at once that Estella took this as encouragement. But this was no kindly smile; it was a heartless grin, the wicked smirk of someone who saw they were about to get what they wanted.

Estella's reaction to the nuts was almost immediate. She didn't even manage a second bite before a flash of surprise passed over her face, closely followed by panic and then fear, as the sandwich fell to the floor and she clutched at her throat with both hands.

Miss Grayson simply stood there and smiled silently down at her. At one point, Estella stretched out a hand towards her, desperately grabbing at the teacher's skirts. Miss Grayson leaned down and, just for a moment, I thought she might comfort the dying girl. But instead she grasped Estella's hand firmly by the wrist, disentangled it from her skirts and took a smart step back.

I didn't want to watch but I couldn't look away as Estella struggled in vain against her death throes. Her legs kicked at the blankets, her hands reached out, her nail-less fingers clutched at thin air. And all the while Miss Grayson stood and watched.

All too soon, Estella's legs stopped kicking, her arms went limp at her sides and her face froze in that same terrible expression I'd seen before. There was the sound of a knock on the door, and Miss Grayson jumped and looked towards it. I knew that this must be the moment when I had arrived.

I watched, my stomach roiling with anger and disgust, as Miss Grayson hurriedly picked up the sandwich and placed it, with precision, back on the plate before going to answer the door.

I didn't need to see any more, I already knew what happened from here, so I turned back to Estella's ghost, crouching down by her side.

"I won't let her get away with it," I said quietly, taking both her hands in mine. "Do you hear me? She'll pay for what she did to you."

The frenzied look seemed to fade from Estella's face. She took a deep breath and then, with an effort, swallowed down the mass of hair and dolls' hands. "Do you promise?" she whispered, finally able to speak.

"I swear it on my soul."

Without another word, she took my hand and led me back through the school to my bedroom, where I could still see myself on the other side of the glass.

"You should go now," she said.

"But what about you?"

For the first time, Estella smiled at me. "I can hear my brother, John," she said. "He's calling my name. I have to go and find him."

"Good luck," I said, giving her one last hug.

She waved goodbye as I pressed my hands against the glass and stepped back out of the mirror.

Chapter Twenty-Nine

Isle of Skye – February 1910

I spent the rest of that day going over and over it all in my mind. What should I do? What could I do? In giving Estella that sandwich, Miss Grayson had practically murdered her in cold blood. But how could I prove it? There'd been no witnesses. There was no evidence.

That afternoon I felt a sudden need to see Henry, so I went searching and found him plastering the wall in the classroom. He greeted me cheerfully enough, but it made my heart ache to see the tension lines that had appeared round his eyes.

I longed to talk to him about what I had discovered but I knew he would never be able to believe that Miss Grayson had been responsible for Estella's death. He was too nice, that was the problem, and it made him believe everyone else was as decent as he was.

But I knew that being nice didn't always work. I had Edward Redwing to thank for that lesson.

His voice seemed to whisper in my ear: *It is not I who has the dark soul, madam...*

"Is anything wrong?" Henry asked, putting down the trowel and peering at me.

"Nothing."

Everything.

I forced a smile. "I just wanted to see you. That's all."

The next day was a Sunday, which dawned bright and sunny. When I went downstairs, I found that Henry had persuaded Miss Grayson to allow us to take the girls for an outing in the carriage after church. The carriage was an extra-long one with bench seats that could just about accommodate everybody if they all squeezed in. The schoolmistress showed no interest in joining us – a fact for which I am sure everyone was glad.

"I thought it would do them good to get away from the school for a bit," Henry told me. "In fact, it would do us all good. So we're going to have an extra drawing lesson at Loch Pooltiel today. You'll love it there, Mim. It's the most beautiful sea loch and it's not that far away."

The girls were eager to leave and piled into the carriage. This was the Sunday that Cassie and Hannah had their day off, so we packed up a picnic lunch to eat on the way. It was a perfect day for drawing, with a clear sky and a bright sun. Loch Pooltiel itself was incredibly beautiful, with crystal waters that sparkled in the sunlight, contrasting sharply with a beach of black volcanic sand. A towering cliff flanked the loch on one side – the tallest cliff on the island, as I heard Henry tell the girls. The snow was melting in the sun and an icy waterfall cascaded over the side of the cliff. Already, just being away from the school made me feel a little better – human, sane, able to breathe.

Bundled up in our cloaks and gloves, with the sun beaming down on us, we were perfectly comfortable sitting on the black sand. The only sound was the soft lapping of the water, the scratch of pencils on paper and Henry's voice as he walked around the girls, tutoring them in their work.

Martha sat beside me with her hands placed listlessly in her lap. Her eyes were still bandaged up and I saw that the white bandage no longer looked very clean. I made a mental note to change the dressing once we got back. To my dismay, I saw a single tear trail from beneath the bandage and run down her cheek. My heart ached for her, and I took her small hand in mine and squeezed it tight.

"I can hear them," Martha said quietly. "They're here."

"Who?" I asked, startled.

Before she could reply, Henry came over and crouched down beside her. "Come on, star pupil," he said. "I can't allow an artist as talented as you to sit out the lesson."

Martha made a strangled sound. "But ... my eyes—"

"There are other ways to create art," Henry said. "You will just have to learn to see the world differently."

He'd brought some objects with him and I watched as he pressed these into Martha's hands one by one. First there was a large, flat pebble, polished smooth by the ocean. Then there was a long piece of driftwood, then a seashell, then a strand of seaweed.

"You can learn to create art through texture and touch," he said.

I smiled at Henry and got up to check on the other girls. Half an hour or so went by and then suddenly the shadow of a sea eagle passed over the beach. The bird gave a raucous shriek. For a moment I saw the gleaming red eyes of Redwing's hawk-topped cane, felt the cold, clammy touch of his fingers round my throat...

Then, from the other side of the beach, I heard Martha give a sharp cry. I looked over and saw that she had clamped both hands over her ears.

"Oh, please make them stop giggling!" she moaned.

I thought she meant the other girls at first and frowned because no one was giggling, they were all working quietly on their drawings. But then I heard it, too – muffled laughter coming from somewhere close. I recognized that sound. I would recognize it anywhere.

"*Shall we play a game?*"

"*Oh, yes! Yes!*"

"*Which one shall we play?*"

The girls could hear the dolls, I could tell by

the way they glanced at each other, their eyes wide with fear. I looked over at Henry but his attention was fixed on Martha and he didn't appear to be aware of anything out of the ordinary.

How could the dolls be back? I had thrown them away, tossed them into the sea… My eyes went out to the lake and then it occurred to me that this was a sea loch.

"We found you before, Mother…"

"And we'll find you again…"

"We know where you are, always…"

"We'll always love you…"

"We'll always find you…"

"Where's Bess?" I said, suddenly noticing she wasn't on the beach.

I stared along the stretch of sand but she was nowhere to be seen. I hurried over to where she had been and snatched up her sketch pad. When I saw the drawing on it, I almost dropped it in shock. Bess had drawn the lake, with a girl floating face down in the water, her long hair trailing around her. I thought of that first day back at school when Bess had stood before me in the classroom, soaking wet, choking on weeds and clumps of black sand.

"No," I whispered, but as the drawing fell from my hand and I looked up, I already knew what I would see. "Bess is in the water!" I screamed, pointing out towards the little figure floating face down in the middle of the loch.

Henry was already removing his jacket, kicking off his shoes and running down the sand. The other girls huddled round me, gathering about my legs and clutching fearfully at my skirts. We made a strangely silent group as we watched Henry swim out to Bess and then bring her back.

When he walked out of the shallow water on to the beach, it was obvious that there was nothing that could be done. You could see it in the heavy lolling of Bess's head and the limp dangling of her hands. Henry was dripping wet, his lips blue with cold, and he was shaking as he covered Bess with his cloak. I wanted to shake, too. More than anything, I wanted to feel shock or horror or grief or even fear. But there was nothing. Simply nothing.

"Take the girls back to the school," he said to me. "They don't need to see this."

"What about you?" I asked.

"I'll take one of the horses and … and take Bess into town," he said. "One horse will be enough to pull the carriage and get you back to the school." His eyes were haunted as he looked at me, expressing the horror that I would surely feel later. "I'll see you back there as soon as I can."

As the girls huddled together in silence, trying not to look at the awful, still shape upon the beach, Henry and I unhitched one of the horses. Henry scooped Bess up and swung himself on to the horse's back, cradling her body against his chest as he clicked his tongue and urged the horse along the path into town.

Without needing to be told, the girls piled into the carriage, shivering and clutching their cloaks about themselves. Their art books and supplies were simply left scattered on the beach. No one wanted to go back on to that black sand. I was just about to climb up into the driver's seat, pick up the reins and take us back to the school when suddenly I froze.

I could hear the dolls whispering behind me, their voices carrying clearly on the still air.

"Where are you going, Mother?"

"Don't leave us here."

"We want to come home and play."

I put my boot on the step. I wouldn't look round, even though part of me longed to.

But then one of the voices piped up. *"We have a special game we want to play with you, Mother!"*

"Oh, you'll be so pleased when you hear about it!"

"It's another murder game!"

"The best type of game!"

"Remember the stab-the-mesmerist-game?"

"Remember it, Mother?"

"This one's even better!"

"Yes! Yes! It's the bludgeon-the-teacher-game!"

"Oh, hooray! Hooray!"

I stood there, my hands gripped tight on the edge of the carriage seat. I could climb up now and never look back. But what then? Miss Grayson would still be there at the school. The girls wouldn't be safe. I wouldn't be free. I could leave the dolls in the sea or bury them in the sand, but what if they got out and found me again, like they promised?

My mind went round in a whirl, searching for answers. I could smash the dolls to bits on the rocks and yet the memory of what had happened when I'd thrown the Frozen Charlotte in the fire was enough to make me baulk at the thought of doing that.

"*It's the only way, Mother,*" the dolls said.

"*Sometimes you can't win if you play nice.*"

"*Take us with you.*"

"*And we'll play a game…*"

"*…that will make all your problems go away.*"

"You're talking about the murder game, aren't you?" I whispered.

For a moment I felt blood, slick between my fingers, as I recalled how easy it had been to kill Redwing. How the act of murder had ended the nightmare that was Whiteladies. Without the dolls I might still be there now, my skin burning and bruising beneath his cruel fingers. My scars itched at the thought.

"*Just one more death,*" the dolls whispered. "*And then it's over.*"

Just one more death, I thought, *and then I win.* It was an ugly thought that seemed to swell up until it filled my entire mind. It must be the dolls making me think in such a way. Surely they were the only reason I found myself thinking of murder with such longing. But I was not a child and the dolls wouldn't be able to control me like I was one. I knew that I must resist their influence with all my might.

They were evil little things, they had blinded Martha and now they'd murdered Bess, and it was my fault they were out in the world to begin with. I couldn't leave them free to infect other children. And yet I was too afraid to destroy them and risk releasing whatever demonic spirit was locked away inside their porcelain bodies.

That left only one option. I would have to hide the dolls away somewhere that no one would ever find them. And that meant fooling them into thinking I was on their side, that they could trust me.

"Perhaps we *should* play the murder game with Miss Grayson," I said under my breath, just loud enough for the dolls to hear.

"*She'll get what's coming to her, won't she, Mother?*" a Frozen Charlotte replied gleefully.

"*The bald, beastly bitch!*"

"*Ha ha! Bald bitch!*"

"*One more game and then you win!*"

"*You win forever!*"

"Wait here a moment," I said to the girls, making up my mind. "There's something I need to do."

A few of them called for me to stay but I ignored them as I took my foot off the step, turned round, and walked purposefully across the black sand, pausing only to pick up one of the baskets of art supplies. I continued on, right to the edge of the lake, the water practically lapping at my toes. From beneath the dark surface, I distinctly heard a giggle.

"All right," I said softly. "This is no time for hide and seek. I know you're in there." I emptied the basket, coloured pencils falling on to the black sand at my feet. "Come out now," I said, "or I leave you behind."

"Don't be cross with us, Mother," a doll piped up.

"We'll do as you say."

I stared at the water as, one by one, the Frozen Charlotte dolls rose to the surface. Soon there were dozens of them, floating on their backs, bobbing about in the water with their little hands held up towards the sky. I remembered how I used to play with my own Frozen Charlotte in the bath as a child. She had seemed so sweet and harmless then. Now, I could only see them as monsters. But sometimes you couldn't play nice and expect to win. Sometimes you had to make a deal with the devil.

The dolls floated across the water towards me in a wave of white. I crouched down at the edge and scooped them up, dripping wet. As I had suspected at the time, the toy chest must have burst open when it hit the water and I saw now that a lot more of the dolls were broken, with many of them missing an arm, a leg or even a head.

Finally they were all contained within the basket, and I straightened up and lifted it. It felt unnaturally heavy in my arms and the giggle of a Frozen Charlotte grated on my nerves as I turned back to the carriage.

Chapter Thirty

Isle of Skye – February 1910

As we got closer to the school, the dolls in the basket beside me became more and more excited.

"*Let's play the murder game again!*" they whispered. "*Let's play the murder game!*"

"Miss Black," Violet piped up tremulously from the back. "The dolls are whispering things. Bad things. Oh, can't you hear them?"

"Don't be silly, Violet," I said, as firmly as I could. "Dolls can't talk."

At last the school loomed into view, the dark patch of charred ground still tainting the air with the smell of something burnt. I ushered the girls from the carriage, set the basket of dolls down on the floor and then tied the horse to a nearby post.

Out! Out! Redwing's voice suddenly shrieked inside my head. *I'll have no horses at Whiteladies!*

The memory was so strong that for a moment it was like I was right back there again.

Vanessa is here, in the house, madam…

Poor little Vanessa Redwing. If only she hadn't fallen from her horse that day, none of this would ever have happened. We would never have gone to Whiteladies. Mother would not have had her head beaten to a pulp, Bess and Estella would still be alive, I would not be here, with the dolls, at this school.

Let that be a lesson to you, Jemima…

Charlotte says the thunder hurts her ears…

You'll speak to your daughter again, Mr Redwing…

They move around in the toy room…

A loss as unspeakable as yours…

Now. Where were we?

"Miss Black!"

I opened my eyes and saw that the girls were huddled together in a little group on the drive. Olivia was tugging at my sleeve and it seemed she'd been trying to get my attention for some time.

"What is it, Olivia?"

"Are you all right?" she asked, giving me a worried look. "You were just standing there muttering."

"Nonsense," I said briskly. "I was merely reminding myself of something I need to do."

"But—"

I picked up the basket of china dolls at my feet. "Come along," I said. "It's time to go inside."

I led the way into the school, the girls following, silent and subdued. We'd set out that morning in the hope of respite from darkness and yet the shadow of death now hung over us all again, like a wet cloak that seemed to grow heavier and heavier.

"Please go to your dormitory," I said, peeling off my gloves in the hallway.

"But it's still early, miss," Olivia said.

"I'm perfectly aware of what time it is, thank you, Olivia," I said. "Now do as I say. Return to your dormitory and say a prayer for Bess. And for Estella. I need to speak with Miss Grayson."

Without any further argument, the girls filed up the stairs. Taking the dolls with me, I followed them to make sure they were all accounted for. Then I fetched the keyring from my room and locked them in. For their own protection, they must stay in there until the dolls were disposed of.

"*Is it time yet, Mother?*"

"*Time to play the murder game?*"

"*Oh, it must be time to play by now!*"

"*It must be!*"

328

"Hush!" I told them. "Yes, it's time. But, listen: why don't we play a different game? A new one that I made up all by myself. One that you've never played before."

Yesterday I'd seen Henry put the bucket of plaster away in the supply cupboard downstairs. Perhaps I could use this to trap the dolls in the walls of the basement, where they'd never be found. The trick would be making them think it was all a game so they'd go along with it.

Before I could say anything more, I was startled by the sound of footsteps climbing the stairs. I walked down the corridor, the basket of dolls still in my hands, to see Miss Grayson, her ubiquitous leather tawse dangling from her wrist.

"Oh, Miss Black," the schoolmistress said, pausing on the top step. "There you are. I'd started to wonder what had become of you. Why didn't you report to me when you arrived? And where are the girls?"

"Bess died," I said, placing the basket on the floor at my feet.

Miss Grayson stared at me. "I beg your pardon?"

"She drowned in the loch."

The schoolmistress's mouth fell open in an

expression of disbelief. Then she glared at me with a look of utter fury. "You stupid, careless girl!" she cried. "How could you allow such a thing to happen? Oh, how could you? Don't you realize that questions are being asked as it is? The trustees want to launch an investigation. And, now, with another death, the police will certainly—"

"Perhaps you should have thought of that before you murdered Estella!" The words burst out of me before I could stop them.

The schoolmistress froze. "How dare you say such a thing?" she finally said. "How dare you?" She was trembling with anger. "You will leave this school, miss," she said. "And you will never come back."

I shook my head. "I won't leave these girls here with you. You're a danger to them."

"I'm the only person in the world who cares about them!" Miss Grayson cried. "Do you think their miserable, drunken, dirty families care? Do you think the magistrates care? The only chance of a decent life these girls have is me!"

I stepped towards her. "You gave Estella that sandwich knowing it would kill her," I said. "I saw you do it. And when she began to choke for air you didn't fetch help or even try to comfort her. You just pushed her away and watched her die. You're a monster."

Miss Grayson closed her eyes briefly, then looked at me and said, "You saw through the window, I suppose."

I could hardly tell her that I'd seen her through the mirror, so I simply shrugged. "I saw you," I repeated. "I know what you did."

"If you saw what happened then you'll be aware that all I did was give the girl a sandwich," Miss Grayson replied. "How was I to know there were nuts in it? Once she'd taken a bite, there was nothing to be done. If anyone is to blame, Miss Black, it is you." She pointed a finger at me. "It was in *your* cookery class that the real crime occurred."

I felt the sudden urge to grab hold of her finger and snap the bone clean in half. Because the worst thing was that she was right. I *was* partially responsible.

"I never meant to hurt Estella," I said, desperately looking for a way to ease my own guilt. "You did. That's the difference between us."

"You will never prove that," Miss Grayson said. She blinked at me rapidly. "However, it remains an indisputable fact that Estella had something wrong inside her head. Dreadfully wrong. I always knew it. I saw it the moment her parents brought her here. They couldn't control her and neither could I. She was always lying, always misbehaving. I tried to deal with her the best I could, to beat the wickedness out of her, but when she blinded Martha I saw that I had failed. Estella's death was an accident, but it was good for this school and good for the other girls, and I certainly won't waste any tears on such a child as her."

I glared at the wretched old hag, hating her with all my soul. "If it's the last thing I ever do, I am going to see to it that you pay for what you've done. I'll find some way to make the police believe me and then you'll hang. The worst part of it is that Estella didn't blind Martha, she tried to save her."

Miss Grayson shook her head. "No other girl in this school would do such a thing," she said.

"It wasn't one of the girls," I said.

"Then who?" Miss Grayson said. "You'll be accusing the servants next."

"It was the Frozen Charlotte dolls."

We both looked down at the basket of broken dolls at my feet.

"You are mad, girl!" the schoolmistress said. "Raving mad!" Her eyes gleamed. "And no one would blame me for protecting myself from a madwoman. Especially one who had just confessed to the murder of poor Estella."

She moved so quickly that I didn't even have the chance to raise my hands as she struck me across the face with her tawse.

The blow sent me reeling back, electric eels of pain shooting out from the places where the thick leather strips had hit me. Blood filled my right eye and for an awful moment I thought she'd managed to blind me. But then I realized the cut was just above my right eyebrow, stretching down towards my ear.

I wiped the blood from my eye but Miss Grayson pressed her advantage immediately, striking me again with the whip, this time across the shoulders. The bombazine crepe of my black mourning dress split beneath the blow and my back became warm with blood as she thrashed me again and again. The agony of my skin splitting apart was unbearable and, at the back of my mind, I marvelled that Estella had been able to take such a whipping without so much as a whimper.

I couldn't think through the hurt; I couldn't catch my breath. Everything was a fog of pain and panic. I could feel Miss Grayson's murderous intent with every blow of that tawse. How many strikes would it take to be whipped to death? Through my panic, I somehow managed to struggle to my feet and throw myself at Miss Grayson.

The impact caused her wig to fall from her head and I found myself staring at a woman who was almost completely bald. My mother had warned me of the dangers of using curling irons but I had never seen such extensive damage before. Only a few straggly tufts of wiry, grey hair remained on her head. The rest was just skin, puckered and scarred from old burns. Without her hair, the schoolmistress was transformed into some grotesque version of herself.

The moment the wig fell from her head, Miss Grayson's face contorted into an expression of pure anguish. She made a strangled sound at the back of her throat and spun away from me to lunge towards the wig. But then she froze and so did I. The wig no longer lay on the floor where it had fallen. Instead it was clutched in the tiny hands of a Frozen Charlotte doll.

"*Nobody hurts Mother!*" the doll piped up in a loud, clear voice. "*Nobody!*"

The schoolmistress gasped and snatched back her hand. "It isn't possible!" she said.

"*I know!*" the doll said. "*Let's play a game!*"

I looked down and saw that more dolls had climbed out of the basket. They went to Miss Grayson so quickly that they were barely more than a white blur.

"*Let's play the push-the-teacher-down-the-stairs game!*"

"No!" Miss Grayson cried. She took a stumbling step backwards, away from the dolls, but closer to the stairs. "No, don't!"

"*Every night when I get home, the monkey's on the table!*" trilled one of the dolls.

"*Take a stick and knock it off!*" cried another. "*Pop! Goes the weasel!*"

And then the doll opened its painted lips to expose multiple rows of impossibly sharp needle teeth. In one swift movement, the doll bit down hard on the schoolmistress's ankle. Trickles of blood ran down her leg, staining her woollen stockings.

Miss Grayson cried out and staggered backwards on to the top step. Her flailing hands were unable to find a purchase on the banister and I heard a groan as she landed part of the way down, and then tumbled over and over, all the way to the bottom. There she lay in a heap, her head twisted at an awful, unnatural angle.

As fast as my throbbing back would allow, I hurried down after her. I knew she was dead the moment I stepped off the bottom stair. Although she was lying on her front, her head was twisted round so far that she was practically staring up at me.

I shivered but felt no regret. None whatsoever. She was a warped, evil woman who had deserved to die. It seemed to me, in those few seconds, that her death had solved all my problems and I smiled at the thought.

But then I looked up and saw Cassie, returned from her day's outing. She still wore her coat and had a basket of milk bottles clutched in her hand. And she was staring at me with an accusing, appalled expression on her pretty face.

Chapter Thirty-One

Isle of Skye – February 1910

"You!" Cassie said, staring at me like I was the devil himself. "You killed Miss Grayson!"

"She tripped," I said. "Cassie, listen, it wasn't me. It was the Frozen Charlotte dolls." Even as I heard myself say the words, I realized how crazy they sounded. Cassie didn't even reply – she simply dropped the basket, the milk bottles smashing where they fell, then turned and ran.

I briefly considered grabbing a Frozen Charlotte and going after Cassie to prove to her that the dolls were alive. But when I looked round, I couldn't see any of them nearby.

From above, I heard a Frozen Charlotte giggle.

"*That's torn it!*"

"*Ripped it!*"

"*Spilled it!*"

"*No use crying over spilled milk!*"

"*Hee! Hee! Spilled milk turns sour!*"

I looked up and saw several Frozen Charlottes lined up at the top of the stairs in a perfect row.

Cassie started yelling as she ran through the school.

"Murder!" she shrieked. "Help! Help!"

I had no choice but to turn away from the dolls and hurry after her, my back throbbing as I went down the corridor.

"Cassie!" I called. "Please! Come back here and listen to me!"

A moment later I heard her thundering up the servants' staircase. I was right behind her, using the banister to drag myself up the stairs. As I went I saw Dolores standing there in the gloom, staring at her duster like she didn't know what to do with it.

I reached the first floor in time to see Cassie look over her shoulder and give a squeak of alarm at the sight of me before dashing into the nearest bedroom, which happened to be mine. Her stupidity seemed to know no bounds. She could just as easily have carried on running down the corridor, taken the main staircase back down to the ground floor and then gone out through the front door. Instead, she had trapped herself in a room from which there could be no escape.

It seemed she had some notion of screaming for help from the window because, as I entered the room, out of breath from the race upstairs, I saw her go straight over and throw it open.

"Henry!" she shrieked. "Help! Help! She's gone mad!"

"Oh, for God's sake, would you shut up?" I snapped, clutching my side where a stitch had developed. "Henry isn't here. He's gone into town."

Cassie immediately started to cry. I glared at her. "Listen to me," I said. "You've got to understand. I did not kill Miss Grayson." I took a step towards her. "It's the dolls. They're possessed. Something happened back at my old home that—"

"Just wait until Henry hears about this!" Cassie spat.

I felt myself go suddenly very still. There had been so much in my life that was truly terrible. Henry was the one chance at happiness that I had left. By God, it was a sobering thought.

"I'm going to tell him!" Cassie threw the words at me, her eyes red from crying. "I'll tell him what you did! And then he'll see you for what you really are.

A freak, glooming around the place with your air of tragedy!"

I closed my eyes and Henry's words echoed round and round inside my head:

The honest truth is that I have loved you from the moment I laid eyes on you...

I know I must have a foolish grin on my face and I don't care...

You have made me the happiest chap in the world...

"No." I opened my eyes. "I can't let you take it all from me. Not when I'm so close to being free."

"Let's play the murder game!"

The whispering of the dolls seemed to fill the entire room:

"Every night when I get home..."

"The monkey's on the table..."

"Take a stick and knock it off..."

"Pop! Goes the weasel!"

"Ha ha ha!"

"That weasel got popped!"

"Henry is mine," I said, taking another step forwards. Cassie shrank away from me but there was nowhere to go and she ended up with her back pressed up against the windowsill. "He's mine.

340

I won't let you ruin it."

Cassie stared at me and I saw real, naked fear in her green eyes. "I ... I didn't mean it," she stammered. "I won't tell anyone what I saw. I promise."

I shook my head. It was too late for that. We both knew that she was lying. The moment someone arrived here, she would tell them everything.

"*It's the only way*," the dolls whispered.

"*It's now or never.*"

"*Winning the game is the only thing that matters.*"

Everything seemed to shrink down to this one moment, in this room, with this choice.

It is not I who has the dark soul, madam...

The dolls were whispering and whispering, urging me on.

"*Remember what fun it was before!*" they said. "*Remember how marvellous!*"

And the dark truth was that it had been marvellous, in a grim and horrible way: the satisfaction of warm blood flowing out over my hands; the joy of the blade scraping over bone; the triumph on seeing that look of pure terror on Redwing's face. I saw it again now, mirrored on Cassie's.

"Please," the girl whispered. "Oh, please don't."

But her words couldn't move me and her fear lit a tiny flame of pleasure, deep in my soul.

"*Humpty Dumpty sat on the wall,*" sang the Frozen Charlottes.

"*Humpty Dumpty had a great fall...*"

Cassie tried to lunge past me but I grabbed her by the shoulders, dragged her back to the window and forced her, face down, over the sill, so that her upper body hung out and she was faced with the sight of a great drop to the flagstones below.

She let out a dreadful scream – a sound loud enough to wake the dead. Her arms waved around but there was nothing there for her to hold on to.

"Please!" she yelled. "Oh, God, I'll do anything! Anything you want!"

"It's too late," I said, lifting her legs up to tip her over the ledge.

Her feet disappeared and she screamed all the way down before there was the sound of a thump and a crunch, and then nothing. Nothing but silence.

I peered over the edge. Cassie lay sprawled on the flagstones, a growing pool of dark blood spreading out from her head.

"And all the king's horses and all the king's men," the Frozen Charlottes sang, *"couldn't put Humpty together again."*

I heard the rattle of wheels on cobbles and looked up at the front gates. I'd acted just in time. Henry had returned and brought the police with him.

Hurriedly I stepped back from the window before they could see me. I could hear the girls calling me and banging on the door of their dormitory but I couldn't let them out just yet. I had only minutes to change into a new dress and pull a brush through my hair. Then I wiped the blood from my face and used powder to cover over the cut before going to let out the girls.

"What's happened?" Olivia cried. "We heard screaming."

I did my best to look astonished. "Did you? I was down in the kitchen and didn't hear a thing."

From below there came shouts and exclamations. Henry and the police must have come inside and discovered Miss Grayson. Soon enough, they would discover that there was a second body round the back of the school as well.

Chapter Thirty-Two

Isle of Skye – February 1910

The girls were removed from the school the next day to be sent off to different industrial schools on the mainland. All except Martha, whose aunt had decided that she would care for the girl herself. When I told the police that I had heard Miss Grayson and Cassie arguing, they seemed ready enough to believe that Cassie may have pushed the schoolmistress down the stairs and then killed herself in a fit of remorse. There was no proof, however, and since both parties were dead they decided to rule both deaths as accidents. The Dunvegan School for Girls was to be closed, they said. Hannah and Mrs String had been told not to return. Henry and I would have to find positions elsewhere but, of course, we had never had any intention of staying.

"It's for the best, Mim," Henry said later that afternoon, once the police had gone. "We just need to start over."

That night, all alone in the school, I didn't sleep. I kept thinking I could hear the girls running up and down the stairs. The Frozen Charlottes, which I had collected after the police left, giggled and whispered together in their basket. And I lay there in the dark replaying what had happened, what I had done, over and over again in my mind. The doubt began to creep in. And the guilt. The horror of it.

"I'm a monster," I whispered.

"*Monstrous,*" the dolls whispered back. "*What fun it is to be monstrous...*"

Finally, towards dawn, I made a decision and got out of bed. I sat down at the desk and wrote a letter to Henry. In it, I detailed every last thing I'd done. I told the truth about what had happened to Edward Redwing, as well as the events of yesterday. I held nothing back. My dark soul was laid bare. He deserved to know the truth. He was good and pure and decent, and all the things I wasn't.

When I was done, I put the letter into a sealed envelope and wrote Henry's name on the front. Then I told the Frozen Charlottes we were going to play a game and I took them down to the basement, along with the tub of plaster from the supply cupboard.

The dolls tittered and fussed as I plastered them into the wall.

"*What are you doing, Mother?*"

"*Is this a new game?*"

"Yes," I said. "It's the new game I mentioned earlier, remember? Just you wait until you find out what it is. You'll love it."

The dolls seemed content with this and giggled to themselves as I imprisoned them in the walls of the school.

"You have to stay here and wait for me to come back," I said. "Then I'll explain the rules."

"*Why can't you tell us now, Mother?*" one of the dolls cried petulantly as I smoothed another layer of plaster over its hateful little face.

"Because," I whispered, "it's going to be a surprise."

"*Oh, we* love *surprises!*"

"Yes," I replied. "I thought you might."

I had to believe it was the dolls' influence that had made me do the things I had done. Such wickedness surely could not have come from me.

The sun had risen by the time I was finally finished.

"Wait for me here," I said. "I'll be back to

explain the game later."

The only answer was silence.

"Hello?" I tried again.

But there was nothing. Perhaps they couldn't hear me beneath their thick coat of plaster. Or perhaps they could hear me but couldn't make themselves heard back. Satisfied with my handiwork, I turned and walked from the room. Then, before I could lose my nerve, I collected the letter, put on my cloak and went down to Henry's cottage. He looked like he hadn't slept, either.

"Let's go for a walk," I said.

He fetched his coat, and Murphy came hopping out, all excited. We walked along the clifftop. Henry took my hand in his and I revelled in the touch of his warm fingers. I tried to commit the feeling to memory so that it might comfort me in the lonely days to come.

Finally we reached Neist Point and stopped to look at the view. It was now or never.

"Henry, there's something I must tell you," I said. Forcing out the words was one of the hardest things I'd ever done. "There's something you need to know. And, once you do, you won't want to marry

347

me any more. You'll never want to see me again."
I held out the letter. "It's all in here. Every last secret."

Every last sin...

Henry took the letter from me and gazed down
at it before opening his fingers. The letter was
immediately plucked from him and went sailing
over the edge of the cliff, dancing in the air for a
moment before it was sucked down towards the sea
and lost in the foam and froth.

"Don't ever tell me," he said in a quiet voice,
gazing out towards the water. "I don't want to
know, Mim." He looked at me, then wrapped his
fingers round mine and said, "What's done is done.
I love you. We're meant to be together. That's all I
need to know."

I hesitated. I could blurt out the truth to him
right here and now. I could force him to listen as
I explained that I had murdered two people and
that some small part of me worried that I might kill
again one day.

It's such fun *to play the murder game!*

I shuddered as a doll's voice rang out in my mind,
as clearly as if there was a Frozen Charlotte in my
pocket. Even if the dolls had influenced me, I had

enjoyed it, just the tiniest little bit. And that was the most sickening shame of all. To tell Henry the truth would have been the decent thing to do. But I also wanted to put all my suffering behind me.

"Are you sure?" I said softly.

Henry's fingers tightened slightly round mine. "I am," he said. "Whatever it is, let's just bury it. We're so close to escaping, Mim. Please don't let anything spoil it now. Please."

"All right," I heard myself say. "If that's really what you want."

Henry's eyes were serious. "We won't ever talk of this again," he said. "We'll leave this place and never look back."

Chapter Thirty-Three

Cornwall – December 1912

Henry and I married and built a new life for ourselves far away in Cornwall. All was well.

Then, one day, I walked into Henry's studio to clean. The moment I entered the room, something felt amiss. I couldn't place it but there was definitely something wrong. I had the weirdest sense of being watched. Several times I glanced out of the window but there was no one staring in at me.

Finally I looked at the work in progress on the easel. At first it just seemed like a rather nice sketch of Henry, Murphy and I in the kitchen together, settled in front of the stove on a chilly winter's evening. A happy little family. But then I looked closer and the vase of flowers I'd been carrying fell from my hands, smashing upon the floor.

Hearing the sound, Henry came in from next door. "Good grief, what a butterfingers you are,

Mim!" he exclaimed, bending down to pick up the pieces.

"What's this?" I asked, in a harsh voice.

"What?"

"This drawing." I pointed at it.

Henry straightened up. "Oh. Just a little sketch of the three of us."

"Don't you mean the four of us?" I tried to keep a lid on my anger, but it was bubbling up inside me, begging to be let out. "After all that we went through on Skye, why ever would you draw such a thing?"

"Mim, I have no earthly idea what you are talking about," Henry said patiently.

"Why the hell," I said, "would you include a Frozen Charlotte doll?"

In the years since we had left the Isle of Skye, neither Henry nor I had once mentioned the Frozen Charlottes. The closest we'd come was on one occasion at an auction house when a box of them had come up for sale. By unspoken agreement we had left immediately, without waiting to bid on the settee we were interested in.

At the mere mention of the dolls, Henry went

visibly pale. "What? I haven't drawn one of those things! Why on earth would I?"

"Then what's this?"

I pointed at the drawing. It was so small that you could almost miss it but there, right in the corner, was a Frozen Charlotte on the icy window ledge, its tiny hands pressed against the glass, peering in at us. And right beside it, as if miniature fingers had drawn on the frosted glass, were two words: *Hello, Mother!*

The colour drained from Henry's face as he stared at the drawing.

"I don't … I don't know what to say," he said. "I don't remember drawing that. I would never draw one of those awful things. I don't know how it could have got there. What can it mean, Mim?"

I closed my eyes and suddenly I was back at the loch two years ago, and it was impossible to tell whether the voices ringing in my ears now were merely an echo from back then or real voices that were here with me now:

"We found you before, Mother…"

"And we'll find you again…"

"We know where you are, always…"

"We'll always love you…"
"We'll always find you…"
"Always…"
"Always…"
Always.

Turn the page for a chilling extract from

Isle of Skye — 1910

The girls were playing with the Frozen Charlotte dolls again.

The schoolmistress had given them some scraps of fabric and ribbon from the sewing room to take out to the garden. They were to practise their embroidery skills by making little dresses and bonnets for the naked porcelain dolls. "They'll catch their death of cold otherwise," the teacher had said.

But there was one girl who wasn't playing with the others. The schoolmistress sighed when she saw her, sat alone, fiddling with her blindfold. The girl complained it was uncomfortable but the doctor had said it was necessary to keep her wound clean. And, besides, the sight of her ruined eyes frightened the other girls.

The schoolmistress got up and went over to her, just as she succeeded in untying the knot.

"Now, Martha," she said, deftly tying it back up again. "Remember what the doctor said."

The girl hung her head and said nothing. She hadn't spoken much since the accident. Not since the physician had come and Martha had made those ridiculous accusations.

"Why don't you go and join the girls in their game?" the schoolmistress said.

The blind girl shook her head and spoke so quietly that the teacher had to strain to hear. "It's a bad game."

"Nonsense. Come along now and play with the others. I'm sure they can help you if you ask."

She took Martha's hand and tugged her, stumbling along, to where the girls were playing in the sunshine. But when she got there she found that they weren't making dresses for the dolls after all. They were making shrouds. And they'd covered the dolls up with them as if they were corpses. Some of the girls were even making little crosses out of twigs.

"What are you doing?" the schoolmistress said.

The girls looked up at her. "We're holding a

funeral for the Frozen Charlottes, Miss Grayson."

"Well, stop it at once," the teacher replied. "I never heard of anything so ghoulish."

"But, miss," one of the girls said, "they like being dead. They told us."

Chapter One

Now Charlotte lived on the mountainside,
In a bleak and dreary spot.
There was no house for miles around,
Except her father's cot.

When Jay said he'd downloaded a Ouija-board app on to his phone, I wasn't surprised. It sounded like the kind of daft thing he'd do. It was Thursday night and we were sitting in our favourite greasy spoon café, eating baskets of curly fries, like always.

"Do we have to do this?" I asked.

"Yes. Don't be a spoilsport," Jay said.

He put his phone on the table and loaded the app. A Ouija board filled the screen. The words YES and NO were written in flowing script in the top two corners, and beneath them were the letters of the alphabet in that same curling text, in two arches. Beneath that was a straight row of numbers from zero to nine, and underneath was printed GOODBYE.

"Isn't there some kind of law against Ouija boards or something? I thought they were supposed to be dangerous."

"Dangerous how? It's only a board with some letters and numbers written on it."

"I heard they were banned in England."

"Couldn't be, or they wouldn't have made the app. You're not scared, are you? It's only a bit of fun."

"I am definitely *not* scared," I said.

"Hold your hand over the screen then."

So I held out my hand, and Jay did the same, our fingertips just touching.

"The planchette thing is supposed to spell out the answers to our questions," Jay said, indicating the little pointed disc hovering at one corner of the screen.

"Without us even touching it?"

"The ghost will move it," he declared.

"A ghost that understands mobile phones? And doesn't mind crowds?" I glanced around the packed café. "I thought you were supposed to play with Ouija boards in haunted houses and abandoned train stations."

"That would be pretty awesome, Sophie, but

since we don't have any boarded-up lunatic asylums or whatever around here, we'll just have to make do with what we've got. Who shall we try to contact?" Jay asked. "Jack the Ripper? Mad King George? The Birdman of Alcatraz?"

"Rebecca Craig," I said. The name came out without my really meaning it to.

"Never heard of her. Who did she kill?"

"No one. She's my dead cousin."

Jay raised an eyebrow. "Your what?"

"My uncle who lives in Scotland, he used to have another daughter, but she died when she was seven."

"How?"

I shrugged. "I don't know. No one really talks about it. It was some kind of accident."

"How well did you know her?"

"Not that well. I only met her once. It must have been right before she died. But I always wondered how it happened. And I guess I've just been thinking about them again, now that I'm going to stay in the holidays."

"OK, let's ask her how she died. Rebecca Craig," Jay said. "We invite you to speak with us."

Nothing happened.

"Rebecca Craig," Jay said again. "Are you there?"

"It's not going to work," I said. "I told you we should have gone to a haunted house."

"Why don't *you* try calling her?" Jay said. "Perhaps she'll respond to you better. You're family, after all."

I looked down at the Ouija board and the motionless planchette. "Rebecca Craig—"

I didn't even finish the sentence before the disc started to move. It glided smoothly once around the board before coming back to hover where it had been before.

"Is that how spirits say hello, or just the app having a glitch-flip?" I asked.

"Shh! You're going to upset the board with your negativity. Rebecca Craig," Jay said again. "Is that you? Your cousin would like to speak with you."

"We're not technically—" I began, but the planchette was already moving. Slowly it slid over to YES, and then quickly returned to the corner of the board.

"It's obviously got voice-activation software," I said. With my free hand I reached across the table to pinch one of Jay's fries.

He tutted at me, then said, "Spirit, how did you die?"

The planchette hovered a little longer this time

before sliding over towards the letters and spelling out: B–L–A–C–K

"What's that supposed to mean?" I asked.

"It's not finished," Jay replied.

The planchette went on to spell: S–A–N–D

"Black sand?" I said. "That's a new one. Maybe she meant to say quicksand? Do they have quicksand in Scotland?"

"Spirit," Jay began, but the planchette was already moving again. One by one, it spelled out seven words:

D–A–D–D–Y

S–A–Y–S

N–E–V–E–R

E–V–E–R

O–P–E–N

T–H–E

G–A–T–E

"It's like a Magic Eight ball," I said. "It just comes out with something random each time."

"Shh! It's not random, we're speaking with the dead," Jay said, somehow managing to keep a straight face, even when I stuck my tongue out at him. "Is that why you died, spirit?" he asked. "Because you opened the gate?"

The planchette started to move again, gliding smoothly around the lighted screen:

C-H-A-R-L-O-T-T-E

I-S

C-O-L-D

"Charlotte?" I said. "I thought we were speaking to Rebecca?"

"Is your name Charlotte?" Jay asked.

The planchette moved straight to NO.

"Are you Rebecca Craig?" I asked.

The planchette did a little jump before whizzing over to YES. And then:

C-H-A-R-L-O-T-T-E

I-S

C-O-L-D

C-O-L-D

C-H-A-R-L-O-T-T-E

I-S

C-O-L-D

C-H-A-R-L-O-T-T-E

I-S

C-O-L-D

"This ghost has a pretty one-track mind," I said with a yawn. "I hope you didn't pay a lot of money for this rubbish? Aren't you supposed to be saving up for a new bike?"

"Yes, but I hate saving money — it's so boring. Maybe I'll get a unicycle instead. Do you think that would make me more popular at school?"

I laughed. "Only if you went to clown school. You'd fit right in there. Probably make Head Boy."

"Head Boy, wouldn't that be something? My mum would die of pride." Jay looked down at the board and said, "You know, some people think that spirits can see into the future. Let's give it a little test. Rebecca, am I ever going to grow another couple of inches taller?"

I giggled as the planchette whizzed around, apparently at random.

N-E-V-E-R

E-V-E-R

O-P-E-N

T-H-E

G-A-T-E

D-A-D-D-Y

S-A-Y-S

D-A-D-D-Y

S-A-Y-S

T-H-E

G-A-T-E

N-E-V-E-R

E-V-E-R

"Do you think I should take that as a 'no'?" Jay asked me.

"Absolutely. Titch for life."

Jay pretended to recoil. "Geez, you don't have to be vicious about it." He looked back down at the board. "Spirit, am I going to pass that maths quiz tomorrow?"

B-L-A-C-K

S-A-N-D

F-R-O-Z-E-N

C-H-A-R-L-O-T-T-E

F-R-O-Z-E-N

S-A-N-D

B-L-A-C-K

C-H-A-R-L-O-T-T-E

C-O-L-D

H-E-R-E

D-A-D-D-Y

Jay and I were both giggling now, like little kids, but his next, and final, question made the laugh stick in my throat. "When will I die?"

This time the planchette gave a different answer. It whizzed around the board aimlessly once again before clearly spelling out seven letters:

T-O-N-I-G-H-T

"I don't think this ghost likes me very much," Jay said, lifting his eyes to mine. "What do you think?"

But before I could respond, we both jumped as a tinkly, music-box style tune started to play from Jay's phone.

"Is that your new ringtone?" I asked.

"I've never heard it before," Jay replied.

"Now you're just messing with me."

He shook his head and gave me his best innocent look. "It must be part of the app. To make it more spooky."

A girl's voice started to sing – plaintive and childish, high-pitched and wobbly. It was a simple, lilting melody full of melancholy, a song made for quiet campfires, lonely hills and cold nights:

Now Charlotte lived on the mountainside,

In a bleak and dreary spot.

There was no house for miles around,

Except her father's cot.

"You are such a wind-up," I said, smiling and giving Jay's arm a shove. The sing-song voice was starting to get us dirty looks from the other customers in the café. "You put that on there yourself!"

"I swear I didn't," Jay replied. "It's just a really cool app."

"Such a dreadful night I never saw,
The reins I scarce can hold."
Fair Charlotte shivering faintly said,
"I am exceedingly cold."

Jay tapped the screen to turn it off but, though the voice stopped singing, the Ouija-board screen wouldn't close. The planchette started spinning around the board manically.

"Dude, I think that app has broken your phone," I said.

It was only a joke. I didn't really think there was anything wrong with the phone that turning it off and on again wouldn't fix, but then the screen light started to flicker, and all the lights in the café flickered with it.

Jay and I looked at each other and I saw the first glimmer of uncertainty pass over his face.

And then every light in the café went out,

leaving us in total darkness.

There were grumblings and mutterings from the other customers around us and, somewhere in the room, a small child started to cry. We heard the loud crash of something being dropped in the kitchen.

The only light in the room came from the glow of Jay's mobile phone, still on the table between us. I looked at it and saw the planchette fly over to number nine and then start counting down through the numbers. When it got to zero, someone in the café screamed, a high, piercing screech that went on and on.

Cold clammy fingers curled around mine as Jay took my hand in the darkness and squeezed it tight. I could hear chairs scraping on the floor as people stood up, demanding to know what was happening. More children started to cry, and I could hear glasses and things breaking as people tried to move around in the dark and ended up bumping into tables. And above it all was the piercing sound of a woman crying hysterically, as if something really awful was happening to her.

I let go of Jay's hand and twisted round in my seat, straining my eyes into the darkness, desperately trying to make sense of what was happening. Now that my eyes had adjusted, I could just make out the silhouettes of some of the other people in the café with us – plain black shapes, like shadow puppets dancing on a wall.

But one of them was taller than all the others, impossibly tall, and I realized that whoever it was must be standing on one of the tables. They weren't moving, not at all. Everyone else in the café was moving, even if only turning their heads this way and that, but this person stood completely stock-still. I couldn't even tell if I was looking at their back or their front – they were just staring straight ahead, arms by their sides.

"Do you see that?" I said, but my voice got lost amongst all the others. I stood up and took half a step forwards, staring through the shadows. I could just make out the outline of long hair and a skirt. It was a girl standing on the table in the middle of all this chaos. No one else seemed to have noticed her.

"Jay—" I began, turning back towards him at the exact moment his mobile phone died. The screen light flickered and then went off. At the same time, the café lights came back on. I spun back round to look at the table where the girl had been standing, but there was no one there. The table was empty.

"Did you see her?" I asked Jay.

"See who?"

I stared around for the girl in a skirt, but there was no sign of her.

Anyone would think there'd been an earthquake or something. There was broken china and glass all over the floor of the café, many of the chairs had fallen over and a couple of tables had overturned.

"Who was that screaming?" people were saying.

"What's happened?"

"Is someone hurt?"

"What the hell is going on?"

"Oh my God, someone's been burnt!"

Bill, the owner, had led one of the waitresses out from the kitchen. She must have been the one who'd screamed in the dark. She was still sobbing and it was obvious why – all the way up her right side she was covered in burns. Her hand, arm, shoulder and the right side of her face were completely covered in a mess of red and black bleeding flesh, so charred that it was hard to believe it had once been normal skin. Her hair was still smoking and the smell made me want to gag.

I heard someone on their phone calling an ambulance as other people moved forward, asking what had happened.

"I don't know," Bill said. He'd gone completely white. "I don't know how it happened. When the lights went out, she must have tripped or something. I think… I think she must have fallen against the deep-fat fryer…"

I could feel the blood pounding in my ears and turned back round to Jay. Wordlessly, he held up his mobile phone for me to see. From the top of the screen to the bottom there was a huge crack running all the way down the glass.

"Did you… Did you drop it?" I asked.

But Jay just shook his head.

The ambulance arrived soon after that and took the weeping girl away.

"In all the years this place has been open we've never had an accident like this," I heard Bill say. "Never."

Bill went to the hospital with the girl and the café closed early. Everyone filed away, going out to their cars and driving off. Soon, Jay and I were the only ones left. Normally, he would have cycled home and I would have waited by myself for my mum to pick me up but, today, Jay said he would wait with me, and I was grateful to him for that.

"Thanks," I said. "And thanks for holding my hand when the lights went out."

He gave me a sharp look. "I didn't hold your hand."

A prickly feeling started to creep over my skin. "Yes, you did."

"Sophie, I didn't. You must have… You must have imagined it. It was pretty crazy in there."

I thought of those cold fingers curling around mine and shook my head. "Someone was definitely holding my hand when it went dark," I said. "And if it wasn't you, then who was it?"

"Well, it wasn't me. Maybe you've got a secret admirer."

"Did you see that girl standing on the table? I thought I saw her outline there in the dark."

Jay stared at me. "Are you actually trying to scare me right now? Because it's not going to work, you know. I'm not that gullible."

I glanced back through the windows of the café. There'd been no time to tidy up before the ambulance arrived and the place had been shut up as it was, with tables and chairs and broken crockery everywhere. A couple of the tables looked fairly normal, with plates of untouched food still on them, which was almost weirder.

I shivered and turned away, not wanting to look too closely in case I saw the girl among the empty tables.

"Look," Jay said. "It all got a bit mad when the lights went out because of the waitress who hurt herself and started screaming. If it hadn't been for that, none of this would be any big deal. It was just a freak accident, that's all."

My mum pulled into the car park then, waving at me through the window.

"We could give you a lift," I said.

Jay's house wasn't very far away and he always cycled home, but I couldn't stop thinking of that final question he had asked the Ouija board: *When will I die?*

"No thanks," Jay said. "I'll cycle back."

I hesitated. "Jay…"

"You're not still worrying about that app, are you? Nothing's going to happen to me," he said.

Then he grinned. "But just promise me one thing. If I *do* come to some appalling, grisly end tonight, I hope I can rely on you to tell the world it was a ghost that did me in."

For once I didn't smile. "Don't," I said. "Don't joke about it."

Jay laughed and put his arm around my shoulders in a friendly squeeze. "I think you really would miss me," he said.

Behind us, Mum honked her car horn to tell me to hurry up. Jay gave her a wave and said, "I'll see you tomorrow at school."

"All right. See you tomorrow."

I turned and started to walk across the car park but had only gone a few steps when I stopped and turned back. "Hey, Jay?"

"Yeah?"

"Will you do me a favour?"

"What is it?"

"Would you take the towpath tonight? Please?"

Jay usually cycled back home using the shortest route, which meant several busy roads. He did it all the time and nothing ever happened to him. I knew I was being silly. But if he went the other way, via the towpath, it would mean he'd miss all the major traffic and would only add five minutes to his journey.

I was afraid that he'd refuse, or make a joke of it, or tease me again. But instead he just nodded.

"All right, Sophie. I'll take the towpath." Then he grinned, blew me a mock kiss and said, "Anything for you."

I got into the front seat of Mum's car and waved at Jay as we drove past, keeping my eyes on him until the car turned the corner and I lost him from sight.

I didn't really want to talk to Mum about what had happened at the café so when we got home I went straight upstairs and had a bath. Before going to bed I sent Jay a text to say goodnight. It wasn't something I'd normally do, but I just wanted to reassure myself that he'd got home OK. He sent me a one-word answer: *Goodbye*.

I guessed he'd meant to say goodnight but that his autocorrect had changed it and he hadn't noticed. He'd replied, though, so at least I knew he was home. I got into bed and went to sleep.

I didn't remember until the next day that when Jay had shown me his phone at the café, it had been broken.

My dreams were filled with Ouija boards and burning hair and little girls holding my hand in the dark. And Jay inside a coffin. I tossed and turned all night. It was so bad that it was a relief to wake up, and I got out of bed in the morning without Mum having to drag me for a change.

With the sun shining in through the windows, the events of the night before started to seem less terrible. So the lights had gone out and someone had hurt themselves. It was horrible for that poor waitress but it had just been an accident, plain and simple. In the light of day, there didn't seem to be anything that strange about it.

I dressed quickly, for once actually looking forward to school. Jay would be outside soon and we'd walk there together, like we always did.

As I got ready I was vaguely aware of the phone ringing downstairs and the sound of Mum's voice as she answered it, but I didn't really pay it too much attention. By the time I went downstairs for breakfast, Mum was just hanging up.

"Who was that?" I asked.

She didn't answer straight away, and when I looked at her and saw her face I knew instantly that something was very wrong.

"What is it?" I said. "Who was that on the phone?"

"Sophie," Mum said, her voice all strained and weird-sounding. "I don't... I don't know how to tell you this... Sweetheart, you need to brace yourself—"

"Mum, *what*? What's wrong?"

"It's Jay. That was his dad on the phone. Something's happened. He... He never made it home last night."

"Yes, he did," I said at once. "He texted me."

But at that very second I remembered that Jay's phone was broken. I pulled my mobile out of my pocket and started scrolling through, looking for his text, but it wasn't there.

"I don't understand. He sent me a text last night. I saw it."

"Sophie, he didn't send you a text. Oh, sweetheart, I'm so, so sorry, but... On the way home he had an accident. They think... They think that perhaps the brakes on his bike failed. He went into the canal. By the time they pulled him out it was too late."

"What do you mean *too late*?" I said, clenching my hands so tight that I felt my nails tear the skin of my palms. "Jay's a strong swimmer. He won almost all the swimming contests at school last year. If he'd fallen into the canal, he would have just swum to the side and climbed out."

But Mum was shaking her head. "They think he must have hit his head when he fell in. Sophie, he drowned."

It could not possibly be true. And yet, it was.

Jay was gone.

ISBN: 978-1-84715-722-0

At least £1 from every copy sold
will go directly to Crisis.

BRAND
NEW
STORIES
&
POETRY
ABOUT
CHANGE

A CHANGE IS GONNA COME

MARY BELLO • AISHA BUSHBY • TANYA BYRNE
INUA ELLAMS • CATHERINE JOHNSON
PATRICE LAWRENCE • AYISHA MALIK • IRFAN MASTER
MUSA OKWONGA • YASMIN RAHMAN
PHOEBE ROY • NIKESH SHUKLA

ISBN: 978-1-84715-839-0

"One of the best anthologies for young adults."
Wei Ming Kam